ADVAN
CONFIDE

"Barbara Fischkin takes us on a transcontinental romp, this time from the heart of Mexico City to guerrilla territory in the Philippines. The adventure is colorful and authentic, fast paced and fun. All the while the bittersweet undercurrent of life is evident and real; optimism and strength carry the day."—Peter Eisner, Deputy Foreign Editor, *Washington Post*, and coauthor of *The Italian Letter: How the Bush Administration Used a Fake Letter to Build the Case for War in Iraq*

"*Confidential Sources* is bright, smart, wildly funny, and one of the most touching novels I've ever read. It's about what happens when two seasoned reporters leave the world at their front door and come home to each other. Barbara Fischkin's observations go very deep, and I found myself reading faster, rooting for her, the man with the all-purpose blue eyes, and their two wonderful sons. Read *Confidential Sources* and fall in love with this family, as I have."—*New York Times* bestselling author Luanne Rice

"With the wit and keen observation of a journalist at the top of her form, Barbara Fischkin takes us to the most foreign and maddening country of all: Marriage. Here is a story told with courage and humor. Barbara has invited us into a rollicking, fictional version of a life shot through with equal parts strength and adventure. In the end, the details may be only Mulvaney-true, but the emotional pitch is true-true."—Ana Menendez, author of *Loving Che,* and columnist, *Miami Herald*

"Witty, poignant and utterly alive, Barbara Fischkin's novel, *Confidential Sources,* is a pacey, original read."
—Marti Leimbach, author of *Daniel Isn't Talking*

"Never mind Tracy and Hepburn, give me Mulvaney and Fischkin any day. Their story will make you laugh and break your heart. I just loved it."—Marcia Wallace, actress and author of *Don't Look Back,*
We're Not Going That Way

AND PRAISE FOR

EXCLUSIVE
Reporters in Love . . . And War
A NOVEL

"As I read this screwball comedy of two insane but lovable journalists, I kept thinking: Hepburn and Tracy. Fischkin and Mulvaney doesn't have the same ring, but you will laugh as hard, and love—just love!—the zany characters Barbara Fischkin has created (or exposed, with a wink).
Exclusive is a joy to read."—Ken Auletta, author of
Backstory: Inside the Business of News

"The dead-on newsroom details are quite the scoop."
—*Entertainment Weekly*

"A crisp read buoyed by a delightfully caustic voice."
—*Publishers Weekly*

"Ireland figures large. . . . This is a tale that will bring a smile to the reader's face, on the beach or anywhere."
—*Irish Echo*

"Required reading . . . A screwball romance . . . as the sparring pair compete for scoops around the world."
—*New York Post*

"A wacky first novel . . . fun."
—Ed Lowe, *Long Island Press*

"A unique, innovative read. Don't miss it!"
—Donna Kauffman, author of *Not So Snow White*

"Two better-than-fictional characters."
—*Long Beach Herald*

"Dynamic . . . Mulvaney and Fischkin are off-the-wall, larger-than-life, and completely endearing. Full of wit, sarcasm, and humor, *Exclusive* gives reader[s] exactly what they are looking for in a romance—and an adventure. Mulvaney and Fischkin's escapades are non-stop and their on-again, off-again romance is as hot as it gets. Fischkin's writing is magic. Never has getting the news out been so sexy! Don't miss a chance to pick up this *Exclusive*—you'll never forgive yourself!"—www.roundtablereviews.com

"Charming and clever . . . the story of a couple falling in love and remaining in love . . . intelligent with a chick lit voice but without the chick lit clichés . . . a story that succeeds on its uniqueness, originality, and strength of the narrative . . . a screwball comedy that is too intelligent to be silly, and too funny to be serious. Highly recommended."—*Paperback Reader*

ENTIAL

SOURCES

A NOVEL

Barbara Fischkin

DELTA TRADE PAPERBACKS

CONFIDENTIAL SOURCES
A Delta Trade Paperback / November 2006

Published by Bantam Dell
A Division of Random House, Inc.
New York, New York

Book design by Carol Malcolm Russo

Delta is a registered trademark of Random House, Inc., and
the colophon is a trademark of Random House, Inc.

Library of Congress Cataloging-in-Publication Data
Fischkin, Barbara.
Confidential sources : a novel / Barbara Fischkin.
p.   cm.
ISBN: 978-0-385-33800-4
ISBN-10: 0-385-33800-7
1. Journalists—Fiction.   2. Jewish women—Fiction.   3. Irish Americans—Fiction.
4. Marriage—Fiction.   5. Americans—Foreign countries—Fiction.   I. Title.
PS3606.I768 C66 2006
813.'6 22   2006048499

Printed in the United States of America
Published simultaneously in Canada

www.bantamdell.com

BVG   10   9   8   7   6   5   4   3   2

For the Real Grandmothers,
now back in cahoots

Again, these tales are less than true
but not entirely false.

CONFIDENTIAL SOURCES

PART ONE

Off the Record

DISPATCH FROM THE WAR AT HOME My husband grins, proud of himself.

I fume.

Silently, we sit in our tangerine Honda Element in the parking lot of an ice arena on Long Island, a place I once swore I would never live or work. But I also swore I would never marry Jim Mulvaney. He says it was fate; that we were meant to be together. Two newspaper reporters finding scoops—or stealing them from one another—living and working in foreign countries. Eventually, we'd come home—to his home, that is; mine was in Brooklyn—and raise children.

Yes, children.

That they are ours is one of the few things in our marriage that *is* indisputable. Two boys, now teenagers. Mulvaneyesque beings, albeit with smoother edges. Those, I'd like to think, come from me.

Jack, he's the hockey player. Defense.

Dan, our older boy, is more complicated. *Lawyers, guns, and money,* we cry out in jest. As if that's what it takes to raise and—even more so—to educate him.

Let's just say that school administrators have been known to bolt the door when they see us coming. Proving, I suppose, that sometimes this marriage does work as a partnership.

At the moment, though, I am not feeling particularly chummy.

"Great game," he says.

"Don't you dare speak to me," I reply.

Through the wide, square windows of our Element, a rank Labor Day weekend rain pours down. Inside the car, water turns into steam. My husband—who will always be

"Mulvaney" to me, never "Jim"—wrings out his rain-drenched, coffee-stained Rangers T-shirt and looks at me with those blue eyes of his. They're lighter now, in middle age, and they water more than they once did. But they still sear too, like no other eyes in the world.

I will not let those eyes get to me. Not tonight.

Less than an hour ago, just as Jack began to play his second game of the season—after losing the first in a stunning third-period setback—my husband turned into one of those horrific sports parents you hear about on the evening news.

In short: He was banished from the rink.

As in: Escorted to the door. Kicked out. Ejected.

The charge? "Parental Misconduct."

Meaning it could have been so much worse.

Allow me to recap:

Early in the first period Jack got a penalty. Not a particularly fair one, but, like a man, he skated graciously off the ice. Behavior long in the making. For this, my father-in-law, a devoted fan of his grandson's, gets credit: *"Complain about the first penalty, Johnny, and you get another."*

A concept some of us are still learning.

"Hey, Ref," my husband boomed as Jack took his place in the box, where, mercifully, kids cannot hear anything their parents say.

"Hey, Ref. Hey, genius! Are we playing ice hockey—or lawn croquet?"

Quickly, a uniformed rink "official" appeared.

"Sir, we do not yell at the refs."

"Yeah, yeah, yeah," Mulvaney replied, rolling those very blue eyes. "Maybe *we* don't. But *I* do."

I watched from an upper bleacher, shaking my head at my father-in-law.

Now, people pay homage to his past by calling him the "*Real* Mulvaney." It's also a handy way to distinguish him from his son. My husband, as you may imagine, would prefer they called his father almost anything else.

"There goes my retirement," he grumbled.

"Your son's gonna need a good attorney," I agreed. "Again."

In his younger days Mulvaney's father wore a straw hat year-round and sauntered across Queens Boulevard from bar to courthouse five days a week. He was, as he will tell you himself, the best criminal lawyer in the borough.

Below us the fracas continued.

"Happens again, sir, and you will be asked to leave."

"And who the hell are you?"

"Security, sir!"

"Rent-a-cop, hah!"

Eyeball-to-eyeball, neither my husband nor the official backed off. Frozen air wafted from all four of their nostrils.

"Well, let me tell you something, buddy. I do not speak to rent-a-cops. I speak to legitimate law enforcement officers. . . ."

"Sir!"

"Do not 'sir' me," Mulvaney yelled back. As their faces turned competing shades of red, my husband pointed his index finger and tapped the goldtone nameplate on the older man's breast pocket.

"Duffy?"

The man took a step back.

"Duffy, that your name?"

Two Irishmen, I thought, and braced for all-out war.

"Well, Duffy, I speak to legitimate Nassau and Suffolk County cops. I speak to the NYPD. I speak to federal agents. I used to speak to Interpol. Still do when the need arises."

Duffy gave him a hard look. He was at least sixty. Even from my vantage point up in the bleachers I could see he was tired. He could have been a big deal cop himself once. "Mulvaney, that *your* name? I've heard about you."

"Fire the ref!" my husband bellowed into the vast expanse of ice, sensing his time was now limited. "Fire Duffy, too!"

"Out!" Heaving his chest, the official gave my husband a polite but firm shove toward the exit.

". . . And I speak to criminals! Lowlifes, blue collars, occasional writers imprisoned on human rights violations. But not rent-a-cops! I'd speak to a *white*-collar criminal before I'd speak to a rent-a-cop! Hell, I'd even speak to a *PR man* first. Now *that's* telling you something."

"That's it!" Duffy snapped. "Out the door now, or your kid's team forfeits."

"Mulvaney," I say, after another five minutes of silence punctuated by the steady beat of rain on the car.

"So you are talking to me, now?" he asks, coldly.

"No," I reply, opening the glove compartment and fumbling for a blue and white pamphlet featuring a picture of a young player shooting, his father smiling from afar. "I am reading to you:

"Zero Tolerance: House Rules for the Happy Hockey Family
Parents who act in a disrespectful manner, which in-cludes but is not limited to yelling at refs and at other rink personnel, will be asked to leave the premises. If such parents refuse, security—and, when necessary, Nassau County police officers—will be contacted, lead-ing to possible incarceration and, in extreme cases, games forfeited. We are here to have fun. Winning is

not everything. Sportsmanship is. Sportsmanship is at
the heart of hockey."

"Need I remind you," I say, "that the kind of testosterone
you displayed in there caused a hockey parent murder not
too long ago?"

At this, he brightens. Jim Mulvaney, former cop
reporter, loves nothing more than a good homicide.

"Two nut-job fathers," he says, as if he is remembering
something sweet from his past. "And it was physical. That
in there? That was baloney. They can't arrest you for
yelling at the ref. In the real world, people yell at refs.
How we gonna prepare our kids for anything if we make
life so nice all the time?"

Is he trying to tell me that the NHL—even in its more
courteous reincarnation—is the real world?

"What you did in there," I reply, "was not funny. Nor
was it necessary."

"Ah," he says, lifting a towel out of the back seat and
drying his face, "in time you will see that it was both. You
will see that the story of this evening, in all of its
versions—true-true and Mulvaney-true and even in the
version that hasn't happened yet, in the stories it will lead
you to imagine, in the jokes and the asides it will
inspire—is just more glorious proof that you and I will
always be together; that we will never run out of stories.
That we will have them to tell into our old age."

A Mulvaney-truth is, by the way, a bold lie, based
though it may be on a tiny grain of fact. Mulvaney truths
are woven into the fabric of our lives.

"Mulvaney," I say. "What happened in there is your
story, not mine."

He tenses. "There was a time when you believed that
my stories were yours . . . that all the stories were ours. A

time when you didn't take the house rules so seriously.
A time when you and I, together, got ejected from entire
countries and you took it less seriously than this. Barbara,
we've gotten thrown out of *countries!*"

Just two, really.

Lately, when Mulvaney wants to make me cry he plays
Bonnie Raitt singing "Nobody's Girl." He claims that
song has always made him think of me, but he's only
informed me of this recently, now that, like most women
in their fifties, I am contemplating flight.

"When you are old you will need someone," he
warns me.

On days like this, when our vintage romance is not
going so well, I wonder why my husband, dashing and
handsome though he may still be, refuses to mellow with
age. There was a time, when our kids were little, when I
thought that he might. He took up golf. Now, though, he
makes scenes at his kid's hockey games—and then plays it
himself. Every Tuesday night. Recklessly. As if he were still
twenty-five.

More often, now, I think, what if I left Mulvaney?
In a snap, everything—all those years of marriage,
cohabitation, competition, love, and stories, too—would
blow up, like the world itself could at any moment. And I
wouldn't care. What was amusing, charming, or, at its
worst, tomfoolery bordering on delinquency when we
were younger does not play that well anymore.

"Just write the sequel," he says. "It will make you feel
better."

"Better?" I say.

"Yeah. You didn't tell half our stories the last time you
wrote a book about me."

That is what I do now, write books about my husband.
Although perhaps I shouldn't.

"The way we had children. The way we prepared ourselves for that."

Trust me, it wasn't in any conventional manner.

"The way we saw how the world changed."

Even if, like most people, we didn't see it coming.

"The way we learned that fighting the war at home can be just as hard as covering the ones abroad."

Danny.

"And now you can tell everyone about how I got thrown out of my own kid's hockey game! The perfect literary touch. And you have me to thank."

Maybe, I think, there *is* more to write.

"But you're also going to have to tell them that I didn't huff off and get a beer. You're gonna hafta tell them I watched him in the rain."

I spot our son Jack through the revolving door by the rink exit. He's the one who, even more than Danny, looks like his father. But he's not merely the younger edition, he's the wiser one, too. He was only seven when he proved that to us, beyond all doubt. Now at fifteen, and with age-appropriate uncombed hair, he can transform himself in minutes from a padded defense thug-on-blades to a sweet, funny kid celebrating nothing as much as pure victory.

He bangs happily on the driver's door—Mulvaney always drives—and the trunk pops open. "One goal! Three assists!" Jack shouts as wind blows through the car. He slams down his humongous—and ripe—equipment bag. "And only one penalty. And it didn't even matter!"

"Maybe you'll be the one," his father says. "You'll be the one to vanquish the Mulvaney curse."

I glare at him. After all he's done tonight, he's bringing up that stupid curse, too!

"Saw the whole game!" Mulvaney continues.

Double glare.

"Almost. Only missed a few minutes."

Jack doesn't react. Possibly, he was playing so hard he doesn't know his father was ejected. Why do we persist in thinking *their* lives revolve around *us*?

"Maybe," says Jack, as we drive home, "there never was a Mulvaney curse at all."

CHAPTER ONE
Deep Background

I didn't meet Jim Mulvaney in a bar or a supermarket or because friends fixed us up or while changing trains at Jamaica. One couple I know met when they crashed on the Long Island Expressway, and although that sounds more like us, it didn't happen that way, either. But while ours may not be a *typical* Long Island love story, it is a Long Island love story all the same. Mulvaney and I may have reported the world together, danced with danger in any number of war zones, and interviewed revolutionaries galore, but, for better or for worse, we met and first romanced here, in this long array of suburbs, Nassau County, then Suffolk, jutting out into the Atlantic Ocean for about a hundred miles east of New York City.

He says it would have happened anywhere.

Fate, I reply, needs a locale.

In our case, it needed several.

Mulvaney tells people that we met covering a murder. But the true-truth is that our acquaintance was at least twenty-four hours old by then and we already disliked one another intensely.

It was the 1980s and Jim Mulvaney was an Irish kid from Queens with dazzling eyes, dreadful shirts, a brand-new job as a *Newsday* cop reporter, and an I-own-the-world attitude. As I would later learn, he'd moved to Long Island at fourteen and was educated, briefly and painfully, at Garden City High School, a local jewel of the public education system, appropriately nestled in the midst of that rarefied, tree-lined, planned-to-perfection village. It was, to put it mildly, not a good fit. After high school he enrolled at a party college in Maine, skipped before graduation, and, ultimately, caused a stir at his first paper in Connecticut, where the readership voted him the second-most inflammatory newspaper columnist, second only to William F. Buckley.

At the time I first laid eyes on Mulvaney—mine are brown—in *Newsday*'s Suffolk County bureau, a city room without a city, I wanted only two things in life, neither of them him. What *I* wanted was to live and work in Manhattan and to find, although not necessarily marry, a reasonably sane man. Like Mulvaney, I was only in my midtwenties, with a lot to live and more to learn. I was a good-looking, if cranky, black-haired young woman from Brooklyn, where I'd been raised Jewish and traditional, although not overly so. My mother's most recent claim to fame was that she ran a barely legal Las Vegas–style fundraiser out of her neighborhood shul. As for education, my own high school career, although better than Mulvaney's, was not nearly as distinctive. I got pretty good grades, acted in a few plays, smoked a little pot, and took subways to "the city," thanking my lucky stars that I wasn't one of those "hicks" from Long Island, the sort of kids forced to beg their parents for rides everywhere.

It didn't mean, though, that I couldn't wait to get even farther away, and I did, to a school upstate. Although, to be honest, my view of college was that it wasn't as much an educational experience as it was a launching pad to my ultimate destination: the Big Apple and thence the world.

Not that I knew what I would do when I got there. Not, that is, until I took a journalism course and fell in love with the idea of that kind of career. Imagine. You just go out and talk to anyone who has a story. And then *you* get to tell it.

A lot of my friends, English majors all, wanted to go to law school. But that wasn't for me. Tell a story according to statutes? Compared to reporting, that sounded like the print version of claustrophobia.

Journalism—all the stories to be told and all the experiences to be had—stretched out before me, limitless.

Yeah, so the stories had to be true. No big deal.

So I got a newspaper job up there in Albany and, with the bravado of youth, figured that before long I'd be leaving for Manhattan and the *New York Times* or, at worst, the *Post*.

Four years later, though, I was still there. Covering the statehouse for the *Knickerbocker News,* a small, faltering afternoon daily that got worse by the week. Even the *Daily News* didn't want me. And although I kept meeting men in Albany, most of them were Irish and, more to the point, certifiable.

Then *Newsday* called out of the blue to offer me a

week-long audition, a tryout that could lead to a job. No way I wouldn't try. *Newsday* was, after all, "Long Island's Largest Daily Newspaper." Its only daily newspaper, too. Which didn't hurt circulation. *Newsday* had ten times more readers than the rag where I currently toiled. At the least, it was closer to Manhattan. At the least, I would meet fresh male blood. All I had to do was ace the tryout, which I figured would be a breeze. What could anyone on Long Island possibly know that I didn't?

My first encounters with Mulvaney, at that *Newsday* bureau in Ronkonkoma, make for a long story, one I've already told. Suffice it to say the ground shook. And not in a good way. The "tryout" I was on? He tried to sabotage it. When it comes to romancing, Neanderthals have nothing on my husband.

I vowed never to speak to him, but somehow we would end up in an on-again, off-again—but always torrid— courtship. Marriage had never really been a big blip on our radar screen. But then, suddenly, in the flow of good stories filed separately *and* jointly, we found ourselves tying the knot on the deck of one of the best dives in Queens: Pier 92, on Jamaica Bay, a bar that embodies the heart and soul of the Rockaway Peninsula. Ours was an "arms-related" wedding, if not exactly shotgun. To make another long story short, we got married after the Brits in Northern Ireland found a pile of guns under reporter Jim Mulvaney's bed.

We married shaded by a *chuppah* festooned with green, orange, and white ribbons. Well, it *was* a Jewish wedding in an Irish bar. The canopy was also decorated with letters from well-wishers who, busy with revolutions at home—in Belfast, the Basque Country, and the Big Apple, too— couldn't make it.

We missed those characters and the tales they told. But

the place was packed anyway. And so, with Rosemary Clooney crooning "Thanks for the Memories" on a boom box in the background—perhaps not the most appropriate of wedding songs—Mulvaney attempted to seal the deal Jewish-style by smashing a glass with his boot. Unfortunately, it was a shot glass and indestructible, footwear notwithstanding. I still think, though, that if he had only tried harder he could have done it.

After the ceremony we celebrated in the company of an international coterie of cops and various in-laws and outlaws, and at least one IRA man-on-the-run. Our editor, who twitched characteristically throughout the entire ceremony, came, too, along with his minions, including The Men Who Did and Didn't Write *Naked Came the Stranger,* a bestselling porn novel penned surreptitiously serial-style, on slow news days. The Brit PR man who had been so instrumental in convincing us to "make the commitment" *was* also there, to ensure all went according to the odd agreement I'd made back in Northern Ireland: If I promised to marry Mulvaney, they wouldn't send him to prison. And yes, "God-fearing" Protestants, one in particular, had something to do with it.

Looking back on this now, I have to ask myself: Was it worth it? My husband might have actually *thrived* covering stories from a dank cell in Long Kesh prison.

DISPATCH FROM THE WAR AT HOME "Those guns were planted and you know it!"

My husband is revisiting the old-alleged-crime that brought us together for good, shouting from the large second-floor deck of our newly renovated house, minutes from the scene of his most recent crime—that skating rink. Long Beach, where we now live, is as far south as anyone can reside in Nassau County and still be guaranteed regular electricity.

Mulvaney and I, we like to go to extremes.

"And you know why they were planted, too. Nice thing. Blaming your husband, as if you had nothing to do with it. Who really got us thrown out of Northern Ireland, Barbara?"

And who, Mulvaney, I say to myself, got us thrown out of Nicaragua, which was really a better story? A new war, as opposed to the troubles that had been going on for about eight hundred years.

I am in my downstairs office, as far away from him as I can be in this house. He must have slithered down to read my laptop when I went to the bathroom.

The last time I wrote a book about him, he stood over me while I typed. This is, oddly, an improvement.

"You'd better fess up to the truth," he yells out so the whole neighborhood can hear.

I reconsider the deck. Maybe it wasn't such a good idea, even if I did finally get my own contractors instead of lusting after the neighbors'.

Not that I can actually pay them.

If only my husband's get-rich-quick schemes—the first of which was hatched in Nicaragua, of all places!—ever worked.

"The truth!" he repeats.

I hear a door slide open with a screech. Mulvaney pounds down the stairs, heading closer.

He stands in the doorway to my office. "They planted those guns under my bed . . ." he says as I cover the computer screen with a hand. "To punish me because . . ."

His hand perches over the keyboard. With my other hand, I push it away.

"To punish me because you sneaked into Armagh disguised as my wife . . ."

Armagh. Yet another prison that figured in our romance.

". . . while you were busy stealing *my* story!"

This, I have to admit, is nearly true. I did say I was "Mrs. Mulvaney," even though we weren't married at the time. Who would believe that Barbara Fischkin had a cousin to visit in a prison for women in *Northern Ireland*?

Often, in war zones, people aren't who they seem to be. Even in peace they don't always turn out as expected.

I stop for a moment to relish those days and stories that mattered. Protestant guards strip-searching Catholic political prisoners twenty, thirty times a day.

"But the guards were broads, too," Mulvaney reminds me. "Just doing their jobs."

Since he left journalism to become a private eye, my husband believes he is smarter than he ever was as a police reporter. Or a foreign correspondent. Or even a Pulitzer prize–winning investigative editor. Nowadays Mulvaney describes himself as a "security connoisseur."

This is his final—I hope—get-rich-quick scheme. Jim Mulvaney, Private Investigator.

Or, as he calls it, *Jim Investigates Privately, Inc.*

For years I have been telling him that he needs to be more careful. To look not only at names but at the acronyms people will inevitably make from them.

"Mulvaney," I said, "its initials are J.I.P."

He is going to charge people more than newspapers ever paid him, to do just what he did as a reporter—and *not* write it down. Not publicly, anyway.

Seems to me like less work for more money.

"Yep," I agree. "Those broads were just doing their jobs. Just like the guy at the rink."

There is a silence.

Bad news. He often is silent before he starts—or escalates—an argument. Gathering ammunition, no doubt. But if we spend the afternoon arguing, I won't spend the afternoon writing.

I smile to demonstrate I was only kidding.

Another long silence.

I smile again.

"I'm sorry," I say. Words he claims he never hears me utter and yet I say them all the time. "Perhaps that was harsh."

Wifely, I am trying to sound wifely. Wifely women get time to write.

Finally, he smiles back. With his eyes. His blue eyes. He never smiles with his mouth. Why would you, if you had eyes like that?

But is he thinking about his exploits abroad?

Or at home?

CHAPTER TWO
Marriage

A good reporter gets better at nuance as the story progresses. Sometimes it takes a few tries. So, if I were to be *absolutely* accurate, I would have to say that while I *agreed* to marry Jim Mulvaney to keep him out of Long Kesh Prison, I didn't actually think I'd have to *go through with it* once we got home to America.

That I did is the fault of only one person: my editor.

Well, what reporter worth her salt doesn't blame her editor for almost anything? Why stop at misquotes, typos, clunky leads, and major factual errors? Why not blame him for my misguided marriage, too?

This particular editor couldn't sit still. But the name we all called him, the name we still call him even though most of us are long gone from *Newsday,* had more to do with the way he dressed than the way he moved.

Leisure Suit. To us he was Leisure Suit.

If any of us remember his real name, we wouldn't admit it. There's a lesson in this: Major sartorial errors made in the flush of youth are hard to live down.

By the time I arrived at the paper—on the heels of Mulvaney—Leisure Suit was already its veteran Suffolk County editor, a job to which he'd ascended quickly. He'd been a reporter, too, but not for long. Unfortunately for us. Just try pitching a *real* story to an alleged human being who hasn't covered one of his own in years. Although back in those days, when newspapers believed they had a future, those were the types that always got promoted. As Mulvaney and I battled it out in Belfast, Leisure Suit, too, ascended. He kept his old title, added a new one, and so was anointed the paper's Suffolk County/Foreign Editor.

In celebration, the advertising department ran a huge photo of him on the buses that traversed Long Island, as if he was already a familiar figure to the poor, carless people who rode them. His mug was also posted on the sides of delivery trucks, and then, noticing something was missing, those busy admen, and adwomen, stayed up all night to write a new slogan:

"*Newsday:* Long Island's largest daily newspaper. At home *and* abroad."

But, alas, as many a reader letter confirmed, the paper was more at home at home. For while *Newsday* covered foreign countries with a greater appetite than it did Times Square, its coverage of the world was random, spotty, whimsical, and heavily invested in the notion that a story couldn't be important unless it had some connection to one of Long Island's two counties, Nassau and Suffolk, and preferably both.

People who wanted the nonprovincial version of what was happening overseas still read the *Times.*

But that didn't bother Leisure Suit a bit. Even better, he believed he owed this accrual of power to us. We were, after all, the only Long Island staffers who were actually overseas when his fortune changed.

In gratitude he promised to make us real foreign correspondents, as soon as the guns-under-the-bed issue was settled. And to let us set up the paper's first Latin American bureau—in Nicaragua, the best international story going. A dream job for me and Mulvaney, even if it was potentially dangerous for the rest of the Western Hemisphere.

So I came back to America with my alleged husband-to-be, figuring we could renege on the whole marriage deal and continue our happy lives as a romantic reporting couple who couldn't stand to be apart—or together. People who broke up with each other often. In retrospect, I should have known this plan wouldn't work when Mulvaney's father, in Belfast to help rescue his son, delivered a typically silly message from Leisure Suit. "No wedding, no Managua," the Real Mulvaney told us. "Too much paperwork otherwise."

To be honest, I thought it was a joke, although to be on the safe side I played along until the plane landed.

But when I spotted Leisure Suit on the JFK tarmac—having crossed what for him was one of life's most perilous borders, the one between Long Island and New York City—I had the sinking feeling my life as a single woman was over.

"I meant it," the editor said as we kissed the ground. "No marriage, no Latin America." He mercilessly twisted the wire on a corked bottle of French champagne until the Real Mulvaney grabbed it out of his hand, popped it, and poured it over our heads.

"You'd better say yes," my Mulvaney warned me.

"Okay," I said, feeling as if people from Northern Ireland to Ronkonkoma were conspiring against my firm resolve to stop this while I still could.

"Louder!" Mulvaney insisted.

"Okay," I yelled, licking champagne from my lips and trying to tell myself this was merely a job-related move, no matter what my mother claimed.

It was, after all, far from the first time a woman got married to advance her career.

Being that we were an engaged couple between war zones, there was no time to make the trek to Fortunoff's—the traditional pilgrimage of the betrothed of Long Island—where silver, china, and other household essentials are selected. There wasn't, in fact, much time for anything, particularly a well-planned wedding.

Some previously unreported true-true facts from the day: The ceremony was about to begin when the jazz pianist Mulvaney had hired in an uncharacteristic fit of romance, and to supplement his boom box, showed up sans piano but with an accordion—and a monkey. Mulvaney, nervous as any groom, but putting his own spin on it, hauled off and slugged him, only to have the guy pop up like a reset bowling pin and swear that his monkey talked—and that it knew things no one had ever heard it say.

I watched as my husband-to-be softened. Even the best of us fall for the promise of an unlikely scoop. Especially when it comes from an even unlikelier source.

Just as peace was restored, the wedding photographer announced that he had a day job shooting subway crime scenes for the MTA.

"Time for one picture," he said. "Then I gotta split."

"Mulvaney," I said, "if you hit him, too, the deal is off."

He looked at me hard with his blue eyes, as if he thought I meant it.

I stared back at him, as if I did.

"They'll send me to Long Kesh if you don't . . ." he said, uttering the very sentence that was supposed to be part of our top-secret, original, handwritten vows.

I put a finger on his lips.

He put his arm around me and, as we continued the ceremony we didn't know we had started, the bar phone at Pier 92 rang off the hook.

Perhaps the solemnity of the occasion—allegedly talking monkeys notwithstanding—got to Leisure Suit. He was as good as his word. As soon as the ceremony was over, he hand-delivered two shiny, new computers from headquarters. Amazing computers. They could send messages to anyone who worked for the large media corporation that owned *Newsday,* the *Los Angeles Times,* the *Baltimore Sun,* and other papers.

All we had in Ronkonkoma was "message pending," which meant that we could talk to one another on our computers. But why bother when everyone was in the same room?

Now we were connected to a large network of reporters. Ones outside of Suffolk County. Leisure Suit really *was* serious about sending us out into the wider world!

I think our editor also hoped that as husband and wife, Mulvaney and I would at least keep an eye on each other.

Why do we assume it is only reporters, not editors, too, who believe their own incredible fantasies?

DISPATCH FROM THE WAR AT HOME Without thinking, I let my hand slip from the screen of my laptop.

"And just what the hell is this?" Mulvaney asks, pointing to the heading above, as if he has found me with something truly dreadful, like a three-thousand-dollar pocketbook or an Ashton Kutcher look-alike.

He leans over, bangs on the keyboard. "There will be no dispatches from the war at home. There will be only the story of my life. Fascinating enough for one book. Or two. No illogical time references like the last time. Beginning, middle, end! That is how all the good ones go. . . ."

My husband, I should mention, has never actually written a book.

"Do not mix up the past with the present. Write one book at a time!"

I shake my head.

"Barbara," he says, softening his tone. "I am pleading with you. As your husband and your protagonist. I don't think any of us can again take the stress of fitting present-day asides into the narrative structure."

He should have thought of that before he got himself thrown out of the hockey rink.

"Can't we just do this one the easy way?"

"Especially not this one," I reply. "It's about marriage."

"So?"

"Marriage has layers."

"Layers?" he asks, as if I mean a cake with white frosting.

"And not just layers. It has complications, tensions, rivalries that make even a tortured premarital romance like the one I wrote about the last time look like a day at the beach."

"If you'd only stop competing with me!"

"Mulvaney," I say. "This book, unlike the last one, is not merely about me and you. Or even me versus you. We are coming at people not as flimsy, short-term partners, but as a man and a woman who have slept in the same bed for more than two decades. This book is about the power of that. That power versus the world, sometimes . . . It's about an entire institution, an institution created by two people who once had—who still have—an itch for each other, and about all the stuff that itch created.

"Marriage isn't a wedding cake, Mulvaney," I say. "It isn't a bakery or even a bread factory. It's all those things, wheat fields included."

CHAPTER THREE
Honeymoon

What if that photographer left because there was some big-deal murder?" my husband waxed dreamily, not too many hours later, as we luxuriated in our bed, and in our new bureau.

Managua, Nicaragua.

Wasn't that the name of a love song?

I sighed and moved closer. We were spending our first night as a married couple in a bed. How normal. And safe. It felt safe. Although you never could tell. We were, after all, in a war zone again. And a Communist one at that.

Well, I thought, with any luck, the worst that will happen is they will read our mail.

"What if he had to leave the wedding to shoot a picture of Son of Sam on the IRT?"

The only thing Mulvaney liked better than a good homicide was a series of them.

He reached under and past the mosquito net that covered us, grabbed an open bottle of champagne, and poured it through the tiny holes so that it streamed, amazingly, right into my mouth. Strained champagne. Somehow he'd managed to do that and keep the fizz.

He did it again.

I loved the way Mulvaney poured, although I did wonder if this would attract the very bugs we were trying to repel.

"Son of Sam," he said, dreamily.

"Son of Sam," I reminded him, "was arrested years ago. He's in an upstate prison somewhere. Attica, probably."

I studied the pink stucco walls of our pretty little cottage, shaded by palm trees and situated in a rich, relatively non-war-torn section of the city, and thought that maybe marriage wouldn't be that bad.

"Maybe there's *another* Son of Sam!" Mulvaney enthused as he poured more champagne through the mosquito net.

God, I hoped not.

I let the champagne swirl in my mouth and realized that it was pretty bad. Even worse than the bottle Leisure Suit had brought to JFK.

"Mulvaney," I said as he turned to do a honeymoon sort of thing, "this doesn't taste French."

"California sparkling!" he said proudly. "And from a Long Island distributor, too! I bought it at the Dollar Store."

"You brought it all the way from Rockaway?" I asked, thinking he meant the 99-cent store near Pier 92. My husband. A man who never missed an opportunity to exaggerate, no matter how small.

How, though, had he found champagne, even champagne this rotten, that cheap?

He looked at me, annoyed. Was this because I had interrupted his romantic overture?

"Not Rockaway," he said. "I bought it here. At the Dollar Store in Managua."

"Managua?" I said.

"Yep. They got a place where the Sandinistas sell American products for American money."

"Mulvaney-true," I said, identifying that necessary small grain of truth.

Was there a dollar store in Nicaragua? I doubted it.

But would the Nicaraguan people love it?

Absolutely.

As I turned back toward him, I smiled.

"They even have that pink stuff you like."

Pink? I hated pink.

I woke before he did and, like many a bride on the morning after, wondered how this had happened.

Getting married to get out of Belfast—and to get to cover Nicaragua—was the least of it. The bigger question was how we had wound up together, period. It was a rare romance that got off to a rockier start than ours had, less than two years earlier.

True, he had all-purpose blue eyes.

What he thought about the way I looked the first time he saw me, he did not say. But I could tell from the way those eyes focused that he thought something, as opposed to nothing at all.

As soon as the romance began I knew it would never last. So why did it?

In the haze of early morning I wondered if Nicaragua *wasn't* the least of it. Tell both sides of the story, I reminded myself. You are, after all, a reporter.

Maybe I really did get married because I wanted to cover Latin America. And if I had, so what? Here were some facts—and if you were a reporter, facts came in handy: I had hated covering Long Island. On my beat, Huntington, nothing ever happened. When Mulvaney left me—for the first time, if not the last—to go to Northern Ireland, I was not only angry over the breakup of the romance. I was jealous, too. Not because he'd meet girls in Belfast but because he'd be getting better stories. And so, I got caught up in a competitive dance with him, and that had spun me straight into marriage to a boomeranging madman, an Irish Catholic kid who walked too fast.

Mulvaney says I was destined for him. If I hadn't been I would have gone to Brooklyn College, married a doctor or a lawyer, or even an accountant like my father, and moved immediately to the suburbs to have children.

"You escaped," he'd reminded me early on. "Just like me."

But not exactly like him. Yes, I'd rebelled. But with logic.

This is not to say Mulvaney's lack of logic lacked charm. When he told me that the nuns at the Catholic school he'd attended as a child all loved him, I believed that. He had an innocence, a trust, an admiration for people who did things better than he could. An intrinsically open nature. Nice qualities in a man.

The net smelled sweet. But no insects had settled. Perhaps mosquitoes didn't like California wine, either.

Perhaps Mulvaney and I did belong together.

Still, that didn't mean we were compatible. But if you listened to another of my mother's many pearls of wisdom, people did not get married because they got along.

His blue eyes opened and I looked at him.

DISPATCH FROM THE WAR AT HOME Why is it that women are always explaining marriage to men, and not the other way around?

"Bakeries, bread factories, and wheat fields!" Mulvaney sneers. "I'd say marriage is more like the New York City subway system. Hot, dark, dangerous, and never-ending. Not to mention confusing."

Question answered.

CHAPTER FOUR
The Honeymoon Is Over

Forget that in the 1980s Nicaragua was America's sworn enemy or that the White House funded the Contras. Everyone in Managua wanted dollars. Landlords, restaurateurs, bodega owners, child guides. Certainly the Sandinista government itself wanted dollars and, to demonstrate this, erected a place where that was the only currency accepted. A simple building in the heart of the city, packed with American-made products. When it came to financing a fracas, the Sandinistas had it down: charge the hand that bites you.

Yes, the Managua Dollar Store was true-true, which ultimately turned out to be all the worse for our very new marriage, although to be perfectly honest I did not see it coming. I went there with Mulvaney and perused the bodega-like shelves, amused by the hypocrisy. With politicians, it's always money that's important. The ones in Managua—their Marxism aside—were the same as the ones in Chicago or Albany or Suffolk County. A reporter's credo if ever there was one. With this in mind, I entertained myself with my own little charade and acted as charmed as a traditional Long Island bride might be on the china- and silverware-buying spree we'd never had. With trembling hands I selected a few things we might need to start our life together in Nicaragua: a bottle of Heinz ketchup, a tube of Bain de Soleil, a bottle of California red that didn't look too bad.

"You want this pink stuff?" Mulvaney asked, handing me a bottle of Oil of Olay.

I shook my head. "My mother sends me plenty," I said. She always had. It was *her* favorite.

The salesclerks, male and female, handled the Dollar Store's products as if they were jewels, wrapping them carefully in brown paper, which they folded and taped neatly so that there were no rough edges. Maids sent to bring home supplies to foreign dignitaries from Ortega-sympathizing countries greeted me politely and without embarrassment, as if we were in the heart of a functioning Communist experiment rather than the Dollar Store it promoted. *"Buenos días, señora. Buenos días."*

But the operation's best customers, by far, were foreign correspondents based elsewhere in Latin America. The "hacks," as they affectionately called themselves, although they were anything but that.

"Everyone comes here," said a reporter from the *Los Angeles Times* whom we'd read but never met before. He was our age but already a legend, even more so than Mulvaney. "It's because they don't sell Pampers in Mexico City. The diapers they sell there leak."

I looked at him with curiosity. He was a notorious romancer—and unattached.

"Greatest babe magnet in the world," he explained, giving the large package a pat. "Get on a plane with these and the women all want to know you."

Mulvaney and I interviewed many Sandinistas, wrote about them, and, in response, got an invitation from Bosco Matamoros, PR man for the Contras. Under the stars of the Nicaraguan jungle we met and interviewed the men he worked for, the other side of the story.

Also interviewing them—for an academic journal, so it posed no competition—was Colm McEligot, whom we knew from Ireland. He was a professor of political science at Trinity College in Dublin, a very tall and renowned "expert" on most regions of the world, excluding his own. When he saw us he pulled a wrinkled cocktail napkin from the pocket of his tweed blazer—too warm for Managua, but Colm didn't sweat—and wrote the name of a woman we should talk to if we went to Mexico City: Doña Venusa Alcalde de Poder. The Doña, he said, was an antediluvian local playwright, a prominent socialite–socialist in her youth, who lived in a large house on the historic and beautiful Plaza de los Arcángeles, most of which she owned.

"And if you want, she'll let you into the mansion next door," he said, winking at me. "Carlos Fuentes once lived there."

Colm and I had had a brief fling once, so I knew that houses occupied by famous people, sometimes even fictional ones, excited him.

Mulvaney gave me a sharp look.

"Don't worry," I said. "If I ever leave you, it will only be for a rest."

*   *   *

"Mulvaney," I asked, when we were alone in our tent, "does either side seem that different from the other?"

"Nah, they both want a better Nicaragua," he said. "And they both want it with American money. But only one side has it . . ."

"So the other side is Communist," I said, and like newly-weds, we laughed together.

"And you talked to that PR man," I continued, thinking, foolishly, that marriage might already be making Jim Mulvaney a more reasonable human being.

"Yeah," my husband replied. "He had a gun. First PR guy I ever met with one."

We lay quietly for a while.

"I've been thinking . . ." Mulvaney said.

"Yes?" I replied earnestly.

"How about a Dollar Store mail-order service for the Latin American foreign press corps? Why go to Managua when Managua will come to you?"

I giggled, thinking he had to be kidding.

But then he turned toward me and, in an austere voice, said: "*This* could make us rich."

I told Mulvaney not to do it. That, one way or another, we would get into trouble big time. Reporters weren't supposed to have businesses, particularly not in the countries they covered.

As a teenager, though, my husband had once commandeered a Garden City golf cart as if it were an Army tank, and ruined the greens, simply because he wanted to.

He messaged everyone he could on his computer, made phone calls to the rest. Within weeks orders were flooding in faster than he could fill them. FedEx trucks arrived several times a day to pick up packages of toiletries, food, and alcohol—*that* part had to be illegal—bound for Mexico and other Latin American countries where American foreign correspondents, in the days before NAFTA, missed not only home but its products as well.

Since we also had to write stories and report and travel—and since I refused to help him—Mulvaney hired a few of our neighbors' maids to cover shipping and handling.

"*A mí no me gusta* details," he explained to them in the half-Spanish he was slowly acquiring.

"The business needs a name," he announced to me. "I considered 'Jergens for Journalists.' Too limiting, though. There's no telling how this could grow."

"Mulvaney," I said, "I want nothing to do with it."

"Ah, but you will. You won't be able to resist."

He took a deep breath and then spat it out.

" 'Sending Toiletries: A Latin International Network.' Very progressive, don't you think? A company for the computer age!"

I repeated it to myself and gasped.

"Mulvaney," I said. "Try it as an acronym."

"Sure," he replied, slowly. "S—T—A—L—I—N."

The Sandinistas, I was sure, were not going to like this.

A Federal Express truck delivered a small package from my mother.

"STALIN! Brilliant name for a capitalist enterprise," she'd noted. "Good work hoisting those commies on their own petard!"

*   *   *

Before long several government gunmen descended on our living room.

"Petard?" one of them asked. "*¿Qué significa esto en inglés?*"

Postcards, I remembered, were the easiest mail for censors to read.

"It's the Mulvaney curse," Mulvaney noted as we quickly boarded a plane to Mexico City to set up a Nicaragua bureau in exile.

"Mexico," Leisure Suit had said, ordering us there. "Didn't you guys have your first kiss at the Taco Bell on Route 110 in Huntington?"

"What curse?" I asked Mulvaney as the plane took off.

"Just when you think everything is going well, it hits you smack between the eyes," he'd said. "Life seems good and then, suddenly, it isn't."

The things one learns after the wedding.

DISPATCH FROM THE WAR AT HOME "Mom," Jack says.

"Honey," I say, "can we talk later? I am trying to remember the quiet, peaceful life I once lived as a foreign correspondent in war-torn and environmentally ravaged places."

"It's time to drive me to hockey," he says.

"You played hockey yesterday."

"That was yesterday, Mom. High school team. Sunday is travel team."

Travel. I never liked that word, not when it comes to kids' sports, anyway.

The local rink is five minutes away. Travel, like the word implies, involves a trip to someone else's rink. An hour away if you're lucky. Worst-case scenario? It's in New Jersey. Worst-worst case? It's a weekend tournament. In Pennsylvania, if not Prague.

I think back to the old days of the high school jock. He played one sport—football usually, which required grass and a helmet. Not ice, not Zambonis, not five-hundred-dollar skates. The rest of the time he walked around being a big jock, letting girls feel his muscles.

Kids today don't have time for this.

They're too busy traveling.

I can smell Jack's bag, filled with aromatic equipment and uniforms I have neglected to launder.

"Isn't your father out on the deck?"

"Just left. Said he had to go save America."

From what? Too many teams?

Jack leans over to read what I am writing. "You're putting Dan and me in this time, right?"

Dan, at eighteen, is three years older. Jack, though, is PR man for the brothers, albeit a necessary one.

"We both want in," he says, puffing out his chest like his father.

"Go make sure you packed your mouthguard," I say, gazing at his teeth and wondering, like any Hockey Mother, if it will be for the last time.

I remember when Jack was a baby. We tried to make Danny feel better about having a brother by saying, "Jack has no teeth."

"Your last book was good," my son reassures me. "I read all 378 pages."

It only had 324.

CHAPTER FIVE
Still Over

One morning months after Mulvaney and I got married—already it felt like years—I spotted him midway through the revolving doors at the Omar Torrijos International Airport in Panama City. Would this, I wondered, always be our way? Spinning in a circle toward each other, before spinning apart again? I hadn't wanted to get married. But now that I was, I worried that it wasn't supposed to be so fragmented.

Perhaps Jim Mulvaney wasn't the right husband for me.

Fast, I said to myself. Run to your connecting flight. Run for your life.

But before I knew it, he'd kissed me fast on the mouth.

"Saw you first!" he said.

When it came to Mulvaney, I never ran fast enough.

*   *   *

The Dollar Store escapade had distracted us. We'd had to move, rent a house in Mexico City, set it up, catch our breath. As a result, we'd lost stories to other papers and now, in an attempt to squelch that competition, we were scurrying throughout Latin America in different directions. We were rarely home at the same time.

I was on my way to Bolivia to interview a Long Island cop who ran guns to Northern Ireland. And Mulvaney? All I could tell was that he'd gone native in a white guayabera, a shirt that did not need to be tucked in. It flapped happily in a tropical breeze he made himself; as always there was a coffee stain. This one was on the embroidered pocket.

"I miss you," he said, smiling, but not with his mouth.

When was the last time I'd seen my husband?

His eyes looked bluer than usual. Canal Zone blue.

He put his hand on my cheek.

Maybe, I thought, the gunrunner can wait.

Funny how that can happen in a split second.

My gaze fixed on a row of souvenir stands, one with a display of thick silver earrings, the kind you can get a lot cheaper in Mexico. Maybe someone had a cousin there who smuggled these down. Mostly the Panamanian airport stands sold *molas,* locally produced wall hangings made from layers of cut fabric. Nice, but how many ways, really, could you depict a rooster?

Rash, I thought. I will be rash. I will buy a pair of those overpriced, oversized airport earrings and wear them to dinner. How long had it been since I'd eaten dinner with my own husband?

We could stay right here in this capital instead of boarding separate flights to the next Latin American city, the next Latin American story. They were all the same story, anyway, weren't they? But eating dinner with my husband, that was unexplored territory. We could dine at the French restaurant at the top of the Marriott. There was talk of martial law. It could make for a romantic view. Escargot. Steak au poivre. A good St. Emilion. And Mulvaney pouring.

I looked him straight in those eyes. He was invigorated. But . . . there was something unsettling about it.

This wasn't over sex.

This was over . . . a story.

I took a minute to consider the facts: I'd had no idea he was in Panama. If I'd known, I might have combed my hair. This could mean only one thing.

Mulvaney had a scoop he wasn't sharing with me.

"Novelist-in-Exile." He nodded, sounding a smidgen guilty. "He just spilled his guts."

Damn.

Mulvaney didn't just have a great story. He had *my* great story. The Novelist, an American on a self-imposed exile, was my source, as well he should have been. A Jewish writer from the city, not an Irish one, not Jimmy Breslin or Pete Hamill. Granted, not I. B. Singer or Philip Roth, either. But Singer lived on the Upper West Side and Roth was in Connecticut, and both those places, unlike Panama, were not on our beat.

Nor, as far as I knew, was Singer or Roth trying to topple a dictator.

The Novelist was, though.

In Panama he'd married a former ballerina and now, in between writing novels about his adopted country's political intrigue, he was going to live the fiction he imagined and depose Manuel Noriega. For better or worse. Not that it was an unworthy goal. Noriega was involved in his fair share of drug smuggling and a political murder or two. He had even, according to some, killed his mentor, Omar

Torrijos, for whom this very airport was named. I didn't believe that. Fog and a drunken pilot was the more plausible scenario. But even the best sources pushed harebrained theories.

Cara de Piña—pineapple face—was what Noriega's own people called him, for his acne-scarred complexion. While among the peasants of his country, the *campesinos,* it might have been a term of endearment, there were a lot of more powerful individuals who wanted him dead.

Still, the Novelist's alleged plan—which he had now apparently coughed up to Mulvaney in its entirety and which Mulvaney could use to make himself look like a genius once the deal was done—had seemed pretty risky to me. Particularly for a *rabiblanco*—literally, a "rich, white tushie." *Rabiblanco.* One of the few Spanish terms I'd ever heard that worked with Yiddish, too. I could see the bilingual headline now:

The *Meshugas* of a *Rabiblanco.*

But the Novelist could wind up getting killed himself in the bargain. And for what? A dictator, true. But a dictator in a region full of them.

"Mulvaney, what did you just tell me?"

He put his hand on my cheek, but I pulled it off.

"Just that he talked," he said casually, getting my drift.

I reexamined that stain on his shirt. Maybe it wasn't coffee. "And what else?" I demanded.

"No big deal. He's just taken a few bucks from some people in Great Neck."

Damn, damn, damn.

Along with stealing my story, Mulvaney had found the Long Island angle for which I'd been frantically searching. When I'd asked the Novelist about funding, he'd clammed up. Was that because he and Mulvaney were in cahoots? Was he saving the story for him? Saving the Long Island angle for him? Leisure Suit still wouldn't run a foreign story without one.

This was really unfair. I'd worked this nutty source, and made friends with him, too. Two different things. Although for a reporter they were often the same. I'd made him laugh when I told him he spoke Spanish with a Brooklyn accent, and he did, even if he was from the Bronx. Hell, I'd even made friends with his wife. Easier to do since I liked her better.

Damn that Mulvaney. My husband and my competitor. He'd probably win some overseas press award this year, with all that the Panama story would open up. Sources, angles, Long Island and otherwise. And I'd even been a little hesitant to get on the plane to Bolivia, since the cop in question was a former Suffolk County homicide detective. Lawmen were Mulvaney's turf.

"On my way to Salvador," Mulvaney announced, interrupting my reverie. "Even better story there."

"Really?" I tried to sound casual, although I felt anything but.

"Wanna come?" he asked.

"And do what?" I asked, genuinely curious.

"Watch me report," he said, dead serious.

He smiled with his eyes.

Blue.

Vapid blue.

"Mulvaney," I said as I scanned the souvenir stands for a piece of pottery heavy enough to throw, "you must be kidding."

Molas only. These Panamanians really liked their textiles.

He put his hand on my cheek again.

I pulled it off.

"Watch you report?" I said.

"Yeah," he said.

"Why would I do that?"

"You're my wife."

"So?"

"So, wives watch."

I put my hand on his shoulder. In contemplating the various perils of war-torn Latin America, I hadn't considered the possibility of my husband's already sizable American-bred chauvinism getting worse with a mere dose of *machismo*.

"My dear boy," I said, sweetly.

Nah, that was too wifely. Something more authoritarian, perhaps. Like those women prison guards in Northern Ireland.

My voice went hard. "If I was going to watch anyone report, it would be someone who actually knows how."

I rolled up the sleeves of my hand-knit Guatemalan sweater.

He tried to do the same with his guayabera, but flared sleeves do not roll easily.

"And you," he said, his eyes ablaze, "couldn't find a Jew in the Bronx."

"Which reminds me," I said. "Keep your grimy hands off Panama."

"And you stay out of Bolivia!"

"Don't you dare tell me where not to go."

And so, I stomped off in the best Mulvaney fashion I could muster.

Behind me, I heard him stomp harder. In the opposite direction.

I stomped hard, again, and wondered how things could change so quickly.

Then *boom,* the loudest stomp of all. Like someone who could—would—cause an earthquake.

Cause an earthquake, and then cover it.

Yes, an earthquake, I thought, wishing one on him.

DISPATCH FROM THE WAR AT HOME Mulvaney is calling on my cell phone.

Has he saved America already? And if he has, will he take Jack to travel hockey in Hauppauge?

"Hello," he says. I hear Ella Fitzgerald in the background. Sounds like Starbucks.

"The children," he says, "cannot be in the book."

"The children," I say, "are in the book."

"It will embarrass them."

"Are you absolutely certain," I say, "that we are speaking about the same children? As in yours and mine . . ."

"It could be dangerous."

"For whom?" I ask.

Jack knew his slapshot before he knew his age. He's played hockey since he was two, and if you asked him how old he was back then, he'd raise three fingers. Maybe, though, that was just Mulvaney hyperbole. Still, in all those years of crash-bang skating, Jack's had no broken limbs and no real injuries, minus a case of whiplash he got from colliding, on purpose, with a kid twice his size.

As for Dan—team sports might not be his thing now. But there isn't a local football coach around who doesn't look at him and hope. Dan is six feet tall; two hundred pounds of pure muscle. His favorite extracurricular activity? Lifting heavy objects.

"You live in a dreamworld," Mulvaney says. "You live unaware of the dangers out there."

This is the flipside of my husband's middle-age madness. He loves cop types. Legitimate ones, anyway. But everyone else is a potential kidnapper or terrorist.

Or is this just another example of his territorial tendencies?

Is he protecting his progeny or his own status as protagonist?

"Mulvaney," I say. "This book is about our marriage. In our marriage we had children. Therefore, the kids are in—"

"Then you will have to make them up."

"My children—" I say.

"Our children," he says.

"Our children," I say, "want to be in this book. Their hearts would be broken if we replaced them with fictional offspring. Besides, people write about their kids all the time."

"Not people with Danny."

Usually, when it comes to Danny, Mulvaney and I are on the same side, even if no one else is with us. We are people in a situation we can't win but are unwilling to abandon. We are George Bush and Condoleezza Rice.

"I gave birth to him," I say. "I took him around the world, too."

Mulvaney sighs into the phone. I imagine my husband's eyes as a deep harbor. Nothing I know has ever made him sadder than what happened to that kid in Hong Kong, although it could have happened anywhere. Living it might have been easier, though, than reliving it in a book.

It was the worst thing that ever happened to me, too. But it happened many years ago.

"You'll either put in too much or too little," he says, trying to regain his status as a bully while his voice shakes. "Tell it serious and it's melodrama. Tell it funny and you sound flip."

This story is neither melodramatic nor flip. And while it is very serious, there are things about it that you can't help but think are funny. That's how we get through. There isn't a day Danny doesn't make us laugh.

No, I can't imagine not telling it. To leave Dan Mulvaney out of the book about us, the funny book about us?

"In our family," I remind Mulvaney, "we have left Danny out of nothing."

CHAPTER SIX
Smog

I woke in the living room on a large couch, one of many in our Mexico City "rental," a mansion at the top of the jacaranda-swamped Plaza de los Arcángeles.

Opening my eyes, I rubbed them. Then I coughed.

This, the world's largest city, was its most polluted, as well.

Even here in historic San Ángel the air was only a few notches better than downtown. Worse some days, if you believed the government's new air monitors, although I didn't. Far as I could tell, the numbers were bogus, a desperate, ineffectual attempt to keep the poor and downtrodden from squatting in the capital's better neighborhoods.

In front of me, on a thick coffee table made from half a tree, sat a stack of old tortillas. I reached out, peeled one off, bit a piece, chewed hard, swallowed, and contemplated life alone in what was, in effect, a glorified stucco airplane hangar set behind mammoth walls in the middle of a yard that could be a park. Too sleepy to move, I examined our garden through an enormous sliding glass door. A patio framed by bougainvillea and, beyond that, a murky kidney-shaped in-ground pool, beside which two geckos sunned themselves like tourists.

Bolivia had turned out to be an okay story. Certainly not a great one. A fact Mulvaney must have known or he would have gone there himself. My Suffolk County cop-turned-gunrunner, like most braggarts, couldn't prove he did half the crimes for which he took credit. After a less than sterling interview, I'd boarded the last plane out of La Paz and filed from home, in Mexico. I'd then sunk into the velvet upholstery, a fading burgundy the color of spoiled wine but comfortable nevertheless. Anything was better than our empty bed upstairs.

Now I stretched, took another piece of tortilla, decided it was not meant for human consumption, and threw it to the geckos. They crawled, in tandem, lazily toward their feast, making happiness look easy. I had a dream job as a foreign correspondent but felt like nothing as much as a deserted wife stuck in a cavernous house I had once foolishly viewed as a possible south-of-the-border love-nest-cum-international-news-hub. That, I reminded myself, was when I was still lighthearted enough to believe that a mere ousting from Nicaragua could do nothing to dampen our reporting. Or our romance, which was now, I reminded myself, our marriage.

Back on the couch I dozed off again, only to be roused by a laconic round of gunshots from the plaza.

"Mulvaney," I said, half asleep, "are we still in Nicaragua?"

But there was no Mulvaney. No war, here, either, unless you counted the one against the environment—and

Leisure Suit didn't. Outside we had neither Contras nor Sandinistas, only Albino, our neighborhood beat cop, who got his jollies by shooting at suspected burglars and car thieves, many of them imagined. Albino, dark-skinned despite his name—victim of the same ingrained national irony that deemed the Day of the Dead a festive occasion—was a genuine Distrito Federal police officer. An honor but not much more, he claimed: "A small salary, señora, a worn-out uniform, and an old pistol."

Mulvaney had, of course, befriended Albino from day one. My husband didn't own a gun, never had. A weapon in the hands of Jim Mulvaney, he'd said himself, had the potential to be one of the most disastrous pairings in the world. And yet he always managed to have something to do with guns, to be around people who had them, to get into trouble over them.

The bell outside our gate clanged.

Albino stood there smiling. "Señora, could you spare some pesos?"

"Sure," I said, checking to make sure law and order reigned on the Plaza de los Arcángeles.

I handed him a few bills. Just like America, cops were always collecting for charity.

"A raffle?" I asked casually.

"No, señora," he said, pocketing the money. "It's for bullets."

"Bullets?"

"*Sí,* señora. We have to buy our own."

For a guy who likes shooting so much, that could be a problem, I thought.

"I only have a few left, señora."

I was back asleep, another twelve hours on the couch, when the phone on the side table rang loudly, an unfamiliar sound since here the phones were more often broken than not. Between the ozone, the gunshots, and these annoying intermittent surges of telecommunications power, how did they expect a foreign correspondent to get any rest at all?

"How's the romance?"

Over a wave of static, I heard the voice of my best friend, Claire Farrell, who was also Leisure Suit's assistant and, given his recent promotions, the editor with whom I dealt the most.

A nearly perfect conflict-of-interest situation.

"It's not a romance," I said. "It's a marriage. Or at least it was. . . ." In the background I heard the familiar noises of the "Gloomroom" (my term for the joyless Ronkonkoma newsroom): Leisure Suit screaming over the latest scoop, the Men Who Didn't coughing over cigarettes as they clacked away at their aging computer keyboards.

"Could be worse," she said. "You could be here."

"Leisure Suit," she continued as the phone crackled, "got your gunrunner story upfront."

"Upfront" meant somewhere on the first seven pages of our tabloid-style newspaper. If your story ran upfront, it meant you'd gotten what we in the news biz—our minds on pulchritude, not headlines—called "good play."

But tonight I wasn't in the mood.

"Yeah," I said, unimpressed. "Bet I know which quote he liked best."

Claire sighed, like someone trying to coax a child to behave. "Okay. You are right. It was the jealous cousin in Patchogue. 'We always knew he'd come to no good. . . .' "

"I have decided that Mulvaney and I are totally incompatible," I said.

"Doesn't mean you don't love him," she said, sounding like my mother.

"I don't!"

Claire sighed again. It was a long sigh, full of static. "Doesn't anything ever make you happy? You have a husband who you never see and you live in Mexico City. Do you know how many people would die to be in your shoes?"

In response I coughed up some polluted air. "The people who live here *are* dying," I said.

She snorted in disbelief.

Lately, I envied *Claire's* life. She had a stable job, a big— but not too big—apartment with a view of Northport Harbor, and a romance with a man who had the same schedule.

"How are things with you and Leisure Suit?" I asked her.

So maybe he wasn't the most dashing figure in the world. At least they both worked in the same country.

Fuming, I began to pace the house. It wasn't just that the rooms were the size of ball fields; there were also too many of them. Living room, dining room, kitchen, den, office suite, master bedroom suite, three more bedrooms, an entire hallway's worth of closets, five tiled bathrooms and a characteristically dilapidated servants' quarters with a bathroom, albeit untiled, of its own. When the new Mexican Revolution—long overdue—came, I could invite a few families to move in and I'd never notice.

The gap between rich and poor was another big story here, but sadly one that Leisure Suit did not understand. In 1985, ten thousand people had died in a Mexico City earthquake. But the place was so crowded and the rich lived so well that you could hardly tell. When we'd first rented this house, I'd thought it might be a good idea for Mulvaney and me to stay put for a while. Get to know each other again. Or, at the least, our better sides. Maybe if we had some time together, we'd be able to figure out the attract-and-repel nature of our relationship and learn to live with it. But to do that we'd have to have stories to write. That wasn't a problem, Mexico had plenty of stories. The problem was Leisure Suit. He liked war stories, mayhem as simple as gunpowder. That's why he'd been so happy to send us to Managua. Contras versus Sandinistas. Black versus white. No gray.

Mexico, however, was more complicated than that.

"I just don't get air pollution," Leisure Suit had said to me.

I'd tried to fill him in on why the faltering integrity of the ozone layer was an issue that should concern a sprawling, car-dependent, traffic-laden suburb like Long Island.

"It's not just a good story," I'd insisted. "It's an upfront story."

As I spoke, I'd pictured our editor engaged in his usual activities, which involved fidgeting with office supplies while vetting all proposed foreign stories to make sure that they weren't, well, too foreign.

"Tell me the Long Island angle again?" he'd replied, coughing himself, into the phone.

DISPATCH FROM THE WAR AT HOME Mulvaney's parents show up moments after I return from a grueling Sunday morning trip to the wilds of mid–Suffolk County, all for the sake of travel hockey. And, of course, my son's happiness.

I sit in the living room facing Mulvaney's father, the Real Mulvaney, and his mother, the former Eileen Goodwin O'Keefe. In truth, she is the former Mrs. Mulvaney, too, having divorced my father-in-law many years ago.

Still, they always arrive at the same time.

"Excuse me," I say when the phone rings, hoping for a reprieve and getting my own mother instead.

"I am trying to write," I say, gazing back at my in-laws.

"It's Sunday," she says. And barely noon, I think. "And I am calling long distance all the way from Boca Raton."

From the same development where everyone from Brooklyn's Congregation B'nai Israel recently moved. They've all purchased cemetery plots next to one another, too. This is a crowd that really likes to stick together.

"Writers write every day," I reply, wondering if it will ever be true in my case.

"Good," she says, changing her tune. She's always been like this, though. "Another book about us! Shirley will be so happy. Brava! More roles for mature women!"

My mother is convinced that the movie based on my first book will be a senior citizen comedy. As for Shirley, I'm not sure which one she means. Shirley Selden is her best friend. But she also says she knows Shirley *MacLaine* from a past life.

Within minutes my father is on the extension, offering to help me "brainstorm."

"I wanted to be a writer before I became an accountant and shul president, you know."

This is news to me. Why did he wait until he was in his nineties to bring it up?

CHAPTER SEVEN
What Was Wrong with FedEx?

Unlike the cop who guarded her plaza, our landlady, Doña Venusa Alcalde de Poder, could not have been more aptly named. She was as imposing as Colm McEligot had warned: beautiful and blonde, with ruling-class white skin. She spoke perfect English, complete with idioms and colloquialisms, and immediately told us that she was descended not from the usual Mexican "riffraff" but from Irish pirates who'd roamed and plundered the Caribbean seas. Mulvaney had just started to chat her up about this when I peered to my right in the immense front vestibule, spotted a portrait of the Doña as a young woman—she'd been quite a looker—examined the signature, and opened my mouth too wide.

"Cousin David," she'd informed me curtly—as in David Alfaro Siqueiros. She rang a large brass bell. "I was wearing pearls that day, but David made me take them off. He said that women with beautiful necks should not hide them with anything as mundane as jewels." She touched hers, unwrinkled still, glared at the maid who rushed in, and, with a flex of her hand, presented us without saying a word.

The Doña's own couches were brocade and flowered chintz. Her furniture was not the heavy Mexican sort but delicate mahogany, imported from Europe.

"So you work for News-*Week*?" She'd lifted a Limoges pot the maid had delivered and poured strong coffee into our cups, her voice hopeful, her amber eyes searing with contempt.

I poked Mulvaney in the side, hoping that he'd adhere to form and tell her anything but the truth.

"Didya know Frida Kahlo?" he asked, sounding more like an NYPD beat cop than anyone *Newsday* would ever hire, much less *Newsweek*.

"*Hijo,*" the Doña replied, frostily, "who do you think slept with Trotsky first?"

Still, she'd rented us the house.

"Of course she did," Mulvaney said later. "We offered to pay with dollars."

For dollars, she'd said, she'd even find us a *muchacha*—a girl, a maid.

"I don't need one," I'd said.

"You will," the Doña insisted, her voice like steel, as she motioned, with her head this time, toward Mulvaney. "Maybe more than one."

A Mexican señora, I said to myself.

What did they do? They ran the house. They ordered the maids around. They got rid of those maids and hired new ones. It could be a day's work.

Slowly I climbed the wide wooden staircase and turned left into the servants' quarters.

"Buenos días, Meni," I called out, coolly, using the nickname the Doña had told me our *"muchacha"*—she hadn't been a girl, though, in years—preferred.

A wedge of peeling paint stabbed my back as I leaned against the wall. No answer from the bedroom. I knocked. The door opened slightly and Amenaza Porvenir slid out.

"Buenos días, Señora Barbara," she said, leaning against the opposite wall.

The morning was smog-choked and cold, but even on a sunlit day, this was about as much as my maid ever said to me. She was austere yet muscular, thin-lipped and prematurely wrinkled. According to Doña Venusa, she'd come from a mountain village so remote the locals spoke their own indigenous dialect. So poor, too, that families pooled what little they had to send their women to the capital, to work for what was a pittance here but a fortune there. The most unfortunate of them, the unmarried, childless women like Meni, were sent first, with instructions to wire home most of their wages to their nieces and nephews.

Those who didn't make it, who got fired or couldn't bear their jobs, the Doña told me, squatted on any empty land they could find and lived in cardboard shacks. "Usually, they deserve it," she'd said, betraying no sympathy, odd for a former Trotskyite.

I hadn't liked Meni from the start. On her first day, she'd batted her sunken, almond-shaped brown eyes, nodded yes and no to all my questions, and then, in what I could already identify as a rare utterance, asked if I could hire her cousin "to help with all the work." In Mexico, I quickly learned, one job always became two.

"¿Como estás?" I now asked her.

She grunted back at me, not sounding even vaguely like a woman whose choice was here or the street.

Then she turned her back and went into her room.

Quickly, before she could clamp the lock, I opened the door, looked at her bed, and gasped.

What we had now was more than a communication issue.

What was that crap on her bed?

I glared at it. Sitting in a rickety chair, she waved a hand, as if she were a señora herself. As if it was nothing.

But it was something.

Packaging from the American toiletries my mother had started sending to Mexico City with abandon, crumpled sheets from recent issues of *Newsday*, and—for structure and foundation—the FedEx boxes in which they'd come. A few bits of orange poked out, too, from DHL, the company to which Leisure Suit had switched after FedEx moved its last Suffolk County corporate office to New Jersey.

And the sum of all these parts? Amenaza Porvenir had constructed a miniature Teotihuacán on top of a faded pink quilt, a crude but identifiable replica of the pyramidal ruins that stood northeast of the capital. And she'd made it all from trash. My trash.

What did *this* mean? From Mulvaney, I knew plenty about beds and junk. But at least he kept his *under* the bed. And it was his junk. Meni, though, was going through *my* garbage? An old reporter's trick. But what did it mean when your maid did it? Was she a witch, a *bruja*? Mexico, I'd heard, had plenty of those.

"You are fired!" I snapped, turning my back and marching out.

"Fired?" she said, rolling the word as if I'd just invented it. Then she slammed her door shut in my face.

Humiliated by the maid! If I was going to live in Latin America, I'd have to get better at this.

I turned away and went downstairs, back to the couch, to contemplate how I was going to survive the life I had once longed for. I gazed at the centerpiece of our living room, the conquistador tapestry, a green silk and gold-thread tapestry of an armored brute and steed, hovering over a throng of shivering Aztecs.

Brakes screeched. I ran outside, looked through the large peephole in the wooden gate of our outer wall, spotted a stream of yellow punctuated by orange letters, and cheered. The DHL truck had arrived. My connection to friends and American newspapers. Even to my mother, whom I missed despite myself. Packages from her typically contained enough provisions—and advice—for a lifetime.

I flung open the gate. But Albino jumped in front of me, waving his pistol.

"Don't waste your bullets," I said. "It's only DHL."

"Feed Ex, señora?"

"Like that," I told him.

Two men sat inside the truck. One behind the wheel and, next to him, his assistant. Two jobs instead of one.

The assistant jumped out while the driver left the motor running, and handed me a box with a return address sticker:

Congregation B'nai Israel of Midwood:

Home of Las Vegas Saturday Nite,
A Great Fund-raising Experience.

Traveling Overseas? Let Our
Congregation Be Your Dollar Store!

The box was wet and slimy, although it didn't smell half bad. I tore it open. Pink goo oozed. I tore more and lifted out a half-open plastic bowl with a Mexican customs inspection sticker taped on top of a sheet of synagogue stationery.

And in my mother's unmistakably overwrought hand-writing—each *i* dotted with a heart:

For my dear, wonderful daughter Barbara who has rarely written to me from either Nicaragua or Mexico. Please note that this Tupperware is filled with multiple bottles of (pure, legitimate, American) Oil of Olay, which I squeezed out by myself over quite a long period of time. I have heard reliable rumors that in foreign countries they try to pass off FAKE moisturizer as the real stuff, often swapping or manufacturing their own labels. Several members of the Sisterhood have been on group tours to Europe and noticed this. I imagine that if they do this in Paris they do it in Mexico. Isn't Mexico, after all, the Paris of Latin America? Or is that Buenos Aires?

At any rate, my dear daughter—yes, you are dear even if you don't write—do not be fooled, particularly in a dry climate like Mexico. If you have any such products, my best advice is to throw them out. Or give them to your maid.

Please tell Mulvaney I loved his story about political unrest in Panama. So much like Israel. But then again, isn't everywhere? It's a shame people can't just get along. Covering dangerous and exciting stories, as he does, must make it difficult to find a rabbi who does conversions. I understand, completely. But if he's ever in Chile, please let him know that Shirley Seiden has a cousin who has a friend whose son is a big macher at the Hillel at the University of Santiago and who I am sure knows someone.

Oh, by the way, I read your Bolivia story. Well, everyone deserves to get a "dud" upfront now and again.

Lucky for you it was a SLOW NEWS DAY!

Your loving mother,
Mom (Ida Fischkin)

P.S. Your father is fine.

"Señora," the assistant said, finally impatient. "There is another."

I wiped my hand on my blue jeans and took an envelope. Inside there was just one postcard.

Exclusive!

Mulvaney's own distinctive, quick scrawl.
  Confidential Sources Reveal: Nicaragua Contras Are Funded by U.S.-Iranian Arms Deals.
  Proof exists. But only in Salvador!

Typical Mulvaney. Too many places and too many plots. And yet another unlikely story. Sometimes I wondered why everyone thought he was such a great reporter, especially when more than half his stories were ridiculous and even fewer than that ever panned out.

Fly here! Many scoops! Under your byline, too!

Ha. I'd heard that before.
  Here's the only advice a woman ever needs: Never share a byline.
  Suddenly, I felt a hard shove from behind and went flying headfirst into the cab of the DHL truck. I pulled myself up on the seat and was shoved again as my maid and the driver's assistant jumped in, slamming and locking the door behind them. It was so tight, I couldn't move. The DHL deliveryman floored the gas pedal, swiftly maneuvering through the quaint cobblestone streets of the plaza.
  "Meni," I choked out, trying not to panic, "that thing about firing you? I was just kidding. . . ."
  I stretched to look behind me and caught a glimpse of Albino waving his—no doubt empty—gun in the air.

DISPATCH FROM THE WAR AT HOME In front of me, in the living room, the Real Mulvaney grouses.

If I try, I can see him in a straw hat, crossing Queens Boulevard from bar to courthouse and back again.

Favoring one hip, he gets up and I feel sentimental. Thanks for the memories.

Then I notice that he is heading for *my* office.

I follow him in and watch as he sits down at my laptop. Even his son doesn't do *that*. "Get offa there!" I shout. But with a white, veined hand, he shoos me away. What am I supposed to do now? Beat up my elderly father-in-law?

Amazed, I watch as he signs on as a guest on my AOL account and then checks to see if any women have sent him e-mails containing dirty jokes. When he gets one, he forwards it to me.

Within minutes, my mother-in-law joins us, although she pretends she has come to look, yet again, at a photograph of her son in the middle of a Belfast fracas. She is keenly aware of her ex-husband and shifts one of her eyes, still startlingly blue, toward the computer.

"Dear," she says to me, "I have no problem with you writing another book about us as long as you mention me minimally, if at all."

She said that the last time and I listened. But everyone else wanted more of her. Particularly after she submitted her own choice for a title: *Yids and Micks.*

"How 'bout if I drive you to Starbucks," I ask the Real Mulvaney. "There's probably a laptop there you can borrow."

My mother-in-law glares at me.

"It has ever seemed to me," the Real Mulvaney says, "that both aspects of that option, cold coffee and women drivers, are subliminal death threats."

CHAPTER EIGHT
For the Price of a Hamburger

Reaching over me, Meni clutched my left hand and pressed hard on my two rings, my wedding band and the Irish Claddagh Mulvaney had given me—love, friendship, loyalty—as she spewed instructions in a language that bore no resemblance to any I'd ever heard.

We raced on, passed an airport taxi speeding toward the plaza and blew past a large plaque honoring the Brigade of San Patricio.

Irishmen who'd fought with Pancho Villa. They'd probably liked his personality.

What were Irish men doing here? Wasn't this Mexico?

The driver's muscles bulged, but the assistant's were bigger. For small Mexicans they looked pretty powerful. I wouldn't be able to wrestle one of them, let alone two.

At the top of the next plaza we capsized an unmanned

churro cart. Sugared sticks of fried dough flipped through the air and pelted the windshield as we sped off onto a wide street and into a torrent of traffic that made the Long Island Expressway look like the highway to Heaven. Bad air pushed its way through the vents.

This city had two and a half million cars. And three catalytic converters.

We hit an intersection and the truck took a quick right down Avenida de los Insurgentes. Tall office buildings, fast-food emporiums, and chain restaurants. Not an insurgent in sight.

We passed a Burger Boy, a Carlos and Charley's, a Pizza Hut, and a Fuddruckers. The driver leaned on his horn and veered right, past a gleaming office building and into a rare open space, an overgrown lot dotted with billboards advertising *pan dulce* and Hennessy cognac. I took a breath, looked up. From here you could still see a smidgen of old Mexico, the blue, yellow, and orange Talavera domes of El Convento de Carmen, a seventeenth-century Catholic monastery.

"Is this a local history tour?" I asked, hoping to lighten the mood.

Editors were always trying to get me to do local history stories.

In response, the truck whipped around the billboards and barreled through a tin gate, which clanged shut behind us as the driver slammed on the brakes.

The four of us tumbled out and I found myself perched on a sandy, garbage-strewn hill, minutes from the old mansions of San Ángel and in the midst of the commercial clamor of Insurgentes. Below us stood a Mexican Hooverville, a sad and dilapidated squatters' village of cardboard shacks. The kind of place Doña Venusa had described. She'd said they could be found all over the city, even in the best neighborhoods, despite those strategically placed government air monitors.

"Paracaidistas," Amenaza sighed, speaking her first words since she'd pushed me into the car. Parachutists, literally. Figuratively, too.

"Down there," she continued, "is one of the best stories in Mexico City."

This woman, I said to myself, should be a PR man.

Only one problem. Poor people in Mexico City—poor people anywhere—were not news. The downtrodden. A story since stories began. More recently, Charles Dickens, Jacob Riis, Jack London, and others had told their tales. And here, as every other foreign correspondent had already written, the poor flocked to the capital in droves, where the rich—citing petroleum prices along with currency devaluation—reacted with about as much compassion as Doña Venusa had. She'd scolded me that I was paying Meni too much. She'd never paid her girls more than fifty thousand pesos a week.

A hamburger at Fuddruckers cost more than that.

And, by the way, Fuddruckers was usually packed.

The driver bent so close to me I could smell his Old Spice aftershave.

"I need a peg," I said. A peg was what got any editor talking to you. Something that distinguished a story from all others like it. With Leisure Suit, of course, every peg had to be followed with a Long Island angle, too.

"Peg, señora?"

"What makes these poor people different from any other poor people?"

"Do not be so impatient, señora!" Meni scolded.

This from a woman who had just reenacted the Indianapolis 500 through historic San Ángel.

She motioned to the driver. He bent even closer and

whispered the name of the man who everyone knew would be the next president of Mexico.

"So?" I said.

"Señora, he owns the land," Meni said.

I tried to act casual, but my eyes opened wide.

Not a bad peg at all.

"Owns that, too," the driver said, pointing to the gleaming skyscraper next door. It was, I noticed, the tallest building for miles. Taller even than the Carmen.

Not a bad story. Hard to prove, though.

But perhaps not impossible.

DISPATCH FROM THE WAR AT HOME When Mulvaney returns, I pull him into the kitchen.

"It's nice to have family around," he says. "We didn't have this when we were foreign correspondents."

He forgets how often they all came to visit.

"Get rid of them!" I say.

"I hope we love each other as much as they do when we are that age," he replies.

"Mulvaney!" I say. "Your parents are divorced."

"Only in writing," he replies, as if that doesn't mean a thing.

CHAPTER NINE
Long Island Angle

Meni and I, the DHL deliveryman, and the assistant walked down the hill, closer to the cardboard shacks. I took a breath and tried not to take another. The subtle, rotting stench of pollution, ever present in Mexico City, mixed with other odors here: burnt charcoal, old sweat, and the sewage that sat in a narrow canal. Tall, splintering wooden poles lined its pockmarked banks, attached to one another by a thin wire laced with more wires. Dozens of them flapped in that rotten air, connecting, eventually, to the shacks. Pirated electricity. Was the water stolen, too? I saw a lone spigot burp out dirty spurts and wondered who would want to steal it.

Meni led us deeper. Some of the cardboard shacks were coated with tar. "The rich," she said, wryly. We were seconds away from one of the busiest streets in one of Mexico

City's wealthiest neighborhoods, but except for a slum in Guatemala, I had not seen worse. Probably I hadn't been in Latin America long enough.

School-age children, some with open sores on their mouths, peered up with interest as we filed past. Small faces appeared in the doorways along our path. A little girl hugged a naked plastic doll that was missing an arm. Ahead of us, at a dusty intersection, a boy threw a ball made from paper bags. "¡*Yanqui!*" said the next boy, the one who caught it without taking his eyes off me. He waved to Meni and, in that strange tongue of hers, she called out instructions.

"Follow him, please, señora," she said, as the boy made his way down the cross path, past more shacks. He looked about ten, but these kids were so undernourished it was hard to be sure. Two younger girls joined him, one of them carrying a toddler with a runny nose, which she wiped with the torn hem of her skirt. They stopped in front of a charcoal stove. A rusty coffee can filled with water sat atop it; a package of powdered baby formula was propped up against a rotting chair.

The boy disappeared behind an old plastic garbage bag, a makeshift door. In a moment, a little woman carrying a screaming baby lifted it open again.

"Meni," she said, and the maid nodded.

"My cousin, señora," she said, introducing us.

The woman had rail-thin arms that swam in the short sleeves of a faded pink polyester sack dress. The baby had arms like its mother.

I searched for something to say.

"What is your little girl's name?" I asked, finally.

"She doesn't have one, señora." The woman spoke in careful Spanish.

I knew I should ask the next question. A good reporter always does. But sometimes, you don't want to know the answer, for purely selfish reasons. Did I want to remember this for the rest of my life? Did I want to remember that when this woman looked at me with desperation, all I could offer was the next question?

"What would you like to name her?" I asked gently.

"Señora," Meni's cousin said, "do you know anyone who will buy my baby?"

"Excuse me?" I said. But I'd heard her correctly and she knew it. I could write this and make it a real tearjerker. But what good would that do this poor woman? What good do most of our stories do?

"What is your day like?" I asked, desperately trying to change the subject. A good all-purpose question. One you can ask of paupers—and princes.

"I work at night," she said.

"All day, too," I said, looking at the children.

She smiled weakly.

And we were quiet.

Then, slowly, the path in front of us began to fill with squatter children and their parents and their wrinkled grandparents, although I was sure those grandparents were younger than they looked.

In a chorus, amazingly synchronized, they called out, *"¡Mira! ¡Mira! ¡Mira! ¡El Ángel!"*

And, indeed, coming from the direction of the Plaza de los Arcángeles and from the old convent, El Carmen, was a white silk arch, one long scalloped wing, sailing toward the open space past the billboards and above the shacks. Well, it looked like an angel, or a magical, airborne swan. A grizzled man threw a weatherbeaten ladder against his shack and climbed carefully onto a rare tin roof. The bubble dipped, and I realized I'd been a bit too taken with the romance of the moment. Just some skydiving nut. They had them in Mexico, too.

"A real *paracaidista*?" I asked Meni.

She nodded. "There's a priest at the Carmen who likes to float," she said, her voice flat.

Well, if there was a Flying Nun . . .

"Sounds joyous," I said.

She uttered a few words I didn't understand, Mexican slang or her own language. Definitely *maldiciónes,* though. Curses. "*Claro,* señora, entertaining deprived people is a lot of fun. He lands, tells them stories, goes away. Never sends food."

The parachute came closer; the crowd cheered louder.

"Let them eat sweet rolls," she continued in loosely translated Spanish. "Is that the English expression?"

I nodded.

"I'll tell you why," she said, as the priest touched ground with a thump, on a clearing beyond the shacks. All I saw was a white parachute—and a white collar. "I'll tell you why he would rather entertain than help. Because in Mexico the politicans and the priests share from the same plate."

The people on the path ran to meet their "angel." Meni stood firm.

But her cousin looked longingly toward the crowd.

Then she handed me her baby with no name.

Nervously, I grasped the kid. This was a person, something of value, which was, I guessed, the point her mother had tried to make. I looked at Meni to see if she would take the baby from me. When it came to maternal instinct, I wasn't sure I had enough to keep this kid happy. But Meni looked right through me.

Well, it wasn't as if I needed my hands for anything else. I didn't have a notebook or a pen; people who get pushed into trucks often don't.

I would have to remember the important things everyone said. Verbatim. Or I'd have to paraphrase—and that never went over well with Leisure Suit, who was, among other things, a direct-quote type of guy.

The baby with no name whimpered and I rocked it back and forth.

"So where do you work?" I asked Meni's cousin, who had by now taken two of her older children in her arms, apparently deciding not to run with the crowd.

"Up there." She pointed her head toward the skyscraper, the candidate's building. My eyes widened. I gripped the baby tighter but loosened my hold when she moaned.

"I clean," Meni's cousin said.

You can learn a lot about people from their garbage.

"Many of us clean there, señora. . . ." she said.

I am, I thought, in Reporters' Heaven.

I was ready to ask the next question when gunshots rippled in the distance. Twice in one day, I thought. Who needed Managua?

The cousin and Meni gasped, grabbed more of the lingering children, and with them we ran into her hut, which was about as bleak inside as it had seemed it might be.

The kids, in all their various shapes and sizes, let out a collective scream, not unlike the adults when they'd seen the priest. People here stuck together; they had to.

"Unhand her!" a voice boomed in Spanish from outside.

Maybe this baby-with-no-name did have a father. I clutched her tighter and, at that, she let out her own yelp, loud for a kid that small and skinny. But there was no place to put her other than the dirt floor. And it wasn't as if anyone else had any free arms.

Suddenly the garbage bag door swung open and two men walked in.

Albino the cop and . . .

"Mulvaney!" I gasped. "What are you doing here?"

"What am I doing here? I am rescuing you. What are *you* doing here?"

"I am holding a baby and conducting an interview," I

said, as if these were two activities that normally went together. "And you," I added, "are ruining my story!"

"Doña Venusa said you'd been kidnapped."

Albino jerked. I still had the baby but rushed him anyway, grabbing his gun. He was a little man, easy to overcome. "No more money for bullets!" I scolded the cop.

"Mulvaney, how did you find me?" I asked, angrily. An ungrateful damsel in nondistress.

"Crack police work," he said, motioning toward Albino, who grinned proudly.

A group of *paracaidistas,* their thirst for entertainment whet by the flying priest, came through the garbage bag door.

"Su esposo!" someone cheered, although that was not exactly my reaction to the sight of my husband.

"Esposo de la periodista!" a few more people cried out.

Why did Mexicans think that if you socialized with a man he had to be your husband?

And why did they think this was socializing?

"Mulvaney," I said.

"Calm down," he said.

"Calmáte," an old man agreed, nodding his head furiously. I wondered how many wives had left him.

"Señor," Meni's cousin said, "where do you come from?"

"Long Island!" Mulvaney announced.

"I hear that even poor Yanquis are richer than us," she said.

I watched as he looked at the skinny infant still in my arms, then looked away as if he couldn't stand it.

"They are," he gulped.

Often, it's not the reporters but their sources—and they don't have to be rich or powerful sources—who ask the best questions.

DISPATCH FROM THE WAR AT HOME It seems that my in-laws have been visiting forever when Jack returns from practice on his own. He greets his grandparents, slaps his father five, and then pulls me into another room, just as I had pulled his father minutes earlier. Maybe if we all said things in the open, everyone would leave.

It is only Danny who gives me any peace, preferring to be out all day with people who help and understand him. I do envy him that.

Jack tells me he got a ride home from a father who lives in Queens but loves—loves—to travel to Suffolk County so that his kid can play more hockey. "He drives two, three times a week," Jack says. "But he can't this Wednesday. Can you?"

"Why doesn't he ask Dad?"

"He says he doesn't want to bother Dad. Dad, he says, is a hero."

A hero?

"Everyone who plays hockey on Long Island thinks that ref is a jerk. They want to give Dad a parent trophy."

For obnoxiousness?

"For courage," Jack says, beaming with pride. "For putting that rink official in his place. And for watching in the rain."

So much for Zero Tolerance.

From outside I hear neighbors stationed below the deck. Lots of them come to gape at it now. I think they assume I paid for it with all the money I made writing about Mulvaney. My husband, as you may imagine, says nothing to dissuade them even though the true-truth is that, like many Long Islanders, we don't live so much off our wages as we do our home equity loans.

The neighbors cry out for Mulvaney. They've just read the first book, can't believe they live near such a fascinating man, and can't wait to hear him tell some war stories. No need for him even to come down from that deck he loves so much. He can just boom out those tales from on high. Like Moses. Or Mussolini.

CHAPTER TEN
Angles

Mulvaney bounded after me through the heavy wooden door of our sprawling Mexican rental, brandishing a bottle of Chilean red. He kissed me hard on the lips as he crossed the threshold, which I had to admit—but only to myself—felt good. Then he pulled a corkscrew from his pocket, opened the wine, and passed it to me. I took a slug and passed it back.

"Mulvaney," I said, "what happened to your guayabera?"

He shrugged. "I came home because I missed you," he said. "Who cares where my clothes are?"

I'd given Meni the rest of the day off. How much maid "service" could one person take? But just because Mulvaney and I were home alone did not mean we were speaking to each other. At least not from my point of view, I thought, gulping again from the bottle.

Encouraged by the wine, my husband moved closer. He grabbed glasses from a large, thick breakfront.

"Mulvaney. I have work to do." I turned toward the office suite, hoping this was one of those rare days when the Mexican phone system worked.

"Fischkin," Leisure Suit said, "I just don't see a story."

Talk about a one-note editor. For a good ten minutes I had described every detail about the *paracaidistas,* every shred of pathos, every nuance about the peg. I'd offered to dress up—or was it down?—as a maid so I could get into the candidate's building with the cleaners at night. And I swore—swore on my mother's life, since she was used to me doing that—that come hell or high water I would dig up a Long Island angle, even if there didn't, at the moment, appear to be even a remote indication that one existed.

The phone line from San Ángel to the Gloomroom was as full of static as ever. Acting more like Mulvaney than myself, I pounded my fist on one of the heavy wooden desks Doña Venusa kept here, instead of in her own home.

"A presidential candidate!" I repeated to Leisure Suit.

Pound!

"Poverty-stricken squatters on his land."

Pound!

"Raw sewage, dirty water, life-threatening electrical connections."

Pound!

"The election is next month!"

POUND.

"It's his land, Fischkin, and they're not paying him any rent." Grinding now mixed with the phone noise; Leisure Suit sharpening a pencil to its nub. "He sounds like a pretty nice guy to me. Maybe he *should* be president."

I put the phone down, examined it. It was shiny and navy blue, a very fancy instrument considering that it hardly worked. I counted to ten, picked it up.

"Boss," I said, "he's a very rich man and he's going to be president and people who live on the land he owns and maintains are so desperate they are selling their babies."

When it came to tyranny, you had to be very specific with this editor.

"What if he doesn't win? Mexico's a democracy, isn't it?"

This from a man who'd learned all that he knew about Mexico at Taco Bell.

"He got the *Dedo*," I said.

"The what?"

"The finger. It's a metaphor," I said, as my insides filled with despair. When it came to understanding metaphors, my editor was even worse than my husband. "The current president picks his successor—he fingers him—and then everyone votes for him." Static filled the line.

"You don't have a Long Island angle!" Leisure Suit yelled.

"I told you, I'll find one!" I yelled back and pointed my own middle finger at the phone. But he had already slammed it down.

I looked up and realized Mulvaney was standing as close to me as he could be in this vast office at the end of this vast Mexican house.

"You want me to fix it?" he asked.

Usually he broke things.

But he did know how to break a story, despite what I sometimes said about him. Particularly when all hope seemed lost.

Sometimes . . . Mulvaney could be ingenious.

"It will cost you," he said.

I really wanted to write this story.

"Anything," I said.

DISPATCH FROM THE WAR AT HOME My mother. Her second phone call of the day. She talks. I listen. Just as I think she's about to hang up, she says, "Oh! I forgot your father." A problem as old as their marriage.

When he gets on, he muses—long and in detail—about the years he spent as the Perpetual President of Congregation B'nai Israel of Midwood.

"I miss them days, toots," he says.

I don't doubt it. He was a big shot. There, at least. And it was fun, even if his wife did start a Las Vegas Nite fund-raising event that just happened to be a little bit illegal.

"I've started to write my own memoir," he adds. It was only hours ago that I found out, for the first time in my life, that he even wanted to be a writer.

"When did you start?" I ask.

"As soon as we hung up, toots. You inspired me."

I feel an unattractive surge of jealousy. My elderly father—an accountant!—has gotten more writing done today than I have.

"Writers write every day, toots," he says. Now, where did I hear that before? "And in my case I don't have a lot of time to waste. Writers age quickly, you know."

"Quicker than accountants," I agree.

He tells me his memoir won't only be about the shul. It will also "depict" his working life as an *upstanding* civil servant—my father was once in charge of reconciling all of New York City's welfare checks—and his experience as a *minor* player in the corruption of Brooklyn politics.

"Leave out the part where you cooked Stanley Steingut's books," I suggest. "Nobody cares anymore."

"Well, toots," he huffs, "if it's not interesting enough for you, I can always fictionalize. Seems to be quite the fashion."

CHAPTER ELEVEN
True-True

"Howyadoin', Doc? And how's The Lodge? All booked up, I hope."

Mulvaney flipped on the speakerphone and static crinkled in the office suite's smoggy air.

Despite its cozy name, the Lodge was not a hotel but a well-known soup kitchen and shelter in Hempstead, a struggling community uncomfortably situated next to Garden City and not far from the mansions that lined Stewart Avenue.

The Doc wasn't a real doc either, at least not the medical kind. He was a genuine Ph.D., though, a retired history professor who had once taught at Boutique U., an expensive, well-attended—and carefully gardened—Long Island bastion of higher education.

He was also a genuine lefty. If the Doc were to decorate

something with a Cortés motif, it would be a conquista-dor's scalp.

"Mulvaney," he said, "doncha read your own paper?"

New York sarcasm flew through the air—it was more than words, it was tone—and I realized how much I missed hearing it from someone besides my husband.

"Mulvaney," the Doc continued, "let me be biblical. There ain't no room at the inn. There ain't even an inn. The Lodge is *officially* out of business."

According to the Doc, the soup kitchen had lost its lease to a Foodtown. Another victim of Long Island's skyrocket-ing property values.

"And ya didn't go out with class?" Mulvaney asked him.

By the time they hung up, there was a plan to do just that.

As a post-final act, the residents and clients of the Lodge—now scattered in underutilized motels through-out Nassau and Suffolk, poor but Long Island poor, not Mexico poor—would hold an unauthorized benefit garage sale in the Foodtown parking lot.

And they would send half their proceeds to the *para-caidistas* of Insurgentes.

"Long Island angle!" Mulvaney said smugly.

"I love it," Leisure Suit cried out, when, after a few tries, we got connected. "Love it. Love it. Love it."

From outside, I heard a guitar strumming *"Cielito Lindo."*

"Write your own budget note," Leisure Suit offered, grandly. This had nothing to do with money. "Budget" was just a fancy name the editors gave to their daily list of sto-ries. Jargon. Or better said, "journalese."

Still, if you got to write your own budget note, instead of the editors doing it, you could position your story your way and hold on to at least a shred of control.

Sometimes.

Ay, ay, ay, ay, canta y no llores . . .

The music got closer.

"I gotta go," I told Leisure Suit. "I have mariachis in my backyard."

Mulvaney pulled me upstairs, past the large canopied bed supplied by our landlady the former Communist—or something like that—and out onto our balcony so we could have a better view of the musicians he'd hired from the Plaza Garibaldi. When had he found the time to do that? In between the Mexico City Airport and my alleged rescue?

"You found a great story," he said as a lone guitar strummed the start of a new tune. "It will get good play." The other musicians joined in. From underneath a golden fringed sombrero, a voice more suited for opera sang.

Good play, I agreed, was as good as good sex.

Mulvaney's eyes turned *azul*—Mexican blue.

Well, good sex *could* be better than good play.

"Una más para la señora," he called out to the mariachis.

I hugged him. "You're learning Spanish!" For a Latin America correspondent, this would come in handy.

From our reheated marital bed, the second of our relatively new marriage, I heard beating thunder, the swoosh of large, wide, strong bands of steel.

Suddenly, a wall of metal adorned with a painted American flag appeared in the balcony window.

As Mulvaney leaned in, I jumped out of bed.

"The U.S. Army is here!" I screamed.

"So?" he asked, trying to pull me back.

I shook Mulvaney loose, wrapped myself in a stiff woolen blanket, and ran out to the balcony as a chopper from the 101st Airborne hovered next to our swimming pool, its two sets of propellers gradually slowing but not stopping. The mariachis had dropped their instruments and were throwing themselves over the wall that separated us from the Plaza de los Arcángeles, as if they'd forgotten that they were in their own country and not illegal immigrants being hounded by American officialdom.

In this case, airborne American officialdom.

Missing a bass guitar by a hairbreadth, the copter landed with a jolt and, as its propellers quieted, a door opened to reveal a short man with a white carnation pinned to his suit lapel: Gary Ackerman! My favorite Long Island congressman, even if he was from Queens.

I pulled my blanket tighter with one hand, waved with the other. Mulvaney was behind me. "You're naked!" I said.

"Why not? Nothing to hide." He grinned and pointed. "Look!"

Behind Ackerman, waving an Irish flag, stood Nassau County Comptroller Peter King, a congressional hopeful himself.

"It's a bipartisan landing." King, like most Long Island politicians, was a Republican.

Ackerman lifted a megaphone decorated with a Star of David.

King raised one with an *Irish Echo* logo.

"Mulvaney!" Ackerman ordered. "Get dressed!"

"We're taking you to Washington!" Peter King added.

So much for good sex unimpeded by the American government.

"Iran-Contra," the congressman roared, "is true-true!"

I remembered the postcard he'd just sent me. *Nicaragua*

Contras Are Funded by U.S.-Iranian Arms Deals. So unlikely, I had thought at the time. Amazing!

"Guess I gotta go," Mulvaney said wistfully. The House
Foreign Affairs Committee was, after all, waiting.

I nodded. Just hours earlier he had, in effect, parachuted
in. Still, we were married now. It wasn't as if we had missed
our only opportunity.

"Mulvaney," I asked, "did you ever actually file anything
about any of this?"

He pulled a pile of dirty clothes from his oversized carry-
on. How could I ever have contemplated firing Meni?

"It started with deep background," he said.

Deep background, when it's legit, lets you in on the big
picture. An idea about what a story might be. Reporters,
the good ones, treat it as information they can't print; information that only exists to help them ask the next questions of the next sources, the right questions from the right
sources.

"Do I have any clean pants here?" Mulvaney asked.

I shook my head.

He took a pair of crumpled jeans from the dirty pile, put
them on, kissed me goodbye. "I needed to get more people
to talk. Finally, someone said something off the record."

Off the record is hope. It's not the real thing, just the
story you might have. You can't quote people by name, although you might be able to quote them as sources, depending on your editor. Any editor worth his salt will make
you get someone to talk on the record, too.

"Just being my usual cautious self," Mulvaney said, as he
threw his carry-on around his neck and climbed over the
balcony and down a trellis to the yard. "I couldn't write it
till someone went on the record," he called back at me.

It's true that once someone says something on the record,
it is the same as shouting it out loud. That person has then

spoken for attribution. Those words, *for attribution*, give a reporter the power he or she needs to tell the truth.

But did a congressman shouting "Mulvaney is right" through a megaphone while standing inside a helicopter parked in a ball-field-sized garden in the middle of Mexico City constitute "on the record"?

As soon as Mulvaney left, I went into Meni's room, borrowed a pair of her cheap Mexican jeans and the flowered apron she wore over them. That would be enough. No sense overdoing it. I left her a note about it, too. She'd probably be back tonight, since except for her cousin's shack, she had, as far as I could tell, nowhere to stay.

I arrived at the candidate's building as the *paracaidistas* began the night shift. They let me in. Showed me where to go. Where to snoop.

It *is* amazing what you can find in people's trash.

The next morning I woke up and started making phone calls. Over the next few days, I went to see people.

And soon, I had enough to write.

Budget Note
Ronkonkoma/Foreign Bureau
Main: Mexican Election

Latin American correspondent B. Fischkin takes an in-depth look at our economically struggling neighbor to the south—and at its economic inequities—by focusing on a desperate squatters' village a stone's throw from San Ángel, one of the richest neighborhoods in Mexico City—and situated on land owned by the man designated to be the country's next president after the charade of an upcoming vote. Interviews ranging from squatters' village residents—

including the woman who cleans the honcho-in-question's private office and is so poor she has considered selling her own child—to opposition candidates who don't have a shot. Venusa Alcalde de Poder, internationally acclaimed Mexican playwright, community activist, and national history buff, speaks about the neighborhood's efforts to help the poor who live in its midst. "We need to do more," she agrees. The candidate, in a statement released by his Hombre Para Relacciones Público, refused to comment on his role as "landlord."

Sidebar: Pennies for Paracaidistas

Fischkin explores a Long Island angle: The Lodge, Long Island's most prosperous soup kitchen and shelter, loses its lease and holds a farewell garage sale to raise money for the squatters of San Ángel. PR *hombre* says presidential candidate is "grateful to the Long Islanders who helped my people."

That done, I had time to reflect.

Marriage is a give-and-take affair, I told myself.

Sometimes, I knew, I didn't give my husband his due.

But the light, constructive criticism I occasionally directed his way was meant only to improve him, to shape his unusual essence into something a touch more stable. To make him a drop saner, more organized, calmer, focused. Just a little fine-tuning. It's a wife's prerogative.

Still, when he did something good, I figured I'd better let him know.

I went back to the computer and sent him an electronic love note.

Iran-Contra, Mulvaney. That is yours!

White House operatives, hoping to be heroes, sold guns to Iran in exchange for hostages. And then they funneled some of that money to the Nicaraguan Contras. I am not sure that even my husband could have dreamed that up. But that he found it—that he spotted it and got it—made perfect sense.

DISPATCH FROM THE WAR AT HOME From Boca Raton, my father is reading me the first chapter of his memoir.

" 'Your Father, the Accountant, by Dave Fischkin (former Perpetual President of Congregation B'nai Israel of Midwood).' "

"Daddy," I say. "It's been a long Sunday here."

He continues:

My only regret is that I wasn't funny.

No siree, toots.

No one I know has ever called me funny and there's no reason to suspect this will change after I am dead. My loved ones are very particular when it comes to comedy.

With more experience, though, I might develop new regrets.

Hey, wasn't that funny?

As you may have guessed, I was an accountant.

I sigh—audibly—into the phone.

"Glad you like it, toots! Such great advice you gave me, too. Years ago. When you didn't even know I wanted to write."

What, I wonder, was that?

"To read out loud to a sympathetic but critical audience."

Are they ever the same thing?

Accounting is not a profession known for its sense of humor. Have you ever heard a good Enron joke?

No siree.

Not even in heaven.

Not even from Arthur Andersen.

*Best I can hope for is that I die a funny death, a hu-
morous morsel for my relatives to chew over with the few
friends I have left.*

Finally, hours later, the house is quiet. My in-laws waited
for Danny to arrive, then left. Separately or together, I do
not know. No one ever does. Dan is now happily asleep.
Jack is IM-ing the last of his thousands of friends, all of
whom claim to have also finished their homework.

"So," Mulvaney says, "now that the shoe's on the other
foot, do you get it?"

"Mulvaney," I say, "what are you talking about?"

"Your father's fictionalized memoir. Don't you just want
to stand over him while he writes it?"

"No," I say.

My husband chuckles. "That's because he hasn't gotten
to the part about you."

CHAPTER TWELVE
More or Less True

I t would be weeks before the details unfolded, years before an Independent Counsel—who, like many lawyers, could have used a few lessons in writing succinctly and on deadline—filed his report. But on the evening that an American helicopter landed in the backyard of our rented Mexico City mansion, I am convinced that my husband knew more than anyone about the government arms fiasco that would go down in history as "Iran-Contra."

Was it Mulvaney who'd coined that phrase?

Days before, still in Salvador, he'd called Gary Ackerman, then Peter King, and told them what he knew. He owed them. They'd been the only American politicians in Northern Ireland when Mulvaney was arrested in his own weapons imbroglio. He needed them, too, to help him find out more.

Understandably skeptical, the congressman and the comptroller launched a very private investigation of their own, only to be interrupted by a newsflash that a cargo plane heading into Nicaraguan rebel territory was shot down by a Sandinista soldier brandishing a Soviet anti-aircraft missile. The plane was only modestly stuffed: 101 machine guns, 100,000 artillery rounds, 70 grenades and launchers. Of the four crew members, only one survived—an American, yet another professional gunrunner, although not of Irish descent. Shaken and scared, he said he worked for the CIA and then coughed up a story remarkably similar to the one Mulvaney had told Ackerman and King.

Hearing that, the congressman and the comptroller had only one choice.

"Plaza de los Arcángeles," they said to the pilot of the Army helicopter they'd commandeered.

On the way back to Washington, Mulvaney wrote what he knew. Ackerman and King told him more. He called the story in to Leisure Suit from a landing pad in Virginia, where he was joined by the Real Mulvaney—who had rushed in once again to act as his son's lawyer, just in case the government tried to pressure him to reveal his confidential sources—and by Dan Tubridy, proprietor of Pier 92, the finest dining establishment in Rockaway, Queens.

Nothing big ever happens in Mulvaney's life without his father's bartender being there.

The story got great play, better than any I had ever seen. They even started the text on the front page, which almost never happens with a tabloid format. In this case, good play was certainly as good as good sex—and considerably better than any my husband had gotten recently.

I hoped, anyway.

He called to tell me that Peter King had rescued his vintage doctor's bag, the one that a group of Long Island medical examiners had given him and which he'd toted all around Northern Ireland, particularly when he wanted to be someone he wasn't.

"My byline in the paper and my old bag at my side," he said, sounding very pleased with that rendition of Mulvaney-style poetry. A line, I realized even then, he would no doubt dredge up again. Hopefully never in reference to me.

I did not think anything could be more incredible than Iran-Contra itself until I heard that Leisure Suit read Mulvaney's story as soon as he filed it—and instantly proclaimed that he understood it.

Iran-Contra he understood. But air pollution continued to elude him.

Riding high on Mulvaney's achievement, the editor then suggested a Long Island angle of his own, which, if nothing else, demonstrated a creative side I didn't know he had.

Unfortunately, what Leisure Suit wanted—what he quickly demanded—was a sidebar scolding Nassau County comptroller Peter King for using taxpayer dollars to travel to Mexico City in a government chopper.

"He came to pick me up," Mulvaney protested.

Irony was also proving difficult for Leisure Suit.

Peter King, still on the Virginia landing pad with Mulvaney and his entourage, laughed, took the phone, and offered a trade. If *Newsday* canned the story of his free ride—his *legal* free ride, he pointed out—he'd give up the honchos of his own party, most of whom he didn't like anyway.

"Property taxes," Peter King said.

Nassau County Republicans—former Brooklyn Democrats with large backyards—were, apparently, not taxing themselves quite enough.

I'm told that back in the Gloomroom, atop the City Desk Without a City, our editor danced as if he had maria-chis in his own backyard, while Mulvaney scurried through Washington, interviewing anyone who would talk. A scandal like this could generate stories for years.

My own exposé did not produce quite as much noise.

Except from me.

When I saw it, I waved my arms like helicopter pro-pellers and slammed the newspaper on the ground, star-tling our formerly tranquil twin geckos. They had changed and had begun to compete mercilessly with each another. Now they battled for space in the empty DHL box that had held the offending copies of *Newsday*. I wondered if they had recently married and then remembered that, in my equivalent human experience, this type of behavior started way before the wedding.

"What's with you two?" I inquired, peering at them squashed together inside the orange box. "Did you fall in love?"

Since there was no answer—what would they say, even if they could?—I lay back on the poolside chaise longue, shaded by bougainvilleas, although it did not improve my mood.

The front page of the latest *Newsday* glared up at me, mocking.

Long Island Homeless Send Aid to Mexico; Presidential Candidate Grateful.

The sidebar was on the front page. While the main story—the real one!—about a corrupt Mexican presiden-tial candidate had been buried alongside department store ads.

How could Leisure Suit let this happen?

How could I have imagined he wouldn't?

Meni appeared with a pitcher of piña coladas and two glasses. I offered her a drink, which she took and gulped. At least I was getting used to having a maid, even if we didn't have your typical employer-employee relationship. In truth, she had led me to a good story, no matter what they did to it back in Ronkonkoma. And wasn't that all I wanted, anyway? To tell a good story? I didn't even need a happy ending. I just needed the story. And I had it.

Someday I might even be able to tell it the right way.

When it came to endings Meni was, I suspected, more like me. Otherwise, why wouldn't she have taken her cousin's baby? There was more than enough room here. Not that I wanted a baby.

The maid picked up the DHL box and shooed out the geckos. I nodded, as if to say she could have it. Using garbage to re-create historic pre-Columbian monuments seemed to be nothing more serious than a hobby that soothed her need to make a cultural statement. I could use one like that myself.

"You can have the newspaper, too," I told her.

"You don't want to keep it, señora?"

Aloud, I translated the headline, even though I was sure she and the DHL deliveryman—and his assistant—had sneaked a look earlier. Those three characters knew more English, more of everything, than they let on.

"Ay," Meni agreed. "Still, señora, the truth's all there. It says he owns the land and the building. It's just presented nicely." *Simpático.*

"But is that the way to do it?" I asked her, thinking it wasn't.

She gave me a dark look. "Señora, it's better than what we'd get here. Our own newspapers wouldn't touch it. I tried."

Sometimes it takes a while to get a story into print. Not that it would be easy. It was no secret that Mexican politicians left envelopes stuffed with cash for any number of local reporters. Some foreign ones, too. But there were a lot of papers in this city and in this country.

One of them might still pick it up.

Mexican reporters, though, did get murdered rather frequently.

Meni left me to brood over the state of international journalism.

Long Island journalism, too.

I began to plot, for perhaps the hundredth time since I had been hired by *Newsday* almost two years earlier, how to escape. At first I hadn't wanted the job at all. But I took it. Because covering Huntington for the Ronkonkoma bureau was the best offer I had? Or because I could sense a romance in the making, a romance with Mulvaney even though our first meetings in the Gloomroom had been anything but romantic? When he'd left me to cover Northern Ireland, I'd vowed to stay at *Newsday* but get my own foreign assignment. Then, true to form, I took a circuitous route that accidentally, or maybe not, led me right back to him. But also to the best story going.

Nicaragua.

Too bad it hadn't lasted long. For me, anyway. He still had Iran-Contra. And I still had him.

All my routes, circuitous or not, seemed to lead to Mulvaney. If only that last one hadn't also involved deportation.

Maybe I didn't want to live in Managua, anyway. Manhattan was the only place I had ever really wanted to live, yet each year it seemed increasingly unlikely that I would ever get there. Life kept getting in the way of that. Maybe that was a sign. What would I write in Manhattan? Or Managua? The same story as so many other reporters in those places?

I thought again about what it meant to be living here, in the world's largest city, filled not only with teeming masses but also Diego Rivera murals, indigenous fertility symbols, great food, corrupt politicians, and apocalyptic environmental problems aplenty.

I could stay here and write a book about Mexico City. Someone from the *Times* had recently done that.

Not, though, from the point of view of a *paracaidista*.

DISPATCH FROM THE WAR AT HOME The rest of the world may dread Monday morning. But for a mother who works at home, it is heaven on earth. The children are in school. Mulvaney is in his office in the city. And because my husband and children are not home, my in-laws do not visit.

Nor does my mother call. Weekday long-distance rates, she says, insult her.

I sit and drink tea, think about writing, read the *Long Beach Herald,* our local weekly, which we depend on to cover the stories *Newsday* misses.

There is an article about our beach city's soup kitchen, the one I remember fondly from my days as a reporter, when it used to be in Hempstead. According to the article, the kitchen is *desperate* for weekend help.

Why not? I think. It's not as if I get any writing done over the weekend. If I am helping poor people, maybe Mulvaney will take Jack to travel hockey.

Homeless people, I remember from my reporting days, can be quite peaceable. Especially when they are fed.

The soup kitchen, I think, will be delighted to hear from me. Helping others, I realize, can be very therapeutic. I should have thought of this sooner.

The woman who answers the phone wants to know if I have "food-handling" experience.

"Well," I say, "I have two strapping teenage sons."

"So?" she says.

"You know," I tell her, a little miffed that they are so particular about a volunteer position, "it doesn't just happen. Little boys don't turn into two hundred pounds of muscle with juice boxes and microwave popcorn!"

She says she will take my phone number.

CHAPTER THIRTEEN
Company Loves Charity

Did anyone ever tell you you look just like Trotsky?"

Our landlady, Doña Venusa Alcalde de Poder, winked at the Doc, as they stood on my bedroom balcony and gazed out at a smog-filled view of the large and famous multi-colored tile mural at UNAM, the Autonomous University of Mexico.

"I thought this would interest a professor," she said to him, and the Doc blushed.

Downstairs, Long Island accents cackled, admired, and wondered out loud if "life could be Easy Street here."

In a pure PR stunt, Long Island's Largest Daily Newspaper, the paper that bragged about its coverage "at home and abroad," had sent its homeless abroad. Or, more specifically, to me.

At a San Ángel election rally for the fingered President-Designee, the former residents and lunch clients of The Lodge, the now defunct Hempstead shelter and soup kitchen, would be honored for their contributions to the *paracaidistas* of Insurgentes. They'd be on Mexican television, too, although the *paracaidistas* themselves wouldn't. As far as the candidate was concerned, they didn't exist, except as vague recipients of American largesse. "We don't want to encourage more to come to the capital," the candidate's PR *hombre* told me. Other people's poor, I guess, always evoke more sympathy than one's own.

In preparation, the clients of The Lodge were freshening up at the Plaza de los Arcángeles.

Throughout the house plumbing sputtered, knocked, and clanged: comparatively rarefied Long Island dirt trying to make its way down Mexican drains. As my houseguests took their second, or perhaps third, bath of the day—we did have five toilets not counting Meni's—Mulvaney called from Washington, puffed up with pride. He'd testified before the House Foreign Affairs Committee that the Contras had been financed with gun sales to Iran and, as a result, Daniel Ortega had asked him back to Managua with an "all is forgiven" invitation, a Hallmark card from the Dollar Store.

"Nicaragua?" I said. "Uh-oh."

But he had already hung up, so I left the office and made my way past our now very clean visiting throngs, into the living room, where, to my horror, Doña Venusa had begun to explain the intricacies of her Cortés tapestry to the Doc.

"It's our history," she said.

I imagined a time hundreds of years from now, in which Hitler was viewed as acceptable German living room art.

"You should take it down," the Doc suggested gently.

"Maybe," Doña Venusa said.

Oh God, I thought. She's in love.

*   *   *

Within a week, though, they were gone. I spent an entire afternoon in which I did nothing but sit alone on my own balcony luxuriating in the vast quiet. No mariachis. No helicopters. Not even a maid. For while it was true that Meni had been great with the Doc and his crew, I'd had enough of her, too. I gave her a week off, to visit the *campo*—the countryside she came from—wherever that might be.

As soon as she left, it felt as if a despot had gone, the story she'd found for me aside. Granted, she was no Cortés. But when it came to domestic matters, it was Meni who made the rules, powerless though she claimed to be. I suspected it was the same in big houses throughout the capital.

How did she exert such influence? Simple. She did her job. She went to the market and cooked, so she decided what we ate and when. And also whether or not the food made us sick; fruits and vegetables all had to be debugged with Clorox. Meni determined what we wore. She was the one who did the laundry, and, since the washing machine never worked, that task involved boiled water and tubs and washboards in the garden. Yes, Meni washed our clothes as if she was down by the river instead of in the middle of the largest city in the world, and, far as I could tell, so did every other maid in San Ángel.

In our case, Meni even had control over whether we filed our stories or not. When the phones and electricity went off, as they often did, Meni was the only one who could cajole the local utilities, such as they were, to work faster to get things turned on again. Those guys there, they ignored all women. But somehow not Meni.

The phone, which hadn't been functioning an hour earlier, now rang and rang, ruining my hard-earned peace.

"Where ya been?" Mulvaney asked. "Leisure Suit's looking for ya."

"How's Nicaragua?" I asked.

But he was already in Salvador.

"Yeah, the gunrunner they found outside of Managua lived here."

The line crackled.

"He also called Washington. A lot."

"What are you doing, Mulvaney?"

"I am," he replied, "at the phone company. I am trading bottles of Tennessee bourbon from the Managua Dollar Store for copies of the phone bills of suspected American operatives who, according to my sources, made a lot of calls to a little place known as the White House."

DISPATCH FROM THE WAR AT HOME The following
Sunday my father calls with an update. Already, he has a
new chapter:

I might not have been funny, but I did have one joke.
Years ago. It wasn't so much a joke as a shtick. But every-
one called it "Dave's only joke." As a man with scant
material—and a balding head—I was in no position to
split hairs. Ha-ha. I seem to have another joke.

My wife, Ida, did not find my only joke/shtick funny.
But Barbara did, even if she'd never admit it.

I would start by putting on a solemn face. For emphasis,
I'd stub out my Phillies Panatela, even if it was my favorite
cigar. Then I'd say: "Listen, toots. I'm not your real father."

"I know," she'd reply, bored and world-weary at six.
"My real father's in jail. Ha-ha."

For a full five seconds she'd feign indifference. Then,
glittering as only a little girl can, she'd run out the front
door to look for her friends.

She was not an only child. But she'd been born to us
late in our lives. So she depended on those playmates.
And she'd return with a gaggle of them.

"Hey, Mr. Fischkin," one of them—always the same
pale, dour child—would ask. "Tell us again about her
real pop. Did he really do all that stuff, Mr. Fischkin?"

Years later, as if she'd been marked for hardship, as
if she herself had been cursed, the playmate with the
questions watched her own father go mad. Her memory
haunts me, although at the time we were all happy fami-
lies in our semidetached—or semiattached, depending on
your philosophy of life—houses on Avenue I, a tree-lined
street in the heart of Flatbush-Midwood-Flatlands.

CHAPTER FOURTEEN
Baby Blues

A car door slammed outside, followed by silence and then a frail whimper, like a sick cat or a door hinge in need of oil.

Then a voice—Mulvaney's, I was sure, but softer than usual.

In a flash, the whimper turned to a wail.

I rushed down the wide wooden staircase.

When my husband looked at me, his eyes were *baby* blue.

The bundle he held, however, was wrapped in a pink blanket.

I looked back at him, as if to say he was beyond belief, beyond even suspended disbelief.

He gently moved the blanket and lifted an elbow so skinny it could have belonged to a bird. It was a limb I was afraid I had seen before.

"I bought arms," he said.

Then he laughed nervously.

For once in his life he knew he had made a bad joke.

"I couldn't help it," he said, his voice shaking.

Wails became screams, filling the large living room, a space I'd thought nothing could fill. How could anything that small make so much noise? Unable to stand it, I grabbed the baby from Mulvaney's arms. Holding her tight, shushing her, I rushed to the kitchen and with one arm, as if holding a baby was something I had done all my life, not just for a few minutes recently at a squatters' village, I pulled a bottle of milk from the rusting refrigerator, poured it into a pot, and turned the stove on low.

"Make it high," he said. He'd followed me in. "To get rid of germs."

"Do not give me advice," I replied as I turned up the flame.

We didn't have any bottles.

Meni's cousin's baby screamed on.

Why would we have bottles?

Someone banged at the front door and I heard a bag drop inside. "Extra if you don't carry your own, señor!" The gruff voice of a *taxista*.

Waving pesos, Mulvaney ran out there and, as the infant shook with screams, he ran back again. He slammed his "suitcase," that old doctor's bag that he'd used so many times for subterfuge, on the rickety kitchen table, dug into it, and pulled out—of all things—a baby bottle.

"I stopped at the *farmacia*," he said, as if expecting to be congratulated.

I grabbed the bottle from him and glared.

The milk was boiling. Milk that hot would kill this kid.

"Great baby, huh?" he said as he took the pot off the stove and put it in the refrigerator.

"Don't you dare speak to me," I said, leaving the room with her in my arms.

I walked up the stairs, headed for a rocking chair in one of the bedrooms we did not use, and sat and rocked that hungry child. Rocked her and rocked her and rocked her more. Still she cried.

Finally, Mulvaney appeared with the bottle. "It's cool enough," he said. "I tested it."

I snatched it from him and stuck it in the kid's mouth. She missed it, screamed, and then got it and sucked ravenously.

"Mulvaney," I said.

"I paid that woman five times what she asked," he said. "That was a great story you wrote about the squatters."

I would have to be a lot more careful about what I wrote.

He looked me dead in the eye. "I couldn't leave her there."

"We have to give her back," I said.

"I put the mother and her kids on a bus back to the *campo*."

"Where?"

"How should I know? You're the one who wrote the story."

"Meni can take her back," I said, seething.

"Caridad," he said, caressing the little girl. "I gave her a name. Caridad . . ." he cooed. "Charity."

Parenthood, I thought, is nothing like you expect it to be.

When I met Mulvaney, I knew right away that he would be a lot of fun and a great risk; that he would be entertaining and that I would pay a price for that. He was a man who would go to extremes. This, though, was not an extreme I had contemplated.

I fed the baby—excuse me, I fed *Caridad*—until she fell asleep. Then I carried her into our own room, gently put her down on our wide canopied bed, and tried not to compare it to her former home, a cardboard shack.

Mulvaney, toting a bottle of Corona, appeared and watched as I checked the cloth diaper she wore under thin, white-footed pajamas. It was dry. Babies weren't supposed to be dry this long, were they? They also weren't supposed to be this hungry.

"She's so cute," he said as I got into bed next to her.

"Mulvaney," I said, "I have nothing against adoption. . . ." I examined the baby. Her breathing sounded uneven.

"I have nothing against unconventional parenthood, either," I continued. "Still, usually, the first step is deciding whether the two of you want a child. . . ." I tried to modulate my voice. "In normal relationships there is usually some sort of discussion. Should we make a baby? Can we? Should we adopt? All followed by an agreement."

"So?" he said, his eyes glowing at the child.

"Mulvaney!" I screamed. "Normal people do not buy children. They especially do not buy children if they aren't sure they want any!"

He looked but did not speak.

"Mulvaney," I said, "this is far worse than anything you have ever done. This isn't some stupid businesss scheme. This isn't profiteering, for a laugh, over a Communist country's love of capitalism. This is serious, Mulvaney. This is a human life. And it's our lives, too. Once you bring children into the picture, Mulvaney, everything changes. You can't be the same person you once were!"

He shrugged, squeezed himself into the small space on the other side of the baby and me, and fell asleep as fast as she had.

I gently repositioned her legs and arms. She moved

closer to Mulvaney and suddenly breathed more freely. Could it be this baby liked Mulvaney? I looked at him. He was peaceful. But he was never peaceful for long, even in bed. He could roll over on this kid.

I got up, turned on a small reading lamp, put my two pillows on either side of her, and turned the light back off. In the dark, I groped my way toward our hall of closets, an amenity many notches beyond the standard walk-in variety beloved by so many Long Islanders. The lights here, unlike the old lamps and chandeliers throughout the rest of the house, were fluorescent, and when I hit the switch they hummed efficiently.

I walked the long, straight line of closets, my head bobbing left, then right. A house like this had to have guest linens, even if we were never here long enough to have any guests, the homeless of Long Island notwithstanding. I pulled open doors, examined empty wooden drawers, tiled counters, and plexiglass containers—imported, no doubt, at great expense. Finally, close to the end, I discovered cedar shelves filled with lush pillows in cotton cases, flowered sheets, and soft woolen blankets and quilts of the department store variety. Not as vivid as the ones sold in the markets here, but not so rough, either. I grabbed a pile, all I could carry at once.

Caridad slept so soundly that she did not, as I had feared, cry when I moved her away from Mulvaney. Once she was settled—safely, I hoped—on a bed I'd made from blankets on the floor beside my nightstand, I got back under my own covers. I dreamed of a baby with ten fingers but woke to a much larger hand softly feeling its way between my legs.

No way, José.

"Mulvaney," I said, as I pushed him away, "I have a headache."

He tried again.

"I was up all night with the baby," I said, pushing him harder this time.

Hours later I woke to hear him grumbling. "Your maid lost all my clothes."

My maid?

"I left them in a pile on this very floor."

I spent one night with a baby—his baby—and already he felt slighted?

"Weeks ago," I grumbled back. "Try the closets."

I woke again, after what seemed like minutes, to more sobbing—grown-up sobbing this time—somewhere off in the far reaches of the house. I checked Caridad's breathing, fell back asleep. A slammed door jolted me awake. The gate clanged, and a taxi backfired and screeched away from the plaza.

I lifted the baby, now so wet she felt twice as heavy, and ran with her down the wooden stairs.

In the kitchen, Mulvaney was cooking his own *huevos rancheros*.

He poured more hot sauce into the pan. "Want some?"

I shook my head.

"The maid came back," he said. "But I fired her."

Each day with him was more unbelievable than the last.

"You bought me a baby and fired the maid?"

What had he said to her? Meni, as I'd learned the hard way, did not fire easily. And it wouldn't have been like her to take a dismissal seriously simply because it was uttered by a man.

Caridad yelped as if she agreed. Would sons, I wondered, be as empathetic?

"I can't find my clothes. My wallet, either," Mulvaney said. This often happened, even when we didn't have household help. "And that maid of yours has some black magic hocus-pocus going on. . . ."

"Mulvaney," I said, yawning, "do you believe in hocus-pocus?"

"Of course not, but all that crap on her bed worries me."

"Mulvaney," I said, "before you married me, you also had a bed full of junk."

"Yes. But I kept it neatly underneath. I think that maid has a lot to do with the Mulvaney curse."

"The curse," I said, "was with us before she was."

I felt a flood soak through to my nightgown.

"There's something wrong with this child," I moaned, exhausted.

"She's just taking a leak," Mulvaney said calmly.

I couldn't imagine why he thought he knew anything about babies.

I held Caridad in the air, away from me. How, I wondered, had her mother managed to take care of her in that horrible place where they'd lived? With dirty water from a spigot? She must have had some kind of secret way.

"Mulvaney," I announced as the phone rang and I picked it up, "I need to go shopping."

"Fischkin," Leisure Suit said. I handed my husband the baby.

"I'll take the assignment," I said. "Whatever it is . . . as long as I have to get on an airplane to do it!"

"Nah. This one's for Mulvaney."

"Mulvaney's too tired," I said, slamming down the phone.

My husband's eyes flashed like a front-page headline.

"You can either be a parent," I said, "or you can go running off to Salvador. You can't have it all."

"Iran-Contra!" he said.

I'd had just about enough. "It's not as if you broke Watergate."

"It's not as if you ever broke anything."

My eyes seared.

His seared back. "Any good story you ever got was because of me."

I eyed one of Doña Venusa's large brown vases. How much could a fake pre-Columbian urn cost?

"Give me that baby!" I said.

He did.

"And never come back!"

He grabbed his bag and ran out the door as Albino rushed in.

"Is the señor going to America?" the cop asked, tickling Caridad's feet, not fazed one bit by the idea that, suddenly, I had a baby. Mexican men thought all women should have babies. What they didn't think about was where those babies came from.

"Because if he is going to America, señora, I need a pair of *esposas.*"

Esposas? He needed two wives? One wouldn't do?

"Mulvaney's gone," I said when Leisure Suit called back.

Caridad screamed louder, into the phone.

"You guys have a baby or something?"

"Mulvaney bought me one," I told the editor.

"Well," he replied. "Congratulations!"

The baby screamed louder. "Fischkin!" my editor said. "Take some time off!"

DISPATCH FROM THE WAR AT HOME An expensive, well-attended—and carefully gardened—Long Island bastion of higher education wants to start a journalism program. There it is, smack in the middle of the Sunday *Times'* Education Job Market page, which I'm reading as my father drones on.

But the last thing I want to be is a journalism professor. I've spent my working life railing against those types and their feeble attempts to turn out good reporters. All the good reporters I know, even the ones who did go to "J" school, learned their craft on the street and then, later, back in their newsrooms. It's a practical, think-on-your-feet occupation. You have to learn by doing.

"No," I say. "I can't do it. You can't teach anyone to be a reporter in a classroom."

Yet the languor of an academic setting—one with, perhaps, a secluded office of my own, a place where I can write without my various relatives interrupting me—is a hard temptation to resist.

That this particular university is located in the elite Nassau County village of Garden City makes it all the more attractive. Garden City, you see, has a thirty-four-year-old All-Points Bulletin out for Mulvaney, based on that little golf cart "mishap." If Mulvaney follows me there and tries to stand over me and watch while I write, like he did with the last book, I can have him arrested. Garden City law, as far as the Garden City police are concerned, supersedes most other laws—state and federal, including any regarding "juvenile" offenders—and statutes of limitations.

CHAPTER FIFTEEN
Dollar Store Blues

I sat on one of the three couches in our vast living room, trying to ignore Cortés and his beaten Aztecs, hoping the phone would ring. But the line was down again. Caridad, her small brown legs flailing against a blanket on the floor, shook her thick mop of black hair and, I think, giggled.

In the kitchen, the sink brimmed with bottles. I took a jar of boiled water from the refrigerator, tested a drop on my wrist, flinched from the heat, squeezed the jar into the small freezer, closed the door, counted to ten. A symbolic act. But at least I'd tried. The water steamed as I poured it into a bottle filled with powdered formula. From the living room, Caridad's laughter developed a staccato edge. I shook the bottle, closed it with a collar and nipple, put the entire contraption back in the freezer, and, with two fingers, plugged my ears against what were now eerie yelps. This couldn't be sanitary.

And her diaper was dirty again! Not merely wet. These Mexican diapers didn't last long. What I needed were some good old American Pampers. What I needed was a Dollar Store.

In less than twenty-four hours I had become a single working mother with no child care. I'd never realized how easily that could happen.

I put the baby on blankets on the floor, but she crawled away. Why wasn't this kid exhausted? We'd been out all day. First to buy supplies, including a large, wide scarf that I slung around one shoulder the way I'd seen Mexican women do it. As if she knew she'd been born to this, that little charity case—as I now called her affectionately—rested inside as we made our rounds. I had hoped to give her back. But when we got to the spot on Insurgentes where the *paracaidistas* lived, I realized I couldn't. It was too horrible. Not that anyone there would take her. Clutching their own sick, disenfranchised children, the *paracaidistas* turned their backs on me and refused to talk. They wouldn't even tell me where Caridad's mother had gone. I'd meant to ask them for the *campo*'s name when I'd filed that story. But I'd been so wrapped up in Mexican political intrigues and Long Island angles that I'd forgotten the most obvious of questions: *¿De donde vienes?* Where do you come from?

The mistakes you make as a reporter, the omissions, do come back to haunt you.

Next, I'd gone to see the police. But the station looked almost as bad as the squatters' village—and the cops wouldn't take Caridad, either, or tell me who would.

"Señora," one of them said, "our people have too many poor babies."

"But I don't want her," I said. "I can't take care of her."

"Impossible!" he said. "You are a woman."

"It's different with Americans," I said.

"Yanquis buy our babies all the time," he muttered, refusing to look me in the eye.

"I didn't buy her!" I protested. "My husband did."

"Señora," he said, "would you like us to arrest him?"

When the bottle finally cooled, Caridad gobbled more than drank. She took full advantage of her paper diapers, even if they were Mexican. I thought I even detected another giggle—did babies this small giggle?—as I tried to clean her up with a thin, barely damp baby wipe that stank of perfumed alcohol. She didn't like it either and began, again, to scream. "Well, what did you expect?" I asked, sniffling from the fumes. You didn't have to be a genius, or even a toddler, to see that my mothering skills were not all they could be.

My own mother was forty-one when I was born. "A surprise," she'd explained. To me. That's how I learned to hate euphemism. I grew up the only child among my mother's circle of friends; the only one in the family, too. My older brother had left for college before I turned six, taking the best kid stories anyone in the family ever told with him. It was only recently that I was beginning to see that maybe my parents hadn't needed to tell me many stories, since they were such stories themselves.

"Shush, Caridad," I said.

"Maaah, Maaah," she screamed, giving me the jitters. I wasn't this kid's mother.

I felt so tired I couldn't move. Tomorrow, I thought, I will find a way to give her to someone. This place must have orphanages.

I examined the polished wood of the ceiling beams, the smooth, brown tile floor. Think positive, I told myself. You can find the good in any locale. Hell, you used to live on Long Island, and all you had there was a walk-in closet. Hoping for optimistic notions to wash over me, I felt, instead, a sudden wave of deep nausea.

Turista! For months I had traveled Latin America without a hitch, eating anything I wanted, breaking all the rules about salad, unwashed fruit, even tap water once in a while. Now that I had a baby I was sick?

Quickly, I put Caridad back on the floor, rushed to the bathroom, rushed back.

As she screamed I flipped on Mexican television. Soon we had the pattern down. Caridad screamed. I put her on the floor and went to the bathroom. I came back, picked her up, she screamed more. . . . And so it went, until an old Marx Brothers movie put her to sleep.

It was the bells that woke her again, although they were muted and distant. Church bells. The Carmen. The same ones she'd heard on Insurgentes. She whimpered, then let loose. The phone, back on again, rang off its hook.

Mexico was like this, I decided.

"Money is pouring in for a new Lodge for the homeless," announced Claire, on the line from the Gloomroom. I tried to balance the receiver between my head and shoulder so I wouldn't drop the baby. "Who says journalism is ineffective? There's even a church in Long Beach that wants to give them a place. For free. No lease."

"Claire, I need stories. Not happy endings."

"Leisure Suit said something about you and Mulvaney adopting a Mexican kid!"

The front door pounded. I must have left the gate open again. In my arms, Caridad screamed.

"Gotta go," I told Claire. "A mother's work is never done."

DISPATCH FROM THE WAR AT HOME Mulvaney, I think as my father reads on, you were wrong again.

> *. . . Speaking of Barbara, did I tell you she became an author! And how proud her mother and I are of her . . .*

This little exercise is harmless. It keeps him busy. It's nostalgic.

That story he tells about not being my real father, I learn from it every time. Even in Mexico I learned from it.

There's absolutely no need for me to stand over him while he writes.

> *. . . But there is one little thing that's been on my mind. It's that latest book of hers.*

Calm, I say to myself. This is probably fine.

> *The one she hasn't finished yet, although only God knows why not. How hard can it be to write about your children? I'm doing that very thing myself, and it's a breeze. I know what her problem is. It's that annoying first person she insists on using. A man can get away with a voice like that. . . . A woman, though, particularly a woman of a "certain age," has to be careful.*

"Dad," I say, "gotta run."
"But, toots, I'm not done."

> *Take me, for example. Or even better, take me and Philip Roth. We both write in the first person, even make our own lives fiction or vice versa and the world thinks we're*

geniuses. Rightly so. A girl does it and it's "chick lit." Only thing worse is when the "girl" isn't a girl—or a chick.

"So what do you think, toots?"

What do I think? I think my worst nightmare has happened. My father, in his old age, has turned into my mother. They say it happens.

"Dad. I have to go."

"So soon? There's more. . . ."

"Maybe next weekend."

"Barbara, I am an old man. I might not live till then. I will call you tomorrow, the rates be damned!"

"Dad," I say, "I have a job interview tomorrow."

"An interview, Barbara? Won't that interfere with your writing?"

"There's a school here that is begging me to be a professor."

Although maybe they didn't know it yet.

But what if I just called Boutique U.?

It was, after all, a journalism class that convinced *me* I wanted to be a reporter. Most journalism professors were reporters themselves at one point. And I hear that they really do kick their students out of the classroom, send them on real stories. They demand real reporting, good writing. It's not as if you can trust newsrooms to be teaching laboratories anymore. You can't count on finding a whole room full of the Men Who Didn't Write *Naked Came the Stranger*—experienced craftsmen, even if they weren't the stars of the operation.

"An all-day job interview," I say, lying more. "Sometimes these schools, they make you try out for a week. A formality, of course. They want to make sure you like them."

CHAPTER SIXTEEN
Real Fathers . . . and Mothers

I opened the door with one hand, balanced Caridad against my hip with the other.

"BWHANOSE DEE-AHS. ¿CUOMO ESSTAR OOOSTED?"

A copy of *Berlitz for Travelers: Spanish Idioms* waved in my face. Under my mother's arm was an old paperback of Octavio Paz's *The Labyrinth of Solitude*. Pretty highbrow.

But with Ida Fischkin you never could tell.

"Mexican politics," she said, "are even worse than Brooklyn's."

"What are you doing here?"

She pinched Caridad on the cheek. "Just wanted to see my new grandchild."

"Mother!" I said.

A Peter Max tote bag was draped across her purple print

cardigan, under which she wore an ankle-length white dress, its low, square collar bursting with embroidered flowers: a garment sold at the airport, exclusively to overeager tourists. The only thing worse than my mother's taste in furniture was her taste in clothes. A mangy wire-haired terrier in miniature native dress yipped at her side, jumping up and down as if it had spent the last six hours in my mother's handbag, which it probably had.

Caridad screamed. The dog bounced on hind legs, dislocating its sombrero.

Could this get any worse?

"Biig Jiiiiim! Hurry!"

Big Jim?

The Real Mulvaney leaped through the gate, an economy-sized package of Pampers in one hand, an Avon sample case in the other.

So, I thought, my husband has called in the troops.

Didn't necessarily mean, though, that he had seen the error of his ways.

"Who needs a Dollar Store?" my mother asked as she took the Avon case from Mulvaney's father.

"Take this, too!" I said, handing her Caridad, who screamed louder.

The Real Mulvaney lifted a hand to his head, ran back out the gate, and returned, straining to carry two stacked cases of Similac ready-to-use disposable bottles, fortified with iron. He dropped them on the tile floor so hard I thought they'd break, opened a box, whipped out a bottle, and stuck it in the kid's mouth. In his coat pocket I now saw *his* reading material: *The Old Gringo*.

"They're convenient. But they won't last forever," my mother warned as Caridad sucked loudly.

"There, there," she cooed, rocking the baby back and forth.

She had never, I was sure, said that to me.

A huffing *taxista* came through the gate, pushing a large box with customs stickers all over it.

A motorized, battery-powered infant swing.

"De-liv-er costs more, lady," the driver said, making a great effort to pronounce the English words.

"NO VALLEY LA PAIN-A," my mother insisted. "It's not worth it!" she proudly translated for me as she grabbed the box out of his hand.

The dog jumped higher and stuck out its tongue. I hated that mutt. Her name was Asta and my father called her "Estuh," but she would always be Queen Asta to me, particularly since it annoyed my mother. This was not the first time Ida Fischkin had smuggled that excuse for a pet into a foreign country, either.

As if she had read my thoughts, Queen Asta yipped happily. My mother brought Caridad down to her and the mutt licked the baby's toes.

Weren't dogs supposed to be jealous of infants?

"There, there," my mother repeated as the baby gurgled and Queen Asta licked.

"Where's Dad?" I asked. At times like this I always missed my father. At least he was sane.

"He'll come down Sunday, after Las Vegas Nite at the shul."

The baby burped.

"There, there," my mother continued to murmur. "Why, she looks just like me!"

"Mother!" I said. "I am not keeping her!"

I do not know how many days I slept alone in the canopied bed that belonged to our Communist landlady. But I do know that it was a sleep that made your typical foreign correspondent's collapse look like an afternoon nap. I got up only to push away the food my mother left on a tray or to run to the bathroom. This was not any garden-variety, short-term *turista*.

Back asleep, I permitted no sound to wake me for long. Not my mother cooing loudly to the baby Mulvaney had bought without asking me, not the DHL truck whooshing away after depositing *Newsday*s that, I imagined, were filled with stories written by Mulvaney and not me. I did not even permit the tinkling of the Real Mulvaney's martini glasses to wake me, tempting though the sound might have been.

"I think I'll have another," I heard him say happily, through the haze.

To find the fixings—we didn't drink martinis, and even if we did he was particular about the ingredients—he would have had to have navigated a foreign city where he did not speak the language, presumably using hand signals to get what he wanted. What was the hand signal for an olive? A little circle? How would you let people know if you wanted green or black? Haunted by these minutiae, I fell back asleep.

I heard my mother and Doña Venusa talking politics. For an anti-Communist and a former Communist, they seemed to have a lot to discuss.

"I could have told you so," I heard my mother say.

I woke again, later, to the sound of Brooklynese Spanish. "EL BANYOS NO SERVEES." Broken toilets? "VAMOOS A TENAIR OONA FEE-ESTAH." A party? Having my mother around was definitely not a party. Not for me, anyway.

Next, the languid voices of Mexican workmen. Pipes banging? Had my mother hired plumbers to come to the house? That didn't sound like something even a native could do on such short notice. But how long had it been? How long had she been here? I began to realize how many sounds floated through this immense house. Must be those Mexican tiles; everything reverberated.

I felt next to me for Mulvaney, but there was no news of him. Not in this bed, anyway.

I wondered about Caridad. Could it be maternal instinct? I hadn't known I'd had any. Still, it didn't mean I was keeping her. No way you could be a foreign correspondent and a mother, too.

And if we were going to buy a baby, I should at least get a hand in choosing it.

I heard my mother cooing. "There, there . . ." And I went back to sleep.

When I woke again, there was singing in the backyard. Not mariachis. There were no instruments, just people crooning their own melodies, all different and all in Meni's language. Each one sounded like its own sigh of relief.

I smelled barbeque smoke. Or was it a Phillies Panatella? Weak, I pulled myself out of bed, walked slowly to the balcony, and gazed down at a crowd of homeless people. But the former denizens of the Lodge had left days ago. These people were dirtier. Thinner, too. And they ate with more desperation.

The *paracaidistas* of Insurgentes were having a party in my backyard. I searched for Doña Venusa and did not see her, but spotted Caridad riding calmly on her motorized, battery-powered infant swing alongside the bougainvilleas that framed the pool. About ten feet away, the Real Mulvaney turned a roasting pig on a spit. My mother, on the other side of the pool, had a lamb rotating on hers. She waved to my father-in-law, trying, I assumed, to keep a friendly distance. My mother did not keep kosher when she went out. But she did have her limits.

I located my father, puffing happily on his cheap cigar and chatting with a small group of *paracaidistas*. At least there was someone down there I was glad to see. He snuffed out the cigar in the grass, picked it up, put it in his pocket, and clanged the pool fence with a large serving spoon.

My mother yelled for attention.

"I'd like to tell a joke. . . ." my father said.

I cringed for him. My father only had one joke. It wasn't really a joke, more of a shtick.

He stopped, looked up, waved to me on the balcony.

"Good morning, toots! Actually it's evening."

People laughed.

"That's not my joke!" my father insisted.

"Daddy," I called down, "they don't speak English."

It was something, though: The Perpetual President of Congregation B'nai Israel of Midwood in Carlos Fuentes's old rental behind the Plaza de los Arcángeles about to address the *paracaidistas* of Insurgentes.

"I'm not her real father," he called out triumphantly.

I groaned.

"Her real father is in jail. I am just taking care of her till he gets out."

A conversation hummed through the crowd until it reached a crescendo.

"Yo también," a voice called out, with reverence.

And then another saying the same words.

And then another and another.

"Yo también. Yo también. Yo también."

Me, too.

A man held up a small girl with long braids. She was clutching a piece of bread. "I am taking care of her till her father is out of jail," he said in halting Spanish. "I feel like her father, though."

So, the *paracaidistas* had a translator. Maybe they weren't doomed.

"*Yo también,*" yet another of them said. And the crowd applauded my father. Cheered him, too.

What had been a lighthearted, slightly lewd attempt at humor in the Flatbush-Midwood-Flatlands section of Brooklyn was serious business for the *paracaidistas*.

My father looked crestfallen, like a man whose joke had failed.

"Daddy," I called out, and he gazed up, "Daddy, they love you."

His face brightened. "You like my joke!"

I shook my head, laughing. But he was already convinced that I did.

"Ida Fischkin," he said, motioning to my mother, "has a question."

She stepped away from her spit and walked toward the swing where Caridad was still riding back and forth. She switched it off and took the baby in her arms.

"It's for the best," she called up at me.

When my mother said this, it usually wasn't a good sign.

The *paracaidistas* chattered loudly. My father handed my mother a spoon and, holding the baby in one arm, she clanged the utensil on the gate.

"Attention! Attention!" She sounded like she was talking to gamblers at the shul.

"Sometimes it isn't possible for children to be with their real parents. . . ." she began.

Please, I pleaded, do not let her tell them I will keep the baby.

I had nothing against Caridad personally. In fact, looking

at her swinging so authoritatively, I had even felt a surge of affection. Wide awake now, I was sure that kid had convinced me I could take care of a baby. But I didn't want a baby just to have a baby. This baby wasn't my baby, although it had nothing to do with whether I'd given birth to her or not. There was a bigger problem. Motherhood was like love. The chemistry had to be there. And Caridad and I did not have any chemistry.

I had seen it, though, in Meni's cousin. She'd loved that kid in a deep, mysterious way. You could see it in her eyes and the way her own skinny arms flinched when she asked if I knew where she could sell her. Sell your baby for her own good? Could I ever love a child that much?

"Sometimes, though . . ." my mother continued, and the crowd stilled. "Sometimes, something can make it possible. At home, I have some involvement with a parish. . . ."

"A parish?" I said.

"A Jewish parish," my mother said.

There was a hush and then whisperings. *"¿Judios? Sí. ¿Como Jesus?"*

"No," my mother said, not masking her annoyance. "Not really like Jesus. But we do have a large fund-raising activity that is making so much money it actually needs a tax shelter."

The crowd murmured. The translator explained "tax shelter" in Spanish and the information made its way around the large group. I stood on the balcony, stunned. Las Vegas Saturday Nite was going to adopt Caridad?

"We'll support her in the countryside with her mother as long as we can afford it, as long as Brooklynites keep playing craps at our tables. . . ."

The crowd cheered while the translator groped for the words.

"Juegos," he said. Games.

"And because charity loves company, I will supplement whatever the shul provides with profits from my new, international Avon route."

"Skeen So Soft," the translator announced, and the *paracaidistas* cheered.

"I only need to know the name of the place where her family is from," my mother said as she sank into a chair. "And no fooling around this time!"

Within minutes the guests gathered around her. They cheered, sang out in unison: *Esperanza. Esperanza. El pueblo se llama Esperanza.*

A town called Hope.

What, I wondered, would Bill Clinton think about that?

Still singing, the *paracaidistas* lifted my mother up in her chair as if she were the bride at a Hasidic wedding. Then, in an utterance Ida Fischkin would later proclaim prophetic, she said, "It takes a village to raise a child!"

My father sat down and was lifted as well, and my parents were celebrated for a good half hour around the outdoor swimming pool of the mansion *Newsday* had rented for us on the Plaza de los Arcángeles.

Weak at the knees and relieved to not be a mother to the wrong kid, I went back to bed, only to have the phone ring loudly in my ear.

"I love it!" Leisure Suit was apoplectic. "Love it. Love it. Love it."

How did he even know what happened?

"The Real Mulvaney called it in!" he said. Why did lawyers, criminal lawyers, especially, always think they could be reporters, too? "He said you'd fix the writing."

Didn't anyone remember I was sick?

"It's a great follow-up to the Long-Island-homeless-help-

Mexican-homeless story," Leisure Suit said. "A shul in Brooklyn is now helping them, too!"

And I thought we didn't cover New York City.

"Brooklyn is where Long Island starts," he said. Although this was true-true, *Newsday* had never acknowledged it. The paper must have done a new marketing survey. "This could be a great beat for you! Long Islanders helping the homeless, internationally. Long Islanders as the true humanitarians of the world!"

And I'd once thought I didn't want to cover Huntington.

After the guests left, I went down to the living room and found my mother packing up the baby swing.

"We'll take her tonight," she said. "Big Jim rented a car. Your father will drive."

I looked at my father, but he shrugged happily. Life, I guessed, was most comfortable for him when my mother did the managing.

"Mother," I said, "you are promising these people too much. Las Vegas Nite won't go on forever."

My parents' neighborhood was, as they say, "changing." Which didn't mean it was becoming worse, only different. This, of course, terrified the people who had lived there forever, as well as the ones who had come with their own strivers' notions. Many of the members of Congregation B'nai Israel of Midwood were either moving or making plans to do so. They would go to the suburbs or to Florida.

The new residents of Avenue I would have their own causes.

"B'nai Israel won't last forever," I continued.

But she shook her head as if she believed it would.

My mother's beliefs were simple yet fantastic.

She believed that everyone should convert to Judaism,

even if they didn't have an interreligious romance going. And she believed in the power of the downtrodden and the oppressed to make new lives for themselves.

As a six-year-old she had, after all, saved her own life during a brutal anti-Semitic Ukrainian pogrom.

"Anyway, there are lots of shuls in America. . . ." My mother waved a long, red fingernail in the air. "And they all need reasons to hold fund-raisers!"

The guests left. In the morning, my mother and father, my father-in-law, and the baby who had almost become mine left, and the house was suddenly quiet again. Mexico City could surprise you with its calm when nobody was around.

I filed my story to Claire. Leisure Suit had wanted me to go to the *campo,* too, but I still needed to be near a bathroom. "No details, please," he'd said. You'd think that as Foreign Editor he'd at least get used to stomach ailments. "The Real Mulvaney can call in to rewrite whatever he finds on the baby-return end." The Real Mulvaney, I thought, would just love that.

As for the other Mulvaney—mine—I did not know where he was or when I would see him again. Or if I wanted to.

The whoosh of the DHL truck broke the silence. A new deliveryman was at the wheel and he had a new delivery assistant, too. He handed me an envelope that, instead of a return address, had only these words written in an elegant script with black ink:

Amenaza Porvenir Presente.

Amenaza Porvenir. When translated literally, it meant "future threat."

Maybe there *was* a Mulvaney curse.

Inside the envelope a thin piece of paper was wrapped around a hammered-metal mirror, a souvenir from a stand at Teotihuacán. I took the paper off—the glass had a small crack—and read the note:

"I had hoped you would help me to create a new Mexico."

Not a reporter's job, I thought.

"Instead you made a headline. And a charity case. America and Americans have done this all too often around the world and it will come back to haunt them.

"Be careful with my ancient city," she continued, *"no good comes to those who toy with it."*

Try to look on the bright side, I told myself. If I had stayed in Brooklyn, I never would have met any of these interesting people.

DISPATCH FROM THE WAR AT HOME Early Monday morning, I make a quick call to Boutique U., rev up our tangerine Honda Element, and speed through the canals of Long Beach, hoping nobody will notice I am not doing fifteen miles an hour.

Even more quickly, I make my way through the glut that is Oceanside's commercial strip and beyond, examine the suburban sprawl, and reflect on all the romances and marriages in all of those houses behind the strip malls.

When I look back on *our* romance—on anyone's, for that matter—it makes its own, complete book. The most detailed story. The one we tell with relish from first itch to wedding. Romance always has only two protagonists, each telling the story in his—and her—own way.

It is a natural tale with a beginning, a crescendo, an end.

Is marriage the end?

Or it is just a slower story?

After the wedding, it becomes a story about days that blend one into the next until they become years and, eventually, part of a whole. In a successful romance, the ignition and the sparks stand out in one's memory. In a marriage, even a successful one, the heartbreaks compete with the fireworks.

It would be nice to blame them on an outside force, a source that no one can quite identify. But the true-truth is that marriage and parenthood are meant to be harder, longer, more enduring, and are only rarely defined by flights of fancy.

But we in the Mulvaney-Fischkin household, as Mulvaney would say, do not have slower stories.

Or at least we once thought we wouldn't.

CHAPTER SEVENTEEN
. . . And the Ground Shook

I had numerous arguments with Claire about the nature of love, all of them punctuated by phone static.

It was her view that an exciting romance was better than a predictable one.

"Yeah," I'd told her. "You also want to live where there is no ozone layer."

I'd vowed never to see Mulvaney again. I only wavered when walking past the house Frida Kahlo had shared with Diego Rivera on the Avenida Altavista. It was actually two houses, his pink, hers blue. A bridge separated them.

That might work, I thought. If it was the Verrazano.

*　　*　　*

"Do not talk to me about love," I said the next time Claire called. It was a miraculously clear fall morning and I was finally starting to feel like myself. Along with the Mulvaney contretemps, my ongoing *turista* had been diagnosed as typhoid by a fancy doctor in yet a different fancy Mexico City neighborhood, *Polanco*. Not a big deal. All foreign correspondents in Mexico got it at least once. Still, the one symptom that lingered was exhaustion.

"Tired or not, you're on a plane to Salvador, *inmediatamente*," Claire said. "Duarte's having a big press conference about right-wing death squads."

"Not going," I said. Mulvaney, I figured, was still in Salvador. Although this was a much better story than a few good ole boy gunrunners who may or may not have some connection to the White House, as if that was anything new.

"Mulvaney is leaving for Honduras," she said.

Now he was chasing his nonstory into yet another country?

"I'm on the next plane," I said, feeling a little better about life.

I knew that Mulvaney thought he was being funny, wry, wistful, and as ironic as a heartsick rock star when he sent a lone mariachi to the front door, not the yard, singing Neil Young instead of Spanish ballads.

"Señor Jim says to tell you: *Just someone to keep my house clean. Fix my meals and go away. . . .*'"

This guy's high falsetto was grating at best.

"But what he really wants to know is: *When will I see you again?*'"

My husband's timing was as bad as his alleged sense of humor.

And I had a plane to catch, the first in a long time. But not the last.

Comalapa International Airport in El Salvador seemed oddly quiet. I found a line of the most solemn-looking taxi drivers I had ever met anywhere. Even in Northern Ireland, with bombs going off, they were considerably more cheerful.

"Very dead here," I said as I got into a car.

"Many dead," he replied.

"Huh?" Maybe I'd gotten too used to Mexican Spanish.

"*Terremoto,* señora!"

"There's been an earthquake, here? When?"

"An hour ago. While you were in the air, señora."

On the plane, even at customs, they had said nothing. But what would have happened if they had? Mass hysteria. In the air—and in the airport, where the officers had guns.

We motored on through the dark outskirts, the city even darker. As we approached, the driver stayed silent, as if merely speaking would move the earth again. Finally, I told him I was a reporter.

He asked me which I preferred to see. Shattered office buildings or shattered hospitals?

"Or the morgues, señora?" he added, tears in his eyes.

"Everything," I said. Leisure Suit, Claire, they would want it all.

The phones were down. I gathered up sights, sounds, descriptions of debris, stones and cement mashed, pipes exposed and bent—and bodies and all the blood I thought I could stomach. Then more. Dead people, the recently dead, even the banged and bruised dead looked as if they were breathing. As long as they still had faces, they looked that way. As if they might come right back . . .

Under me the ground shook. Not imagination but after-shocks that rippled, echoing the worst of what had happened. People jumped at each one: nauseous, petrified, experienced jumps.

But what good was any of this if you couldn't get it in a newspaper? If you couldn't let the world know, and quickly, how bad it was here? How where they lived, where our readers lived anyway, had to be better than this. The quicker this got in, the quicker the money would flow from Long Island, too. Send money, I thought.

Send a phone line.

A mother lit candles around her dead child. That, too, was more than I wanted to see. But each time I thought that, there was more. Lots of mothers, many altars.

And Mulvaney? He must have boarded a morning plane to Tegucigalpa before they closed the airport. I'd looked for him as we drove, as I walked through the scenes I would write about and then, hopefully, forget. Forget and not have dreams. File the story. Forget.

But I couldn't file anything.

The taxi driver—years later he would simply and sadly become just one of many drivers in many foreign countries—stayed with me all day and into the night, past midnight, into the early-morning hours. When he stopped for gas, I noticed that the pumps looked like the ones on Long Island, except they had hand cranks like a Model T.

"I need to take another plane out," I said.

"I don't think there are any tonight, señora."

Or in the morning?

What was better? To leave and file or to stay and report? Report out stories that would be old before I filed. Even these stories got old when it came to newspapers.

"Take me to the Marriott," I said finally.

"*Los hacks se quedan allá,*" he said.

"Yes," I agreed. I couldn't help but smile. "The hacks do stay there."

They'd boarded up all the front doors to the hotel. The revolving one had been smashed.

A lone worker pointed to the backyard garden.

It was darker than the street, yet I spotted him before my eyes could adjust. He was closest to the gate, lying on a metal chaise longue, and it did not look good. A torn white sheet covered his head and shoulders but not the rest of him; a paper tag with a string through a reinforced hole was tied around his toe.

All day, with all I'd seen, I had not let myself think this could happen.

"Oh my God," I said, not moving. I would have had our own children with him, no matter how they turned out.

A skinny bellhop shoved me aside and peered over Mulvaney's toe with a flashlight, staring at his death tag.

"Stop that!" I said.

"*Señor Jim, buenos días,* seeks in the morning," he said, speaking Latin American Hotel English. Then he pulled the sheet off his face. "Please to do me favor to wake up now!"

Wake up?

He shook him, but Mulvaney didn't move.

"Please to wake up now, Señor Jim."

One blue eye, then another.

I breathed out and realized that other bellhops, in other, far-flung reaches of the garden, were shining lights on other toe tags. Shaking most of the bodies awake. Of course. No phones. The toe tags were requests for wake-up calls. The overseas press corps after an earthquake. Resourceful as ever.

As the sun rose, the garden came to life with barely awake hacks, sleeping ones, too. Nightmares now interrupted. Men and women I knew from one country or another.

He saw me.

"Mulvaney," I said. "Who sleeps through an earthquake?"

Slowly, he got up.

"I didn't," he said, looking the way I imagined some long-ago soldier once gazed at a woman from another time or place, appearing out of the blue, in the midst of a battle. "Not the aftershocks, either."

We were able to get into the hotel through a side door. We ran up the stairs to the second floor, the UPI office, where *Newsday* had its phone. A few reporters had beat us to it, but we all sat around and stared at the silence. The lines were dead, too, as dead as they had been, everyone said, the day before. Outgoing and incoming. Nothing rang. Silence.

We all had notebooks out, streams of stories to tell and no way to get them out.

Then, RING. Ring, ring, ring. A lone phone.

Ours!

Newsday's!

Mulvaney and I looked at it as if it was possessed. "You take it," he said.

"I had it on speed dial for nineteen hours!" Leisure Suit said, from Ronkonkoma, bursting with pride.

Well, he had earned it. Now we'd be the first to file.

"Rewrite is sitting here," he said, and another voice came on.

One of the Men Who Didn't Write *Naked Came the Stranger*! Hooray for the Men Who Didn't!

I read everything in my notes, trying to turn loose facts and observations into coherent sentences. The rubble, the pipes, the bodies, the children and their altars. I didn't know if it made sense. But I also knew it didn't matter. This particular Man Who Didn't—Demo, we called him, short for a longer name no one could spell—could take your babble, your rubble, too, and make it sing.

Mulvaney filed to Klein, who might have been A Man Who Did but nobody was sure. As a rewrite man, he was as good as Demo, maybe better. Along with newspapering, he was also the president of a shul in Smithtown. Perpetually, I hoped. In his youth he'd been a television reporter in Vietnam. One of the first. To him an earthquake was still something, even if it was nothing by comparison.

Mulvaney's stories were different, too. A little schmaltz but mostly hard-core reporting, dazzling in their specificity and in the way they insisted on unmasking corruption, even when there was so much "easy" drama. A jeweler who had been trapped for hours in the Rubén Darío building, acid dripping on his face until it ate through the skin of his cheek to the bone, was really a story about the Darío building itself, knocked to the ground into nothing but a heap—and condemned twenty-one years earlier in the last quake. But no one had paid attention. There was money to be made by letting it stand. Money to be saved by not making repairs. And now hundreds were dead, many still inside.

Mulvaney then announced to Klein, and to the reporters who remained waiting for their own phones to ring, that he had—and he stopped for emphasis—he had found tourists from Syosset in a pizzeria in the heart of downtown San Salvador.

Thank God for this, too, I thought.

I'd completely forgotten about the Long Island angle.

*   *   *

Again, the earth shook. The door slammed shut. Mulvaney and I looked around. The other hacks, their phones still silent, had left. We were, for the moment, locked in. Our phone went dead, too.

There was a Marriott couch, though.

A good scare cannot only quell thoughts of separate planes, separate stories. It can also make you want to have your own baby. Insurance, that's what it is. If someone dies, someone will be left.

Daniel Mulvaney, the first of the next generation of Mulvaneys, was born in the American British Cowdray Hospital in Mexico City, a soupçon more than nine months after the Salvadoran earthquake.

Nine pounds, one ounce. *El Gran Yanqui,* they called him there. Presents from home, though, arrived addressed to *The Large Mexican.* He got two passports. We were instructed that he would have to relinquish the Mexican one when he turned eighteen. Either that or join their army.

"Ay no!" Doña Venusa laughed when she heard. "You just buy your way out. *Barato.* Cheap." She kissed Daniel on the head. "Best to keep both in case of revolution."

Mulvaney liked this. "They won't be able to pin him down."

My mother-in-law offered to get Daniel an Irish passport, too. "He qualifies through my grandparents," she explained. "And the Republic is a neutral country. It doesn't even fight wars with itself anymore."

Who could blame us for feeling safe?

*   *   *

Albino, our neighborhood cop, came to see the baby and to ask Mulvaney's mother if, the next time she came, she could bring him two *esposas* from America.

"You'd think," she declared, "one wife would be enough."

Esposas, I told her, showing off my newly acquired grasp of Mexican colloquialisms, meant "handcuffs." One *esposa* might be a wife, but two were a pair of handcuffs. Both—according to Albino—better when made in America.

My own mother, of course, stayed longer than any of the other grandparents.

"He's almost perfect," she said. "All I ever dreamed, except . . ."

"Mother," I replied, "isn't it time you went back to Brooklyn and shipped me a case of Pampers?"

As she started to cry, it occurred to me that I was supposed to be the one with postpartum depression.

"He'll never be president of the United States," she wailed. "He'll wind up unfulfilled . . . like poor Henry Kissinger."

I tried to explain to her that it wasn't the same thing; that being born to American parents who live abroad was different from being foreign born. But she refused to go home until she had "official confirmation."

Fortunately, we knew a PR man at the American embassy.

FIRST DISPATCH FROM THE WAR AT *WORK* As I get closer to the university, I begin to review my goals. Educators, I'd heard, like goals.

These are mine:

1. To teach
2. To write without anyone bothering me
3. To hide from my relatives

At the entrance I stop to read a bronze plaque:

Boutique University
A Theory for Every Human Emotion

CHAPTER EIGHTEEN
Articulation

While parenthood might change your life, it does not change you. Intrinsically, you remain the same.

Even more so, in some cases, since there is ample opportunity to project.

And some of us have enough pathology for two.

Danny had just begun to walk—quickly, I might add—when Mulvaney's own congenital restlessness reappeared, big time.

"We have to move the kid," my husband announced. "Deadlines loom!"

Deadlines?

Danny had a dozen years until his bar mitzvah, seventeen until he had to buy his way out of the Mexican army.

But as our toddler began to use more words, in both languages, his father spoke only of change. I had hoped he would like having a wife and child—and being settled in one place. But I was only half right. He liked us. He just wanted to take us somewhere else. "Together," Mulvaney assured me. I believed him, I just didn't want to go anywhere. Wasn't Mexico far enough? Wasn't this weird enough, interesting enough? It wasn't as if we were raising a child on Avenue I.

"*Juntos,*" Danny translated.

I examined my son and wondered if life would be easier for him since he did not have blue eyes that flamed. His were brown, like mine. But with a painted-on mustache, dressed for a saint's day that celebrated children and their natures, he looked like a little Pancho Villa, which made sense. Sometimes if you had the genes, you didn't need the eyes.

"*¿Cómo le hace el gallo?*" I asked him.

"Quiquiriquí," he replied, delighted with himself.

"And the rooster?" I asked, repeating the question in English.

"Cock-a-doodle-do!"

"Mulvaney," I said.

"*¿Sí?*" Danny replied.

"Not you, kid," I said softly.

This was just what I needed, two Mulvaneys. In two languages!

I bent down to my son. "You are Mulvaney Fischkin, sweetie. That is how we do it in Mexico. Daddy's name. Mommy's name."

A surprising system for the land of *machismo*. If only they took it seriously.

"I think that first maid of yours put a curse on us," Mulvaney said. I had long stopped thinking about Meni, having been through several maids since her, each with a unique set of quirks. But one thing I knew: I had to have a maid. It wasn't negotiable, not with a baby and stories to write. "And the curse is why we're moving," Mulvaney continued, undeterred. "We're moving to China."

"We're moving to China to shake a Mexican curse?" I asked in my usual state of Mulvaney-induced disbelief.

"I want to be an Asia hand. I want to live in Hong Kong and have an office in Beijing."

Seemed like a long commute.

"Mulvaney," I asked, "does Beijing have a Dollar Store?"

"It could," he said as he pulled a penknife from his pocket and opened a Dos Equis.

How long has it been, I asked myself, since the Fall of Saigon? That's when we would have wanted to go. Or even better, during the war. But we'd been too young.

Latin America was where the story was now: Communism flashing and re-creating itself, the way it was doing in Nicaragua. The American Right trying to circumvent American law. What more could a reporter ask for? Why would you want to go anywhere else? Japan was already rich.

"Asia is over, Mulvaney," I said. "All you are going to find is a pack of has-been hacks, sitting around the bar at the Foreign Correspondents Club in Hong Kong."

Danny ran into our backyard park, jumped on the swing, stood and rode it swiftly back and forth. I did not flinch. He was not a child who fell. In fact, he looked particularly at home on the swing. It was off it that he got into mischief. *Danielito el Travieso* was what Doña Venusa called him, after the Mexican version of the *Dennis the Menace* comic strip. Our landlady, the former Communist, only wanted to make sure he hadn't been named after Daniel Ortega Saavedra, whom she considered the real Danielito el Travieso. She said he made trouble for his people because he was "not as pure as Trotsky."

"I once knew a dog named after Ortega," I had told her. "But my kid is named after his grandfather's bartender."

"The Foreign Correspondents Club . . ." My husband muttered. His eyes glowed a Sapphire Martini blue, as if he might like this idea, as if he was ready to change to his father's cocktail of choice, too.

"Mulvaney!" I said. "You are not ready to retire!"

"I will be if I stay here. There are no stories left in Latin America."

Like I said, there were plenty.

"Whoever put the curse on us took the stories away."

"What makes you think they won't do the same there?"

"Too hard," he said. "China is having a revolution. . . ."

"Had one," I corrected. "Mao's dead."

"The Philippines is going to be important in the Arab world. . . ."

Where did he get that from? The only story in the Philippines at the moment was the ousting of Ferdinand Marcos (over) and the presidency of his successor, Cory Aquino. True, she was one determined broad. And who could blame her? Years earlier, Marcos had murdered her husband when, after a stint in America that included a Harvard fellowship, Benigno Aquino came home and tried to run for president himself.

Still, it wasn't enough of a story to make me want to move.

I put my hand on my husband's forehead to check for fever, delirium. "Mulvaney," I said, "you have your geography all mixed up."

Coldly, I plotted to stay in Mexico City. I had pages and pages of notes for that Mexican book—the one from the point of view of a *paracaidista,* or maybe a maid. But my concentration, the railroad of thoughts that led me to find stories, shape them, write them, had been interrupted, first by a husband who had bought me a baby I didn't want and almost got himself killed in an earthquake, and then by the baby we finally did have. Not that *that* baby had been forced on me. I'd wanted Danny. He and I had that all-important chemistry. In the mornings, he'd look at me and I'd look back and think two conflicting thoughts: Who was this strange new being and how had I ever existed without him?

Who could write with all that on the brain?

Each story was a struggle, and I knew it would be even harder to write while moving a kid entering the terrible twos.

I seemed to be at my best when composing lists.

DANNY LIST
Diapers for night (look again for American brands)
Wipes
Ointment
Better potty seat (ask Ida to send one)
Toys that look like they don't have lead
Get shots

ADVANTAGES OF STAYING IN MEXICO
I can write my book
I can get divorced (Divorced women have less money
    so they write faster.)
I can raise my son in a country that does not have a
    Toys "R" Us

DISADVANTAGES OF MOVING TO
HONG KONG
I can write my book but can't reinterview anyone
    in person or see the things I want to see again
    without booking an expensive, long flight that

> I probably can't take anyway because I have a
> little kid
> I won't be able to fake "fluency in Cantonese" the
> way I did with Spanish
> I will not get divorced
> Hong Kong has the largest Toys "R" Us in the world

In the end, though, as before, it was Leisure Suit, a man who went nowhere himself, who decided where I would go. How did I let this happen? Although our editor continued to refuse to leave Suffolk County, he did suffer from vicarious attention deficit. He couldn't stand it when any of his reporters stayed too long in one place. He reassigned Mulvaney to Beijing, me to Hong Kong.

"That setup is only for the accountants," the editor assured us. He was proud that he now knew ways around the moneymen. Years later, as competing forms of news media grew like fungi, causing print circulation to plummet, those moneymen would do him in anyway. But now he was still hopeful about newspapers, still ebullient, still sure that nothing mattered more than a good up-front story written by his own reporters.

"Being that you are married . . ." he began.

Being that he made us get married to go to Nicaragua because there would be less paperwork, I thought.

". . . you can live together in Hong Kong—you'll like it, it's just like Long Island, it even has malls—as long as both places are covered."

Mulvaney assured him that being in two cities at the same time was not a problem.

I said I wouldn't go.

Mulvaney begged me.

"Asia's great," he said. "You don't want to get bogged down."

We hadn't been in Latin America three years. True, we'd been thrown out of Nicaragua, seen Iran-Contra close up, bought a baby, covered an earthquake, had a kid of our own.

But, I still hadn't gotten a book contract.

And neither of us spoke enough Spanish to prove we'd ever been here.

Even Manuel Noriega hadn't been deposed. We still had all those stories the Novelist-in-Exile had told us to write.

"It's also too far for your mother to visit," my husband said.

This, I had to admit, was compelling. Although she would, I figured, find a way.

"I think I'll take Mandarin," he said. "You take Cantonese and we'll have the world made."

I tried to stay in Mexico by proposing a different book, one more newsworthy. A book about Nicaragua and its Communism.

But when it came to wanting what you don't have, to ignoring what is at hand, to guessing at the next big thing, the publishing business was worse than Mulvaney.

"Nicaragua already is Communist," one rejection letter scolded. "Too bad you can't write about China taking back Hong Kong in '97."

That, I noted, was eight years away.

Still, I hid the letter from Mulvaney. A wife needs her secrets.

And on a typical day in Mexico City, a day in which the world's largest city was full of the smog that couldn't hide its splendors, Mulvaney and Danny and I left the Plaza de los Arcángeles, never to see it or any of its characters again.

At least not so far.

DISPATCH FROM THE WAR AT WORK Although the semester has just begun, it is half an hour before I find a legal parking space. If I want that faculty job, I'd better act fast. At the end of a sprawl in which too many new Ford Explorers are parked perilously close to too many beat-up Volvos—those are the ones with faculty stickers—stands a squat, three-story Georgian building.

Can a building take itself too seriously?

At least some designer had the sense to lighten up the heavy wood and marble of the lobby with sleek modern sofas instead of Chesterfields.

Nothing worse than a cliché, even in office furnishings.

When I called that morning, I'd been told to see the president. Of the entire university.

Someone at this school, I think, really wants a journalism program.

There is no secretary, so I walk down the hall toward the sign that says "President" and, for good luck, touch the red velvet wallpaper.

Inside the "oval office," a tall, thin janitor in an orange knit jumpsuit, his back to me, scratches furiously at a speck on the window. They need to give this guy a rag, I think, not to mention a uniform that doesn't make him look as if he's doing ten to twenty-five for manslaughter.

I myself am wearing black pants and a black cotton sweater from The Gap. Best I could do on such short notice. I sink into the first chair I see, feel the leather against my skin, see the studs. I knew they had to have a Chesterfield somewhere.

"Welcome to Boutique U.!" The janitor speaks without turning.

His voice, though—screechy as a sideswipe—sounds alarmingly familiar.

"You're late," he says, and I am suddenly transported back to my youth. All the way back to Ronkonkoma.

But it couldn't be him, could it?

Leisure Suit? A janitor?

"No parking?" he asks. "We pride ourselves on our overcrowded lots."

My former editor turns to me and forces a grin. For the first time ever, I feel sorry for the guy.

Newsday, I'd heard, had finally fired him, but not, amazingly, because of anything he'd actually done. He had even been promoted to executive editor, second in command of the entire newspaper—not counting the board of directors.

Then, within weeks, he was gone.

The paper, according to prosecutors, had been inflating its circulation figures. By tens of thousands of copies.

So much for the sanctity of truth.

And so much for Leisure Suit, too, who, as the highest-ranking editor, was told, after three decades at the paper, to pack up his desk and never return to the Gloomroom. Didn't matter that it was the business guys, not the reporters or editors who had padded all the numbers.

Claire, somehow, had been saved, although she claimed that she and a whole slew of other editors were next—and that the circulation scandal was just a pretext. *Newsday* had been sold off by one large corporation, purchased by another—the second even leaner and meaner than the first. There was a union contract expiring, too.

And like most corporations, like almost everybody these days, the new owners had no idea what to do with newspapers in the Age of the Internet.

"Overcrowded lots mean enrollment is up!" Leisure
Suit now says, preening.

How sad, I think. He still speaks like someone in a
position of power.

"I hope it's easier to count students than readers," he
adds, a bit wistfully.

"I'm sorry," I say.

"Yeah," he says. Then brightens. Too quickly, I think.
"Still, this is a great job!"

"You're the janitor," I say softly, wondering if this
campus has a mental health clinic.

"Fischkin." He glares at me. "I am the president of
Boutique University."

The school, I knew, had troubles of its own. Its last
president was, to put it mildly, a crook. And worse. When
the student newspaper got the goods on him, he shut it
down.

But Leisure Suit as his replacement? They couldn't be
that desperate.

"Okay, it's only a temporary position," my former
editor says as he tries to jiggle open the rolltop desk in
front of him. Frustrated, he pounds on the speakerphone
and demands to see a secretary. He is, I think, going to get
us both thrown out of here.

But no.

"Mr. Interim President," says the middle-aged woman
who promptly arrives. She hands Leisure Suit a gold letter
knife and he pries the desk open, pulls out a pile of blank
diplomas, and throws them in the air.

"Wheeeee . . ." he says. "I like this job. I don't even
have to dress!"

As if he ever did.

"And I now appoint you, too—on a temporary basis, of

course—as a Visiting Professor of Journalism. First on the agenda: You'll need to meet your crackerjack colleagues in the Communications Department. . . ."

The theorists.

I should have known.

Maybe, since I was the only journalism professor at Boutique U., I could work for the English Department instead. Writing. English. It made sense.

"You *could* work for English," Leisure Suit says, "if any of them ever returned my phone calls."

PART TWO

On the Record

CHAPTER NINETEEN
Fast Forward, Hong Kong

In the narrow hallway of the thirteenth floor of The Manhattan Luxury Residence, I held my breath and examined the teak front door of our duplex for signs of bullet holes, nuclear attack, and/or a Crusade, the things mothers worry about when they go on business trips and leave their husbands in charge.

I'd only been away a week. But you never could tell.

I put my ear against the wall—flimsier than you'd think considering the rent *Newsday* paid—and heard Danny giggle as he swooshed down his plastic PlaySkool slide, the centerpiece of our elegant but cramped living room.

I exhaled.

Maybe everything *had* gone well.

Still, it was Sunday, the amah's day off, meaning Mulvaney was in there completely alone with the kid.

Our first and, so far, only child, if you didn't count Caridad.

Tentatively, I put my key in the lock, slowly opened the door, craned my neck around the small foyer.

There, atop the slide again, stood my two-year-old son, clutching our imitation Ming Dynasty umbrella stand with all his might.

"Danny!"

"Your turn," he said to the large blue and white vase.

CRASH!

I ran to him as Mulvaney pounded down the stairs.

"It went boom!" Danny said.

As I lifted him away from the shards, he wiggled his bare toes, a kid delighted by every loud noise, scared by none. His father's son.

Together, the three of us took in the extraordinary views from the place we now called home.

We also called it "The Manhattan," to distinguish it from *the* Manhattan.

Through floor-to-ceiling windows we gazed at sampans and junks on Tai Tam Bay, our own turquoise expanse of the South China Sea. On the left was a new luxury apartment block, designed differently from ours, but the aesthetic—and moral—equivalent. We couldn't wait to hear what they'd name that one. Chinese men, resembling flies on the wall, balanced on rickety bamboo scaffolding that rose for stories. Stronger than it looked, at least we hoped so. Those workers were building flats of 2,800 square feet and more, while they lived, with their families, squeezed into homes as small as a tenth that size.

To the right stood the American Club—more teak— and, alongside it, its pool. Not as big as the one we had downstairs at The Manhattan, although prettier. The whole club was pretty, but not for us. Too tony, or maybe just too straight, filled as it was with Midwesterners trying to re-create home, and its country club atmosphere, abroad. Too expensive, too. So we hadn't even asked Leisure Suit if the paper would pay.

"I see a cement mixer," Danny said. "And a big car." The road in front of the club was a collage of the extravagance, construction blitz, and odd demography of the territory. Behind the cement mixer glided a Rolls-Royce, a Jaguar convertible, and a bevy of bicycles pedaled by old men in pajamas, each moving as if it knew it had its own place on the road. You couldn't look down from our apartment and not wonder what China would do to this place once it got it back.

"And I see a mess," I said. This was the view inside, below us on the floor where, now, shards of imitation Ming Dynasty pottery mixed with the detritus of a morning without Mom—or the maid. Multiple pairs of mismatched socks, large and small, a cluster of apple juice boxes, a mass of LEGOs, all unattached, and—finally—the most damning evidence of all, a bowl of contraband Froot Loops. Stray bits of this beloved but nearly lethal American breakfast cereal, courtesy of Ah Yick Groceries in Stanley Market, made a trail to the steps where, on the next floor, the fourteenth, we had two bedrooms, two bathrooms, an office, and—now—a decorative swatch of torn-up Hong Kong dollars, glued back together, of course.

Glued to the teak floor, perhaps.

You'd have to be a foreign correspondent on an expense account to dream up that arts and crafts project.

I could see the invoice now: research on building foreign currency.

Was it possible that Guli, our amah, had only been off since last night?

"I missed you!" I said, hugging my son hard.

Mulvaney looked at me with what could best be described as relief.

"Hello," he said.

Since we were not only parents but reporters, too, the phone rang.

Mulvaney, desperate for escape, ran up to get it. I heard him chatting up Claire, but it was me she wanted. He came down and I went up.

"How's everything?" she asked from an opposite time zone, sounding grumpy.

"Excellent," I said, ignoring her mood. "The trade conference was boring, but the sushi was great."

"It was Tokyo," she sneered. "Would you get bad spaghetti in Rome?"

She was, I knew, in need of a heavy rewrite on a story Mulvaney and I had reported and written together—not an easy task under any circumstances. This one, though, had been especially tedious, a Leisure Suit–assigned "thumb sucker" on an event that wouldn't happen until 1997: the British handover of Hong Kong back to China—and the considerable local opposition to it. If only we could have written it from the perspective of the view from our window and our visceral reaction to it. And our fear that it would disappear.

"Don't give me any of that visceral crap," Leisure Suit had said when I'd proposed this. "I want pundits! Pundits pontificating on what the place will be like when it goes back to the Chicoms," he'd insisted, snapping his fingers into the phone.

Pontificaters. Great. Just the people we wanted to interview.

Not that we couldn't find them. If you were a reporter, those types found you.

Now I scanned the portable computer we used to receive

the suggestions Claire made from Ronkonkoma. Cranky, cranky, cranky. Maybe what she and Leisure Suit needed was a baby. Some real problems, instead of the ones they imagined.

"Is this opposition a fight to preserve Democracy? Or merely Capitalism?" Claire had written in capital letters for emphasis.

Hard to tell, I thought. That's what happens when you let the noisiest politicians here, or anywhere, talk. In this case it was three short guys from Wan Chai versus the British Empire, the People's Republic of China, and a done deal that was more than a hundred years old.

"No shoes!" I heard Danny exclaim.

I dropped the phone and rushed to the stairs, but all I saw were father and son and Teenage Mutant Ninja Turtle sneakers. And a lesson in tying laces. No blood. Danny had been told to stand back from the shards—or he had done that himself.

For an insane human being, Mulvaney was an excellent father.

An hour later, the Manhattan Luxury Residence shuttle bus let the three of us off in the heart and heat of Stanley Market and, sweating happily, we walked through a labyrinth of alleys shaded by awnings over stalls filled with American clothes, all made in factories here, and more fake Ming pottery than a kid could break in a lifetime. At our favorite small café, we sat at a table with a pink Formica top remarkably similar to the one my mother had in her kitchen before she fell in love with mosaics and replaced it with a giant ashtray.

Still, here, at the other end of the world, it felt a little like Brooklyn—although the Chinese restaurants were better.

"How 'bout some 'guys,' Dan my man?" Mulvaney asked.

The boy nodded.

His father ordered raw jellyfish.

Danny liked them with hot sauce. We didn't know why, but he was the one who had started to call them "guys."

"Next ride, Daddy?" he asked when we were done.

"It's called a taxi."

I bent down and reminded him how to hail one. "Could be useful if you ever live in the real Manhattan."

"Tai Tam Park," Danny announced to the driver.

Up high and green, it was a secluded country getaway with leafy paths and hidden expanses of woods, just minutes from the crowded, throbbing cacophony of the harbor and its environs. There, Danny could run without waiting for the traffic to pass. It was the main island's most unlikely locale.

But, like all places here, you could always get a taxi out.

An hour later, the three of us walked as if we shared one secret, Danny positioning himself in the middle, his hands reaching for ours, taking them, then dropping them so that he could feel freedom, too. We spotted the "double bus" that rode to the Peak Tram, ran to it, shot up that small mountain as if we were in a rocket.

"Slow down," I said. But nobody heard.

Back down the peak and in and out of another taxi, we hopped onto the Star Ferry, a double-decker green and white boat that over the years had transported millions from one side of Hong Kong to the other. One of the mates offered Danny a bag of "crisps," cheese snacks that reminded me of Cheez Doodles, which we never saw here even though Ah Yick made a small fortune selling processed American food.

Between Mexico and Hong Kong, Danny was growing up without Cheez Doodles. He inhaled the imitations, nevertheless.

We rode across to Kowloon Side and Tsim Sha Tsui for the inevitable stop at Toys "R" Us and back, then into Wan Chai and a subway ride that ended at—where else—another taxi stand.

"Let's not get out," I said when we passed the beach at Repulse Bay. Hong Kong's shoreline, heavily polluted, was the only thing here that made me miss Long Island. Outvoted, I watched as Danny, his clothes on, ran in, jumped at the waves, and came out the same color as he had gone in, convincing me that we were truly blessed.

We took another taxi to Ocean Park, a real amusement park in a city that was one itself. There, we rode the cable cars as many times as we could until the park closed.

"It's a Mulvaney tradition," father noted to son. "Last to leave the party."

"Yep," the kid agreed, yawning—finally—as we walked through the revolving door of The Manhattan.

But he brightened when he saw the doorman.

"Hello, *Pungyow!*" Danny called out, mixing Cantonese and English. That, I'd heard from other foreign correspondents, was called code-switching. Kids learning more than one language at once sometimes spoke two of them in one sentence. Supposedly it was fine. All the languages would ultimately come together.

"Hiya, pal!" Danny said in English.

The thin-lipped, bespectacled man at the front desk smiled weakly, as if it was a chore. He was not one of the usual *pungyow*s, the doting, rotund doormen who worked in shifts—but rather their boss, Mr. Henry Yip, Estate Manager of the Manhattan Luxury Residence. A man who made Deng Xiaoping look like a softie.

"Working late, Mr. Yip?" I inquired.

He growled in Cantonese and patted Danny on the head. Blond hair brought good luck, no matter your mood.

"Very bad," Mr. Yip said, waving a red pamphlet with a white plastic binding and gold lettering. The dreaded tenant handbook, which he, as he proudly told anyone who would listen, had written himself.

"Really?" I asked. "How so?"

"Amahs!" he said, putting down his plastic-bound epic so that he could shake a fist in the air. "Amahs in the pool, again! Last night! I am here to make sure it does not happen tonight. Or ever!"

"Amah" was what people here called their maids, most of them Filipinas who had been arriving in droves thanks to Ferdinand and Imelda Marcos. In the years before their deposition, the Marcoses had plundered their country and most of its people, too. A maid in Hong Kong made more than a bank teller in Manila. Oddly, "amah" was not a Cantonese word but a Portuguese one, its adoption here something to do with the proximity of Macau.

Well, Hong Kong *was* international.

Even if Mr. Yip wasn't.

"Amahs!" he shouted, waving the red pamphlet again.

Respectful Residencies:
House Rules for the Happy Manhattan Family
Estate Facilities

Tenants will be issued residents' cards which will enable them to enjoy all the privileges and facilities provided by the Management. Please be respectfully advised that servants may not use the clubhouse, fitness center, tennis, squash and basketball courts, car park. Or the pool. Particularly not the pool. Not even the kiddie pool, even if they are watching the children of Manhattan residents.

Servants may use the Shuttle Bus, but only when embarking on job-related errands.

The Management would be grateful if our European tenants, particularly our German and British residents, would convey this to their American neighbors who do not read house rules and, due to the "unconventional" nature of their own nation, not to mention their historical involvement with the Philippines, may not appreciate that class distinctions are what uphold the fabric of society.

DISPATCH FROM THE WAR AT WORK I follow Leisure Suit out of the building, past those sleek sofas in the lobby. We walk down a path choked by flowers on either side and into another smaller but equally pretentious Georgian building. Since there are no executives here, merely students and faculty, the walls are an institutional green.

Leisure Suit leaves me at a forbidding metal door.

"Gotta go," he says, snapping the button on the sleeve of his orange jumpsuit. "But don't worry, it'll be a breeze."

The Communications Department Conference Room is devoid of communications devices except for a television tuned to Fox News.

The three professors all have cartons of Chinese food in their hands.

"Manipulation!" one of them shouts, slamming his moo shoo pork so that it scatters over the indoor/outdoor carpeting.

Well, yes, I think. It is, after all, Fox News.

The other two professors are women.

One of them is about sixty with fashionably cut gray hair. She wears a lot of jewelry, even more makeup—odd for a woman with such a good haircut—and introduces herself as the department chair.

The other woman offers a weak hand. She, frankly, could use some makeup.

How well, I wonder, do these two communicate?

"So," says the chair, who I now see also wears false eyelashes. Can't say I'd seen those in years. "You must be the new journalism professor?"

"Yes," I say. "You want me to teach the kids to write?"

"Not yet," she says.

What, I think, are we waiting for?

"We need a school newspaper, too," I remind her.

At this she huffs and rubs the rouge on her cheek.

"Well, my dear, before they can write—for publication, no less—they need to know the history of communications. They need to understand the background and the theory of all we do today. They need to know how precious are all the vast and varied communication outlets and portals of today. They need to know *anime!*"

"Anime?" I say. Cartoons. In a journalism program? Please tell me she means political cartoons.

"Like Doug Marlette?" I ask, trying to sound sincere and wondering how he'd feel lumped with all those Japanese.

"They need to know how cave paintings evolved into the animation of today."

They need, I think, to know how to craft a simple news story.

"They need to know about drum signals. That drums were the first telephones."

"Uh," I say, thinking that my career in academia could be very short. "How about we teach them how to call people up and write down what they say?"

And get it right.

I contemplate a world with fewer theorists and more reporters who can still get it right.

Outside, I walk past the clumps of fine horticulture that seem to be another hallmark of this place. Theories and flowers. The kind that bloom all summer and into the fall, just as the students and their parents—their parents who pay—arrive. Marigolds, geraniums, dahlias, zinnias, cosmos. Each variety more perfect than the one before it.

Do they tend to their students as well, I wonder?

CHAPTER TWENTY
Tiananmen

I spotted Mulvaney at the bar of the Foreign Correspondents Club—the FCC—an aging building on Lower Albert Road in Central, the downtown business district of Hong Kong. It was lunchtime on a slow news day and he was drinking Armagnacs—cheaper than cognac and supposedly more fun to say in Cantonese. Perched on the stool next to him was his new best friend, a Netherlander whom everyone called "Vanes."

"*Ying, ying,*" Vanes said with mock impatience. The bartender, a local, poured him a shot of smooth, golden liqueur.

Vanes—the Perpetual President of the FCC—was also a photographer who had taken the most widely published shot of the Fall of Saigon, a helicopter evacuation brimming with emotion.

The most widely misidentified shot of the war, too.

I wiped beads of sweat from my forehead. The club was as overchilled as any in this steaming territory. But the June air outside was so humid it felt more like August in Miami. It defeated even the best air-conditioning.

"Ying, ying!" Vanes said again, gesturing toward Mulvaney, as more Armagnac flowed.

The photograph that Vanes shot those last days in Vietnam was of a helicopter taking off from an apartment building where CIA employees worked. But for years editors got it wrong and, despite our friend's caption, insisted on saying that the helicopter was leaving the American embassy. Better, perhaps, to evacuate bureaucrats than spies. Spies can get themselves out. Better still to evacuate them from the embassy. One small distortion in a war full of them.

"Ying, ying," Mulvaney agreed. That couldn't, I thought, be real Chinese. But the bartender just kept pouring.

"Ying, ying," I asked.

"Means enlightened," Vanes said, taking another sip.

I looked at my husband. Happy, his eyes a frothy blue, the rest of him good-looking still. Above the bar, a new large color television flashed a tape of students protesting in Tiananmen Square in Beijing, clamoring for democracy, even as a gigantic poster of Mao loomed over them. They'd been there for days, starting with a hunger strike to commemorate a visit by Mikhail Gorbachev. Now they'd constructed a fake Statue of Liberty made from scraps of tin.

In Hong Kong, the locals were ignoring them, as if they weren't all fighting for the same thing.

The world, including *Newsday*, was ignoring them, too. Most of it, anyway.

As we drank another round, a Western Union messenger rushed past and handed a telegram to Vanes, who glanced at it before handing it to me. "From some broad named Ida Fischkin. You related?"

> *Dear Internationally Famous Foreign Correspondents Who Do Not Call Home for Good Advice STOP CNN all over students in Square STOP Why aren't you? STOP Organizing shul forum STOP Fighting for Democracy. STOP Then STOP And Now. STOP And Always. STOP LOVE MOM.*

"Mulvaney!" I said, as he hailed a taxi to the airport.

"She's right," he said. "Gotta go. Wanna come?"

I played with my two wedding rings, Irish and American, moving them up and down together on my finger. There was no story there.

"I do not," I said, "get my assignments from Congregation B'nai Israel of Midwood."

"Leisure Suit's dropped the ball on this one."

And my mother, I thought, is a sentimental fool when it comes to the Statue of Liberty.

"Maybe he decided that disenfranchised, ineffective protesters do not make a story," I said.

"Coming or not?" Mulvaney asked me, his eyes red, white, and blue.

I kissed him goodbye. "Have my own stories here," I said.

Not to mention a two-year-old, our son.

I tried, though, to concentrate on the stories.

One of the outer islands was teeming with Vietnamese boat people who, years after the end of the war, were arriving in droves with no place to go, no place that would take them. I may have missed the war, but I'd be damned if I'd miss its aftermath, too.

And then there were the caged men of Kowloon, destitute refugees from the mainland who worked for peanuts and got locked into bamboo cells at night.

Why follow the television cameras—and my husband—to a media event when I could cover my own tales of injustice right here?

DISPATCH FROM THE WAR AT HOME I am back from my first day at Boutique U., trying to write as Mulvaney stands over me. The days are getting shorter and the deck, he says, is dark. (And therefore unlikely to attract admiring neighbors.)

Yes, they did give me an office at the school. But it wasn't as if I could get anything done there. The communications professors kept bringing in textbooks they had written, insisting that I assign the latest edition to all my students. *From Drums to Directories* had, for example, been changed to *From Drums to Digital* by the addition of a chapter and was now offered at a new, higher price.

As he scans my screen, Mulvaney puts his hand on my shoulder. "I still think there is a curse, you know."

"Mulvaney," I say, exhausted from the events of the day. "On the slight chance that there is, it would only mean that all families are cursed. Each in its own special way. Nobody ever really gets their curses lifted, and it is useless to try to find the source."

Midway through a novel based on your fictional life is probably as good a place as any to own up to the truth.

There have been times when I thought there really was a Mulvaney curse.

I have made lists of all the people who might have put a curse on us. I try to go way back.

There was that sad little girl, my childhood friend, the one who had to hear my father tell his only joke as her own father was going mad. But wouldn't she have just cursed me and my father?

Maybe we were cursed because Mulvaney bought a baby from the *paracaidistas*? But we gave her back.

Were we cursed because we never took Cortés down from the living room? Had the Aztecs put a curse on us?

Had Manuel Noriega? Did Mulvaney ever really explain that the Panamanian "strongman" was far from the worst of the villains in his region? He'd gotten the first George Bush angry and lost power. It had more to do with American politics and political money than it did with America saving the world from tyranny.

But isn't that usually the case?

Still, we were newspaper reporters there. We should have explained.

How about Oliver North? Had he cursed us? If we'd written good things about the Contras taking money from weapons sold to Iran—my mother says you can find the good anywhere, if you only look—then he might be a senator now.

Or was it Amenaza Porvenir? Had she cursed the Mulvaneys on behalf of Caridad because, with that particular baby, we had taken the easy way out? It is much easier to raise money for a child than to actually live with one. Or because she gave me a story and got a distorted headline instead?

Was Amenaza merely casting a simple, selfish curse, because she had so much less than we did? The real saying is that "*misery* loves company."

Perhaps Amenaza's name was also her destiny. Amenaza Porvenir. Future threat. Was she put on this earth for the sole purpose of cursing people?

I suppose someone has to do the dirty work. Who better experienced than a Mexican maid?

CHAPTER TWENTY-ONE
The War at Home

The Cantonese of Hong Kong Island had no desire to live with the people who had come there to make money. Those people were *Gweilos*—white ghosts. An ugly word, but no uglier, perhaps, than the image of Europeans and Americans on corporate expense accounts.

And the feeling was mutual. Most Westerners in Hong Kong didn't know more than a few words of Cantonese. And why bother? The Chinese all spoke English.

Everyone, though, did want to rent to or from one another. In the late eighties, an era was ending in Hong Kong. People were trying to make as much money as possible before the Communists took the territory back, and consequently, real estate prices were sky-high.

Gweilos, basically, had two choices. They could live in overpriced apartments—called "flats," British-style—on the main island, or in undersized town houses in suburban Discovery Bay.

"Disco Bay," a predominantly white enclave on distant Lantau, was Hong Kong's answer to Suffolk County, albeit without pizzerias, Pathmarks, or even a whole lot of back-yards.

Even out there, though, rents would have shocked a Long Islander, or even a Manhattanite.

Our own "flat" in Tai Tam, on the north side of Hong Kong Island, was considered a steal at $6,800 US a month.

When we first arrived, I had toyed with the idea of buck-ing convention and "going native," of moving even farther out on Lantau or to one of the other outer islands, Lamma or Cheung Chau, cheaper places untouched by the revolu-tion, the technological one, anyway. I was charmed in a dis-tant way by the old Chinese women who lived there and tended their rice paddies, their stone faces half hidden under pointed straw hats. Former Communists, I thought, feeling some surprising nostalgia for Doña Venusa. Missing her, even.

But what would I do, I thought, if I needed to borrow a cup of rice?

A look inside one of their amenity-bereft cottages didn't help, either, nor did the tour I took of the stolid housing blocks in the Northern New Territories, another place where the real people of Hong Kong lived.

As for Cantonese, and Mulvaney's dreams of our linguis-tic prowess, that never happened. We had stories to do throughout the region. If we learned Cantonese and Man-darin, we should be learning Tagalog and Thai and Viet-namese, too.

Somehow, I couldn't see myself speaking any of those languages. Not, at least, until I mastered Yiddish, and I was a long way from doing that. I had made it to my thirties without being able to figure out what my parents were saying when they didn't want me to understand. *"Fershtayts?"* my mother would ask my father. Do you get it? He'd nod, but I had no idea.

And yet the farther I moved from Brooklyn, the more I saw myself as I had once been. What would a rice-paddy mama and a girl from Flatbush-Midwood-Flatlands have to talk about, anyway, even if I did learn the lingo? Creative renting was starting to feel uncomfortable, particularly as a repeat performance. Even our house on the Plaza de los Arcángeles, a mansion though it might have been, had never felt like a place I wanted to call home. More than once it had occurred to me that we might have been better off in Bosques de las Lomas, a Mexico City suburb filled with corporate executives from Houston and Chicago.

I, of course, did not dare to mention any of this to Mulvaney. I could barely stand saying it to myself.

What was it? Was it motherhood? Was that what made me say "temple" and think "shul," not Buddhist shrine? I liked it that Hong Kong Island had a synagogue and its fair share of Jews, even more so when all the garmentos came on business trips from New York. There were years, I'd heard, when there'd been so many Jews here they held Yom Kippur services in a ballroom of the Grand Hyatt.

Except for Filipinas in his swimming pool, there was nothing Mr. Yip disliked more than a Gweilo. Zero Tolerance for Gweilos. He would have liked that term, too, if it was in use back then.

True, he tolerated Gweilo children and made allowances for Gweilo Germans and Brits when they could be of use to him. But, generally, he wielded his house rules as weapons of mild torture. If you broke them, he wasn't going to throw you out of the complex. That would mean losing rent for at least a month, and his aim *was* to make money. So instead of ejecting you, he would fine you as a condition of continued residence. And moving could be quite a nuisance in Hong Kong.

Mr. Yip was no dummy. To make his Gweilos behave, he'd fine them in a manner that ensured they would have to pay for it themselves. His receipts were the kind that would never pass muster with the accounting department of even the most liberal of corporations.

After careful investigation, Mr. Yip told us, he had discovered that *our* amah was the ringleader of those late-night, illegal swims.

I could just imagine asking Leisure Suit to explain *that* to *Newsday*'s accountants.

"The rule book says I can add to your rent for doing this, Mrs. Mulvaney," he noted, patting Danny on the head again. "So keep her out of the water."

"Mr. Yip," I said, "I am Ms. Fischkin. I only use 'Mulvaney' at the dry cleaners."

Why should I take the blame for my husband's stains?

Letter to All Residents of the Manhattan Luxury Residence
Re: Willful Destruction of Properties at the Manhattan
  Luxury Residence

Dear Residents:
  We are forced to appeal for help to all tenants because the destruction has reached a disturbing proportion.
  Two fire extinguishers were found missing. One (1) was thrown down the stairs of the clubhouse and eight (8) small padlocks used to secure fire hose nozzles were rendered worthless by the use of metal cutters. We believe these acts were committed by children of indeterminate

age, and we will be keeping a very close eye on them.
Their parents should be aware that fines will be levied.

Sincerely yours,
Henry Yip
Estate Manager

"I just wish we had a viable backyard," I told Claire, after I'd filed the rewrite of our Hong Kong story, a bevy of additional business briefs based on my Tokyo reporting, and extensive notes on both the caged men and Vietnamese boat people. It was amazing how much I could get done when Mulvaney wasn't around. "If a person can't live in Manhattan—the real one—they might as well have a backyard."

"I thought you had a maid!" she said, as if this discounted the need for a lawn.

"We do," I said.

Aside from her acts of aquatic civil disobedience, Gulo Bawas—she liked "Guli" better—was a pretty good amah. She looked like a sweet, young Imelda Marcos, who had once been the Rose of Tacloban. She loved Danny and, as far as I could tell, wished us no ill. Even better, the literal translation of *her* name was "less mess."

In the evenings, she retreated, like all the amahs did, to her own room and bath in the back of our flat.

Now, though, as I tried to talk to my editor, the noise downstairs grew: laughter, tears, snapping LEGOs, children swooshing down the slide, more tears. From the stove, I could hear the sizzling of *lumpia,* Philippine egg rolls made with shrimp, pork, and vegetables. The sizzles mixed with *chismis*—good-natured gossip—and there was a lot to gossip about. The Manhattan amahs now took quick dips in the pool almost every night, always minutes ahead of whichever security guard was on duty. It had gotten so bad that Mr. Yip had stationed himself there most evenings, in between watching out for teenage vandals.

But even Mr. Yip had to go to the bathroom sometimes, And when he did—SPLASH!

Throughout the Manhattan Luxury Residence, the house rules were being strictly enforced, which also meant that the amahs couldn't sneak into the spacious air-conditioned, second-floor "clubhouse" with the kids, as they sometimes did when Mr. Yip wasn't looking.

In China, the students were still in the square.

And party officials, according to CNN, were getting testy. "You've gotten away with enough," they'd said in an official statement. Or words to that effect.

It was still morning in Hong Kong, but very late back home.

"You have a view of the South China Sea!" Claire sounded as cranky as if she was tending a rice paddy herself. "Why can't the kid go to the beach?"

"Polluted. And you have to be a sherpa to get down there."

"Sherpas go up. Don't you have a playground?"

"The amahs say the playground is too hot."

"Hotter than Manila? Well, there's always the pool."

Claire, I was now sure, would never understand what it was like to be a mother.

"Gotta go," I said as the doorbell rang twice. "Ah Yick is here."

I ran down the stairs in time to see a thin, pleasant, gray-haired man standing at the door, two white cartons in his arms.

"Ah Yick!" Danny said, and within minutes the other children had joined him. "Ah Yick!" they shouted, jumping up and down. "Ah Yick!" Soon he was in the living room and they were dancing around him.

"Ah Yick!" the amahs shouted, too, as if the entire Philippines had just been saved.

Mr. Sammy Chow, who owned Ah Yick Groceries in Stanley Market, nodded his head in delighted recognition. He was perhaps the most beloved deliveryman in the history of the world. If you wanted Raisin Bran or Edy's Grand Ice Cream or Stouffer's French Bread Pizza, then Mr. Chow—who hired helpers to stay in his store while he made the deliveries "personally" and without a delivery assistant—was your man.

Suddenly it was peaceful again, the way it usually is before full-scale war breaks out.

After we put the groceries away, Guli had agreed, albeit reluctantly, to take Danny to the playground—and that's where I thought they were.

I wrote for a while, called Claire back. I was explaining the pool rules to her when the downstairs door crashed open.

"Boom, Mommy. Did you hear it?"

"Ma'am, I am so sorry." Guli was out of breath. "The management wants to see you. . . . The big pot in the clubhouse . . ."

"BOOM! Mommy!"

I bent down. "Did you break the pot, Danny?"

He nodded vigorously.

I tried to picture it.

"The blue and white one, ma'am."

More imitation Ming. The place was drowning in it.

"The one with the plant in it, ma'am," she said. Excepting for matters of housework, Guli could read my mind.

"How . . . ?" I began, as she rushed past me.

She got busy rummaging in the freezer and grabbed a pizza.

"Ma'am. He was playing behind the screen and it fell on the plant."

"Boom!" Danny said.

Guli put the pizza in the microwave. "You'd better go see, ma'am."

In a far corner of the clubhouse, a Polaroid camera flashed and clicked in tune with a round of harsh, Cantonese instructions. Mr. Yip snapped photos while one of Danny's real *pungyows,* looking far less cheerful than usual, carefully lifted another shard of blue and white imitation Ming porcelain and held it for a close-up. Although the air-conditioning was on full blast, beads of sweat dotted the lenses of Mr. Yip's gold-rimmed glasses. He took them off, cleaned them with a handkerchief. The next time he snapped, I waited for the flash, bent down, and quickly put a small shard in the pocket of my jeans.

"Mrs. Mulvaney!"

I flinched. But he hadn't seen.

The shard poked against me. A family heirloom? Or—finally—concrete proof of a Mulvaney escapade?

"Mrs. Mulvaney? Have you read my latest notice on vandalism, Mrs. Mulvaney?"

Upstairs, Guli looked like she needed a rest, so I offered to take Danny to the playground.

"It's okay," I told her. "I'm not doing anything important."

Danny ran to the swings as I settled in with the other

sweating Gweilo mothers. We sat on molded plastic benches set on a comfortable rubber floor and looked not at one another but at our children playing amid shiny metal in bright primary colors. Our topics ranged from sales at Toys "R" Us to the used rompers at Tot's Trading in Stanley, to the waiting list at the local Montessori Play School.

Nobody mentioned the students in Beijing. Nobody even mentioned Beijing. Or Peking, as some of the mothers, even here, still called it.

A Hong Kong Chinese woman, one of the few who lived in The Manhattan, appeared with her small twins, a boy and a girl in very clean clothes. All the Gweilo mothers stopped talking.

Danny ran back to announce that he would now be attempting "the climber."

The sun shone on a red frozen pizza stain on his toddler-sized plaid shirt. Well, at least the Mulvaney name would live on for another generation of dry cleaners.

"Do you have an amah?" the Chinese woman asked me as she stood at a distance.

Later, I dialed Mulvaney's number in Beijing. *Newsday* kept an apartment and office there, in Jianguomenwai, a bleak, rotting set of buildings with no pool and a utilitarian, although serviceable, playground. As good as it got, though, and, not surprisingly, restricted to foreigners. Easier to spy on them that way.

But Jianguomenwai also had a view of Tiananmen Square.

"It's fantastic here," he said. "They're all still down there and nobody is doing anything about them. And this is China. This really is China. Or it was."

I didn't tell Mulvaney that he was a dreamer.

"I got a great interview with Wu'er Kaixi."

The young Mr. Wu'er was the Western press's Chinese Student Dissident Superstar. Probably because he spoke the best English.

"He was drinking a Budweiser!" Mulvaney announced.

DISPATCH FROM THE WAR AT WORK Boutique
University. Day two.

I am teaching my first class. The Broad History of All
Communications II.

"So how was part one?" I ask the students, some of
whom are trying to eat raw cauliflower and broccoli from
the cafeteria salad bar with flimsy plastic forks.

"Irrelevant," says a student named Mark. "Irrelevant" is
a word I haven't heard since the sixties.

"Did you do Hemingway?" I ask hopefully. This seems
to be a kid who notices more than his own generation.
Hemingway might work for the others, too. Guns, war,
women, and intoxication. They'd grown up on video
games. Why wouldn't they like Hemingway?

"Part one," he says dryly, "only got as far as pre-
Gutenberg. We are supposed to pick up there."

"A lot of drums?" I ask, contemplating a semester in the
fifteenth century—not exactly my forte.

The student's fork breaks over a stem and he picks up
half of it and begins beating his desk.

"So start a school newspaper," I say.

"But how?" asks another.

"Couldn't we just do it for class?" Mark asks.

And ignore the curriculum? Just pass over all those
ancient modes of communication?

"Those who forget history are condemned to repeat it,"
I say, trying to sound professorial. I might be a reporter,
but journalism is, as many have said, the first draft of
history. You can't tell the present without knowing the
past. History, though, without practicality—without
knowing how to write—would get them nowhere. Not to
mention the damage it would do to the world in general.

If these kids didn't learn to write, where would the next generation of historians come from? And where would we get our next reporters? Every story, even Gutenberg's, needs a first draft.

I remind myself that this university no longer has a student newspaper.

"What," I say, unable to resist, "if we try to do both?"

CHAPTER TWENTY-TWO
Tiananmen Two

I was nursing a hangover when Mr. Yip came to call.

The night before, I'd left Danny with Guli and gone to the FCC. First, though, I'd walked around the city, my favorite thing to do in Hong Kong, starting at the Star Ferry dock, where from behind a small booth local students had started to collect money for their counterparts in Beijing. The ones in the square.

"Pray for them," a gray-haired woman in black pajamas had said as she flung money into a large red tin.

"My *pungyow*," Danny now said happily when he saw Mr. Yip at the door to our flat.

"*Josun, josun!*" Good morning, Mr. Yip said, as he tapped Danny's head.

"Have a seat," I said, and sat down opposite him on the living room sofa, holding together a black silk robe from the Stanley Market. Too late I'd noticed its label: "Made for the Asian Figure."

"So what do you think about those students, Mr. Yip?"

"China isn't supposed to be a democracy, Mrs. Mulvaney," he said, handing me a bill.

"We paid the rent," I said, glancing at it. This was almost two months' worth. Twelve thousand US.

"Ming vase," Mr. Ying noted, as he lowered his glasses on his nose.

He was trying to pass that thing off as real?

My head throbbed. I would never drink Armagnac again.

"The Manhattan Luxury Residence expects restitution immediately, Mrs. Mulvaney."

Okay. If he wanted Mrs. Mulvaney, he'd get Mrs. Mulvaney.

"My husband," I said. "He pays all the bills. He's away. . . ." I bent closer. "Tiananmen," I whispered, trying to look modest, unassuming—and not let the robe slip.

Mr. Yip's chin quavered ever so slightly.

Then his walkie-talkie buzzed. "The landlord will want the money soon. He can, you know, double your rent over such a matter."

Mulvaney called to say that if the students didn't leave they might get shot.

On the television, CNN reported that the scene was "grim."

Mr. Yip came for the second day in a row to ask when I would pay for the vase. I made him a cup of tea, which he sipped.

"My husband says it could get very bad."

He took another sip. "Mrs. Mulvaney," he said.

"Yes?"

"Is West Los Angeles a safe neighborhood?"

"Mr. Yip?"

"I have a cousin who lives there."

I nodded. Strategically located cousins continued to be a motif I couldn't escape.

"Mrs. Mulvaney, do foreigners teach their children manners?"

"Foreigners?"

"I mean Americans."

"Well, we try, Mr. Yip. We try. But our children sometimes have minds of their own."

As the tension built in Beijing, Mulvaney spent hours in the square talking to students and as much time as he could writing on his portable computer in the Jianguomenwai apartment. Correspondents from the other papers did the same. Lady Liberty seemed to have gotten to everyone.

The students said they didn't want much. A vote. A say.

From the Central Communist Committee, according to Mulvaney, you could practically see the smoke.

The People's Liberation Army—China's army—was a force of kids, too, much like any other force throughout the world. The soldiers were the kids who didn't make it into college, who were fighting not as much for their people or liberation as, really, just to keep their own heads above water.

According to the rumors that substituted for real news in China, the PLA would be called in soon. To quiet the protesters. Nobody said how.

*   *   *

"Fischkin," Leisure Suit said. He'd called himself, this time, instead of deploying Claire. "I need you there. Now."

Mulvaney called. "You need to be here."

"Mommy," Danny asked, "are they going to shoot people?"

My mother called from Brooklyn in the middle of the night.

"It's very hard to get the time zones straight," she said. My mother had a gift for finding me at my weakest moment.

"You shouldn't go," she said. "It's not that great a story."

"Mother!" I said. "You were the one who assigned Mulvaney."

My mother had been the first woman on the Congregation B'nai Israel Board of Trustees and she'd gotten there by threatening the shul's Perpetual President—her husband—with a discrimination suit if he didn't appoint her.

"Maternal instinct," my mother warned. "It won't ward off any curses. But go against it and you won't be able to fight any, either."

I gave Guli the next morning off, took Danny down to swim. I put his water wings on.

"Jump!" I said. He did, laughing as he plunged, barely getting his head wet. I looked past him, up to the faces of the maids in the window of the over-air-conditioned clubhouse. Then I looked down again and imagined the brown body of Meni, of Amenaza Porvenir, the Mexican maid with the ominous name, snaking through the water of our Hong Kong pool, bringing the Curse of Tiananmen on everyone. Everyone except, of course, the amahs.

"Jump in, Mommy!"

As I plunged in, Meni disappeared.

*   *   *

"Mommy? What's that? Truck, Mommy, a truck."

Danny called me in to see the television.

"Go boom, Mommy."

I had to sit down when I saw it. The tanks rode into Tiananmen Square. Tanks that didn't look particularly Chinese. They looked like tanks anywhere.

The tanks rode in, manned by teenagers mowing down other teenagers. Shooting them, too. A lone man waved his arms, trying to stop them. It was a Chinese station, but I thought I heard them say it fast: *Geeonuhmenwhy.*

Jianguomenwai. The foreigners' flats?

I switched to CNN, where they announced that a tank was outside Jianguomenwai, aiming at a sniper on the roof.

Mulvaney, I said to myself, will be okay.

I'd left the door open and Mr. Yip walked in. He looked at the television.

"I am ashamed to be Chinese," he said, shaking his head.

As a group, the Hong Kong Chinese finally came around in full force and supported the students. They marched for them. They hung pictures of the dead at the Star Ferry.

More than a decade later, few would know how many really died.

I am ashamed to be Chinese. In Hong Kong, this was said many times.

Even as the tanks withdrew, that honest, responsible humility prevailed. People did not disown the men who had sent in the tanks. They were our own. Very wicked, but yes, our own.

Americans would have simply identified with the students. Case closed.

Americans, in fact, did—including one in particular.

"Killed like our own colonial forefathers," my mother noted, during one of what were now her daily phone calls.

"Mother," I said, "your forefathers were from a shtetl in the Ukraine."

Mulvaney had called when tanks were still in the square. He told me, quickly and quietly, that a gun was put to the back of his head. A young soldier . . .

My husband had been wearing a black stocking cap. When he turned, the soldier saw his face and, petrified, perhaps, by a Gweilo face or by Gweilo blue eyes, shot a Chinese man instead.

Or maybe it was just luck.

"I need to laugh," Mulvaney said.

I took a very deep breath. "Tell me a funny story," I ordered. My voice shook. "You always laugh at your own stories."

There was a pause. "Yesterday . . ." he began. "Yesterday," he said again, slowly. ". . . they flew in one of the Men Who Didn't Write *Naked Came the Stranger*."

My substitute was an old single guy from Ronkonkoma.

"And he came," Mulvaney said, "with an inflatable travel toilet seat."

Amazing, I thought, the things they sell in a democracy like Suffolk County.

DISPATCH FROM THE WAR *ABROAD* Later, when it was all over, I understood why it had been my mother, Ida Fischkin, not me or Mulvaney, posted in Asia though we were, who predicted that no matter the outcome, the world would have to pay attention to Tiananmen Square. She had seen it coming from thousands of miles away, from Avenue I in Brooklyn to be exact.

Or had she seen it by looking back?

Since coming to America in 1919, my mother's ear had been cocked toward any number of improbable pleas for democracy. And her radar, long before Ted Turner became a household name, took in the international—and the image-driven.

Was that because she had witnessed a pogrom, not merely heard the horror stories? Or because, in the midst of those horrors, she had also seen the faintest glimmer of hope? As she hid in a haystack, she heard the horses riding over her. Then silence. She peeked out and saw the backs of red jackets. She saw the Cossacks riding away.

So much has been written about "survivor's guilt" that perhaps we forget to give "survivor's optimism" its due. In my mother's aging mind, there are still pictures of people scrambling in terror, packing wagons with all they could, leaving everything else behind. But she saw some of those people again. And they saw her. In a place that was better, immediately, and better still over decades and generations. My mother had seen the impossible. Why wouldn't she think that a gaggle of college students could turn the world's largest Communist state, the world's largest country, into a democracy?

At first it looked as if my mother had been wrong about

the students. Instead of democracy they got massacred. Or put in prison.

But there were some who packed up their wagons and got lucky. Wu'er Kaixi hid, survived, made it to Harvard, dropped out to do the lecture circuit.

And, almost a decade after the Communist takeover, there are places in the People's Republic that more resemble Long Island than Hong Kong.

From the *New York Times,* June 3, 2005: "Suburban housing compounds have now sprouted around Beijing, and the city has added more than a million new cars. Many of the city's wealthiest people, as well as many foreign expatriates, now travel down the city's Airport Expressway through the greenish morning haze toward the ramp to the Third Ring Road."

Still, it isn't really democracy that has triumphed in China, as much as capitalism. The gap between rich and poor grows and the recognition of human rights is nowhere near as predictable as a rush-hour traffic jam.

As for Hong Kong itself, after nearly a decade in Chinese hands I am told it is still very much the place we knew. A capitalist success if not, entirely, a democratic one.

From the *New York Times,* May 31, 2005: "The arrest of the journalist Ching Cheong . . . represents the latest in a series of arrests of Hong Kong citizens on the mainland during the past several years. . . . [Mr. Ching] had been trying to obtain documents on conversations that Zong Fengmin, a retired party official, had with Zhao Ziyang, who was purged as general secretary of the Communist party after the killing in Tiananmen Square in 1989."

Mr. Ching, the *Times* noted, had attended an elite Hong Kong Anglican secondary school and then Hong Kong University. After college he worked for a newspaper that had close ties to Beijing. But he quit to join the protest in Tiananmen Square.

CHAPTER TWENTY-THREE
Make Love, Not War

Mulvaney left Beijing without telling me he was coming home. He arrived stealthily, too, as if he was looking behind him for a tank. Instead of letting himself in at the bottom of our duplex, he rode the elevator to fourteen and knocked at the door no one ever used, the one just outside our bedroom.

I opened it to find him leaning against a rolled-up Chinese rug that smelled a little mildewed.

"Carried it here myself," he said as he threw it over the threshold. "It's blue and silk."

I kissed him.

"Where's Danny?"

"Out with the maid," I said. "They're letting them into the clubhouse. But they still can't go in the pool."

Mulvaney kissed me back, hard on the lips. We lay down

on our large bed. Through the windows on my right I could see the South China Sea. Small but wily sampans and junks scouted carefully around rich Gweilo windsurfers from Europe and America. Yachts, some owned by corporations, others by the richest of the Cantonese, went where they wanted. Hong Kong might be close to mainland China, and the takeover might be coming soon, but this place still reeked of capitalism and the prospect of more.

"We should go to the Philippines," Mulvaney insisted, sounding absolutely MacArthur-esque. He hadn't been home from Beijing more than a few hours.

"People Power!" he said, referring to the successful revolution that had toppled the Marcoses and brought Cory Aquino to the top, where she more or less belonged.

"They sent tanks after people in the Philippines, too," I said, hungering for a place where the taste of war was, at the least, less recent. "How about Kyoto?"

"No stories in Kyoto."

There were, we both knew, stories everywhere. Still . . .

"We should go to the Philippines, because there, when people stood in front of tanks, the soldiers stopped driving them," he said calmly, as if logic played any role whatsoever in this discussion.

DISPATCH FROM THE WAR AT HOME "Is that it?" Mulvaney asks. "Where's all the sex you promised me in this book?"

"Mulvaney," I say, "this is a book about marriage and parenting. Why would you think it would have any sex at all?"

By writing it clean, I tell him, I am also performing my patriotic duty. Not long after my first Mulvaney book came out, I received a note from Congressman Peter King:

"Barbara: I look forward to the next one but implore you to keep the sex scenes with Mulvaney to an absolute *minimum."*

Like most unclear government mandates, this one was probably related to national security.

"What do Republicans know about sex?" Mulvaney yells. His eyes widen. They turn military blue.

"Or security?" he booms.

His pupils are now massive enough to invade an inconsequential country and blow it up.

"Well," I say, "when it comes to Republicans, in general, I tend to agree. But if it wasn't for Peter King, Dubai would be running our ports . . . and long before that he brought peace to Northern Ireland."

Indeed, the congressman was there when Gerry Adams ordered the IRA to get rid of all its weapons, all the while insisting that he was never actually in that outlawed army, much less its commander.

Mulvaney-true is not necessarily limited to Mulvaneys.

"Peter King," Mulvaney shouts, "would not have gotten anywhere in Northern Ireland without me!"

It is true-true that Mulvaney had introduced the congressman to Ian Paisley, creating a shaky but serviceable bridge between American Republicans who are also Irish Republicans and various Protestant paramilitary organizations, none of which Ian Paisley ever commanded, either.

But let's look at precisely *where* that introduction took place. In Stormont Castle, to which Mulvaney was confined because the Brits found guns under his bed.

Suffice it to say that Peter King had not come for tea.

"After all I did for that guy. You think he'd at least help my alter ego get laid," my husband says.

CHAPTER TWENTY-FOUR
Too Tired to Do It

After his homecoming, Mulvaney slept for days, or at least he tried to.

His own screams woke him. I put a cold towel on his face, turned up the air conditioner, rearranged his feet, covered him with a light blanket, kissed his face.

"I want bad American food," he cried out.

"Jell-O?" I offered. "A tin of SPAM?"

He sat up. "More emblematic!"

"Velveeta?" I suggested.

But he shook his head.

I was running out of processed-food groups.

"Talk about what happened there," I begged him. He had told me only the barest details.

"I can't talk about it," he said. "And it is a horrible way to feel."

"Packaging," he moaned. "I want great packaging. The kind that shows American ingenuity. Something that we grew up believing in, something that made us know democracy would always triumph, even when it falls short."

With Ah Yick Groceries as my only resource, this was not going to be easy.

I caught Mr. Sammy Chow at his shop, preparing another delivery, and explained my predicament.

He told me he was ashamed to be Chinese. Then his eyes brightened. He was, after all, used to Gweilo wives and their weird requests.

"Take this," he said, handing me a package of Wonder Bread as he lifted a carton with Cheerios on top and carried it to his truck. "On the house, Mrs. Mulvaney," he said.

I went home and made scrambled eggs on buttered white bread.

"This is what I meant," Mulvaney said, kissing the red, yellow, and blue balloons on the wrapper.

Danny stared at them quizzically.

He looked inside the bag, pulled out a slice, and asked me what it was. Tortillas he knew. Rice, too. And, recently, he had even seen a close approximation of Cheez Doodles.

"American bread," I told him.

The wrapper, though, interested him more. "Can people ride on those balloons?" he asked. Then, "Lunch with Daddy!" he insisted. "Guys, not Wonder Bread."

Would my son's wife, I wondered, have to find raw jellyfish to calm *him* down?

We all went to the market. When we came home, Mulvaney went back to bed.

*   *   *

My mother sent American toiletries, supplemented by health-care products. "Rub things on Mulvaney and he will revive," she promised. She sent Vicks and Ben-Gay. He said that all he could smell was the morgues he'd been in. I bought Hong Kong–made Tiger Balm, but he didn't smell that, either.

"I only smell formaldehyde," he told me. In just two morgues he'd counted more bodies than the Chinese had admitted killing altogether. "I can write it. I can't talk it," he said.

He fell back to sleep. I woke in the middle of the night and, restless, went to examine the rug he had brought home from Tiananmen Square. It had been propped in the upstairs hall since he'd arrived and smelled worse with each passing day.

I checked Danny in his bedroom. He slept soundly. I checked his breathing and his head. Never know when a kid could have a fever. Then I maneuvered the rug down to thirteen, shoved it into the crowded living room, moved Danny's slide to the corner, and, holding my nose, unrolled Mulvaney's latest contribution to our ongoing, alleged domesticity.

Silk, yes. But not my type. Too many flowers ruining a perfectly nice blue and white background. Next to them were strange, crude figures in moldy green. The best Chinese rugs, the ones that took a more conventional route off the Mainland to Hong Kong, had well-balanced colors and well-designed geometric shapes. Rugs that reflected the style of Hong Kong harbor itself. The rugs left in China were musty. Too flowery and traditional, too reflective of too many years of repression.

I moved my finger over the design and felt a chill.

What were those green things? A cross, its bent arms

stretched into a circle. Shaking, I rolled the rug up, stood it on its end, opened the door, and shoved it into the hall. I put in a doorstop, rang for the elevator, pushed the rug in, and rode with it to the lobby. The *pungyow* for the day had left hours ago. I rolled the rug down the marble lobby floor, out a back door, and heaved it onto the garbage heap.

DISPATCH FROM THE WAR AT HOME Back in Brooklyn, when I was a kid, everybody at Congregation B'nai Israel of Midwood worried about intermarriage. Las Vegas Nite aside, they were stuck in the *Fiddler on the Roof* mentality when it came to this. Marry "out of the faith" and you were considered dead. Your parents sat shiva for you.

Oddly, though, it was the boys who got most of the lectures, as if they thought girls were not up to such acts of rebellion.

Or was it the lure of the blonde, long-legged, flat-chested *shikse,* so different looking from all those Jewish mothers? Was that what made the Jewish mothers apoplectic?

Sometimes a blonde who looked like she might be Christian had only to walk down Avenue I for the furor to begin.

"Feh," one of the women would say. "Marry someone like *that* and she'll turn around one day and call you a dirty Jew."

At this, the boys would look at one another to see who'd given it away. Who'd looked with a little too much interest at that blonde?

When I married Mulvaney—unconventional though the reasons may have been—I surprised a lot of people from the shul. They couldn't imagine that the daughter of their Perpetual President would do such a thing. My father, though, he wasn't surprised. Nor did he buy into my mother's prediction—the one she made because she loved Mulvaney—that eventually he would convert.

My father never thought Mulvaney would do that. Still doesn't. And doesn't care. For my father, the shul was politics, not religion. As for the rules, well, as soon as the

rabbi walked past our house on Shabbos, he'd light up a
Phillies Panatella, in defiance, I believe, of all ancient
Judaic law. It is from my father, David Fischkin, that I got
my spirituality. Or my particular brand, at least. People
still ask me about religion as a factor in my marriage.
They want to know how we "work it out."

"Atheism," I reply, which, I suppose, is as good an
answer as any when the two people in question can't work
out much. Why would anyone think that we, of all
people, could solve the two-thousand-year-old Judeo-
Christian split? Christ couldn't do it. Why does anyone
think Mulvaney and Fischkin can? I should, I suppose, be
flattered.

But let me go on the record and say that Mulvaney has
never called me a dirty Jew.

I think he's afraid of the things I might say about the
Irish if he did.

Or the Catholics, even though it is true-true that some
of my best friends are priests.

We don't fight much about religion. If we do, it usually
has more to do with being careful about history, and
about symbolism, too. On the big issues of both our
religions—issues current and time-honored—we agree.

We are pro-choice. Pro–birth control. Pro–meat on
Friday. We think that the Palestinians have a right to their
homeland, but that throwing Jews out of their settlements
on that land was a mess, created by politicians, one in
particular. And yes, we think that gays and lesbians should
march in the St. Patrick's Day parade in Manhattan. Why
the hell not? It's Manhattan, isn't it?

"So how are you raising your children?" people ask.

"With much difficulty," I reply.

Danny's religion is waves at the beach, wind in the
trees, the magic of inconsequential objects.

And Jack? Well, he's as happy as can be with the religion and/or ethnic group that suits the moment. He has used religion—presumably the ones he has a claim to—to get out of going to both Hebrew School and church. He has an all-purpose background, an all-purpose answer for almost any ethnicity-related question. He will tell you, tallying up all sides, possibilities, and antiquities, that his bloodline is, in alphabetical order: Anglican, Arabic (Esau), Celt, Cossack (shtetl-dwellers consorting with the enemy?), Gaelic, Maccabean, Norman, Polish, Russian, Swedish, Viking, and Welsh. Recently, a teacher asked him if he had a British passport, since he was born in Hong Kong before the Communist takeover.

"Nope," he said, gearing up for Mulvaney-true. "The Brits wouldn't give me one because I am Irish."

CHAPTER TWENTY-FIVE
World War Two at Home

Mulvaney woke up for good a few days later.

He had, I guessed, finished covering Tiananmen Square.

He kissed me and said, "I have a great idea. Let's find a place for the new rug."

I said nothing.

"Well," he asked, walking into the hallway. "Where is it?"

"Mulvaney," I said, "I threw it out."

"You what?"

"It had swastikas on it!"

"Swastikas? Are you nuts?" His eyes flared betrayal blue. "I carried that rug out of Beijing in my arms! After having a gun to my head, after seeing bodies piled on top of bodies. What did I think of? The state of the world?

Repression? My own damaged psyche? Nope. Nope. Nope. All I thought was that my darling wife might like a rug."

"Mulvaney," I said. "The rug is cursed."

"Then, at the airport, they didn't want to let me through. Wanted to detain me as a smuggler! But did I let that get in the way of my mission to bring a new, beautiful, handmade, silk rug home to my allegedly devoted wife? Nope. Nope. Nope. I risked my life, yet again, and told them I would not give up the rug."

"Mulvaney," I repeated, "it has swastikas on it!"

"Swastikas! I sat next to that rug on the plane out of Beijing! The rug," he said, "does not have swastikas."

"Well, what would you call them?"

"What would I call them?"

"Yeah, what would you call them?"

"Fylfots!" he shouted. "All Chinese rugs have them."

"Fylfots?" I shouted back. "What the hell are fylfots?"

He stormed out the door and banged the elevator button so hard I heard it on fourteen. Even with air-conditioning. Hours later he returned, smelling of Smithwicks beer, which they had on tap at the English pub in Stanley.

"Mulvaney," I said, "I thought you didn't drink with Brits."

"I do now," he railed. This was the first nice thing I had ever heard him say about the English. "They—like the Chinese—fought the Germans!"

He flung a gold-embossed brown book in my direction.

"Read this!" he ordered.

Angrily, I picked it up. *Funk & Wagnalls New Encyclopedia,* copyright 1972.

"Antique store in Stanley Market is selling them by the volume," he said, testily, as he grabbed the book back and read aloud: " 'Fylfot: Cross with equal arms, the ends of which are bent either clockwise or counterclockwise. The extensions of the arms of the cross are sometimes joined to form a complete circle. This design, one of the earliest-known symbols, was associated with the worship of sun gods in many areas of the ancient world, including Egypt, Greece, and Scandinavia. It still survives as a religious symbol in India among followers of Buddhism and Jainism and in China and Japan, as well as among the Indian tribes of North America. . . .' "

I sighed. Danny and Guli came bounding in.

"I want *lumpia*!" Danny demanded. The maid smiled and ushered him into the kitchen.

" '. . . that continue the practice of aboriginal religion and medicine. The fylfot is the ancestor of many decorative motifs, from the classic Greek meander, or labyrinth, to more elaborate forms. In medieval Europe it was used as a device to fill the foot of stained glass windows, and the word *fylfot* probably was originally "fill foot." ' "

Suddenly he stopped.

I grabbed the book back. " 'The most recent use of this symbol in Europe was the German Hakenkreuz, or swastika (fr. Skr. *Svasti,* "good fortune"), the emblem of anti-Semitism since 1918, and established as the symbol of the Nationalist Socialist German Workers Party under the German dictator Adolf Hitler.' "

"Barbara," he said, "the arms of the German *swastika* are bent clockwise. The *fylfots* on that rug you just threw out were bent *counterclockwise.*"

"Mulvaney," I said, "is this how the Irish justified neutrality during World War II?"

He stared at me and I stared back. There it was, the elephant in the living room, the marital issue that could come between us, that could blot out all the other "insurmountable" issues that we had—so far—surmounted. It could trump a bought baby, stolen sources, missed stories, and forgotten bylines, even guns under the bed.

It had bothered me so much that up until now I had not dared to discuss it.

"No, it is not how the Irish justified neutrality during World War II," he said, mimicking me as if he thought I was some silly little girl. As if we were Ralph and Alice discussing a late night at the Raccoon Lodge. "The Irish were neutral during World War II because it was the logical step for a new, small republic that wanted to survive."

"Ireland," I said, "was neutral over the Holocaust!"

"No," he replied, his blue eyes flaming green. "Ireland was neutral over the *war*."

Was this the cultural divide people said would kill our marriage? Was this why my mother wanted Mulvaney to convert, so when he took a geopolitical side it would always be mine?

And why was I finding this out now? After we'd had a kid?

"Context," Mulvaney said. "Before you go dumping expensive rugs that your husband carried through a war zone in a Communist country, you should, at the least, consider context!"

"Mulvaney," I said, "you are an Irish Catholic. In a million years we could never have the same context."

DISPATCH FROM THE WAR AT WORK For the first issue of the newly revived Boutique U. newspaper, my students say they would like to write an editorial condemning the dreadful food in the school's cafeteria.

I yawn, but part of me is amazed that at college some things never change. We wanted to do a "meal exposé" in my own college newspaper. But that food really was bad. Fresh vegetables? Forget about it. These kids don't know how good they have it.

"You can't write an editorial until you have a news story," I tell them.

"They put Ex-Lax in the hamburgers," a young woman in pink sweatpants proclaims.

A story so old, I heard it in my day.

"Someone in my dorm got sick," she continues.

"Did anyone else get sick?" I ask. "Did any doctors confirm an overdose of laxatives? Did anyone *see* anyone do it?"

"Wow," she replies. "I didn't know you had to ask so many questions. What if we set up a hidden camera in the kitchen?"

"Expensive," I say. Particularly for a newspaper that didn't have a first issue, much less a budget.

I am surrounded by disappointed faces. *"Don't disappoint them,"* Leisure Suit had warned. *"This is a business. They are customers. Consumers."*

"A lot of work for a rumor," I say. "Don't fall in love with one unlikely fact. Don't make it into a big story if you don't have more. One single, vague illness does not make a story."

Mark, whom I now call Reporter Mark, raises his hand.

"There was a demonstration about the food," he says, making me yearn for the days of real student activism.

"There is," I moan, "a war going on in Iraq. And some of you know people who are there . . . or going." Long Island, despite its prosperity and inflated housing market, is far from immune to the war. And it isn't just the odd spurts in gas prices. There is a human cost here; *Newsday*, still doing at least one of its jobs well, puts the Long Island war dead on the cover each time there is a new body.

"Even if you think you don't, someone from your high school, or someone you once saw from another high school, at a football game or a basketball game—or at a hockey game . . ." I feel my own stomach coming undone. "Someone like that is there now. Why don't you find out who? Talk to their parents."

Now they really look queasy.

"Food is easier than war," Reporter Mark says. "What if we practice on food?"

There was a war going on when we complained about our college food, too, at the State University of New York at Albany in 1971. And there were boys we knew there who, shivering over their low lottery numbers, feared at any second they might be shuffled off to Vietnam.

Big international stories, though, do not mean that local news shouldn't be covered. Newspapers are supposed to report out everyday life, too.

I ask if anyone in class was at the demonstration.

"Too early in the morning," one says, and they all nod.

Wouldn't it have been more effective, I wonder, to protest after lunch?

"Well," I say, trying to sound understanding yet professorial, "it's hard to cover an event you did not attend."

"Well," replies another eager young woman who, unlike the others, is what we used to call dressed-for-success, "can't we just make it up?"

Stay calm, I say to myself. Do not throw anything. You are here to teach them. It's not their fault no one has.

"Can't we just pretend we got it from unnamed sources or confidential sources or official sources, or something like that?" she continues. "Lots of my friends will say they heard that this is true. Newspapers do stuff like that all the time, right?"

"If you make anything up," I say, "then you must call it fiction."

"I have an idea," says Reporter Mark. "Why don't we just talk to people who were at the demonstration?"

This kid, I think, has a future.

If only journalism did.

"Reporters who are late for press conferences," I say, "do it all the time."

CHAPTER TWENTY-SIX
Long-Distance Marriage Counseling

T his is over a rug?" my mother asked. "You are leaving him over a rug?"

I should have known she would make this into a home decor issue. And with her terrible taste, she probably couldn't imagine any rug bad enough to ruin even the worst marriage.

"You're coming home to live with me over a rug?"

"No, Mother," I said. "It is not over a rug! It is over history! History, culture, interpretation—and sensitivity!"

"Tell me again what a fylfot is?" she asked.

DISPATCH FROM THE WAR AT WORK Encouraged by the A that I gave him on his food story, Reporter Mark calls Mulvaney to gather information for a "Faculty Profile."

"Any good anecdotes about Professor Fischkin?" the student asks.

At my husband's suggestion, Reporter Mark calls the Long Beach soup kitchen and discovers that due to "impatience, rudeness, and a marked insensitivity to the needs of the poor displayed during a phone conversation with a staff worker," I was recently rejected as a "mealtime volunteer."

The hopeful cub reporter then calls every other soup kitchen on Long Island and finds they've all been known to reject volunteers. But only those convicted of felony offenses. Misdemeanors are, apparently, okay.

Finally, in an investigative flourish that would bring tears to the eyes of any journalism professsor, Reporter Mark checks my criminal record and finds, amazingly, that I don't have one.

The headline blares across the front page of the students' now not-so-underground publication, *Boutique U. News and Views:*

Teaching and Community Service, an Historic Case Study:
At Least She Tried.

CHAPTER TWENTY-SEVEN
A Broad Abroad

The officer who called said he worked for the Macanese police force.

I'd never met anyone who had.

Macau sounded like such an odd, compelling locale, too—a Portuguese/Chinese territory just a ferry ride away. People said that the small hotels felt like Lisbon; the big ones, too. *Vinho verdi* was plentiful and cheap, and they even had gambling. Where there was gambling, there was organized crime. And where there was organized crime, there were stories. My mouth watered.

"Vice squad," the cop said, making it water more. Too bad I was in the midst of leaving my husband.

"If you're lookin' for Mulvaney," I said, "he's not here."

Just as well, since I was packing.

I'd told Danny he'd have a great time visiting Brooklyn.

And I'd told Mulvaney we might not come back.

And yes, I knew how unappetizing it sounded. Going back to Mother. Especially *my* mother. But, as she herself always said, you can find the good in anyone. In any place, too. Flatbush-Midwood-Flatlands. My next exotic assignment.

If only my mother would ask the mob to help her with Las Vegas Nite.

"Too bad he ain't dere," the cop said. Even in Macau, cops sounded like cops. "I got a broad here lookin' fer him."

"A broad?" I said. What was that about? "If she has a story, she can tell me."

Stealing a scoop from Mulvaney. One sweet, final gesture. He deserved it.

"She's got quite a story. You the missus?"

"Not for long," I said, wondering why his type was never able to view me as just another reporter. "Not even at the dry cleaners," I said. "Not anymore."

"Listen," the cop continued, "I hate to tell you dis, but it's over some loot."

"Ah, we don't pay for stories," I said, trying not to jump to conclusions.

"Missus, yah ain't gettin' my drift. Da broad lost all her money."

"I am sorry to hear that," I said.

A harridan yelped in the background.

"Ma'am," he said, "dis is poisonol. . . ."

"Personal?"

"Yep, pois-on-ol! Dis broad is demanding to talk to Jim Mulvaney. Says she loves him. Ain't life sweet?"

Great. Just what I needed. Here I am trying to leave

Mulvaney over an argument that has some intellectual heft—at least we can tell our grandchildren that we split over a major travesty of the twentieth century—and he goes out and has an affair with some young Asian sweetie.

Yellow fever. That's what the Gweilo women here called it. As if it was some childhood illness. There were women who talked about it constantly, as if they could ward off infidelity with whining:

"Check your husband's clothes, regularly, for long, straight black hairs" was what they always said.

How, I'd wondered, fingering my own, would I know the difference?

Oh, you can always tell, they'd said.

Happens all the time.

"What's she wearing?" I asked cautiously, praying it was not mink, a local status symbol. It was never cold enough in Hong Kong, but minks still came out at the slightest breeze. Macau, I imagined, was no different, particularly at the casinos.

Downstairs, I heard Guli and Danny return from the clubhouse. Danny swooshed down the living room slide once, then stopped.

"I don't want to go to Brooklyn," my son announced, running up to fourteen and stamping his Ninja-Turtled foot.

"Cheong sum," the cop replied.

"Cheong sum!" I said, picturing tight-fitting silk, a slit up the side, pert little sleeves. "Suzie Wong," I muttered, unable to control myself.

"Nah," the cop said. "Dis one's an old broad."

"Old?" I repeated incredulously. Mulvaney was having an affair with an elderly Chinese woman?

"Yeah, some old Jewish broad . . ."

"Excuse me." I paused. "Did you say Jewish?"

"Yeah," he said. "An old Jewish broad."

I put the phone down. Picked it up again.

"Officer," I said, "what color *cheong sum*?"

"Hard to tell," he replied. "Kinda purple with dots . . ."

DISPATCH FROM THE WAR AT WORK I receive a terse note from the overdressed Communications Department professor, mailed in a fancy envelope engraved with an address in an exclusive North Shore neighborhood.

The cover of her notecard is decorated by a fluttering three-dimensional eyelash.

Not exactly anime. That would be a thin, arched eyebrow. This, perhaps, is the Long Island version.

Just what I need, another character.

Temporary Professor Fischkin:

There is to be no, I repeat, no newspaper until midterms on Gutenberg are completed. No communications until they understand what Communication is. I repeat: Cease publication! Furthermore, we are a Communications Department with an eye toward the future, and newspapers run the very real risk of obsolescence. If your student newspaper is anything ever, it will be a radio station. Perhaps you have missed our bulletin board listing of famous Communications Department alumni, headed by the illustrious Gary Dell'Abate, "Babba Booey" of Howard Stern Show *fame, who was not only one of my best students but is now a national icon. We are all very proud of Gary/Babba, even if we won't let our students intern for Howard. Please send me a follow-up explanation on paper, as I cannot work my e-mail.*

Sincerely yours,
Dr. Fluttering Lash
P.S. Might I suggest that tenure is at stake here.

Tenure?

I'm having enough trouble deciding if I want to keep one husband for the rest of my life, let alone one job.

CHAPTER TWENTY-EIGHT
Escaping Destiny, an Attempt

My mother. Just across the Pearl River Delta in Macau, on an unauthorized (by me, anyway) visit. Yet again. But this was different. I didn't need her this time. I was a real mother now, not someone with a bought baby I didn't want and a husband I still thought I could humanize, or at least tame. True, I was about to become a single working mother. But by choice this time, not by surprise.

I'd planned. I'd sent resumés. I'd even been offered a job at the *Times*. A place I'd thought would never have me.

Okay, so it was a job working for the Long Island section. Hard to do from where I was going to live—back on Avenue I in Flatbush-Midwood-Flatlands—but not impossible.

Okay, so it wasn't really a job but an offer to write freelance.

At least it wasn't *Newsday*. It was better than that.

And it wasn't with Mulvaney.

If you stop working to have a baby—and then get divorced on top of it—it would be only reasonable to expect you'd have to take a step backward. Maybe not a man. But then, a man wouldn't have a baby. Not most of them anyway, despite *Kramer vs. Kramer*. Now, there was a fantasy film for you. Couldn't have been more unlike real life if they'd had it animated.

One step backward, one forward. I could do it. It was better than living with a man who couldn't tell a fylfot from a swastika.

I had a lot of stories left from my days in Huntington, stories Leisure Suit hadn't wanted. The Doc's soup kitchen, I'd heard, was getting thrown out of the church in Long Beach. That had to be worse than being thrown out of a supermarket. That story, though, was only the beginning. Just an exercise to get my juices flowing again en route to my repository of so many great stories. Long Island. How was it that I had never appreciated it for the reporter's paradise it is? Great sources there, too. And I knew enough people to, for example, bring the Nassau County Republican Party to its knees. Peter King would fill me in on everything. He'd be *my* source. I'd steal him from Mulvaney.

Or I'd get him in the divorce.

"Mulvaney," I'd say. "You can keep the rug. I want Peter King."

Mulvaney. What good was he anyway? Here I was with my mother calling from Macau—I could only hope she'd get arrested for having an expired passport or, more likely, sneaking in an unexpired dog—and where was he? Drinking.

Where else? Even worse, with Brits. He was drinking with the Brits in Stanley, unmovable on the fylfot issue. If he'd only said he'd been wrong about the rug, that he shouldn't have bought it. Or that he should have looked at it more carefully. Or that having had its design deficiencies brought to his attention, he was ready to acknowlege its unsuitability as a focal point of our home.

Our former home.

If he'd only made one move.

But he was steadfast on this issue. He'd bought the rug for me, struggled with it through China. Therefore it should not give me the creeps.

As for my mother. Well. She could spend the rest of her life as a broke party girl in Macau for all I cared. I'd simply take over her house and her life in Brooklyn. Why not? I could be my father's hostess. As the shul's Perpetual President, he couldn't be without one, could he?

If Thomas Jefferson's daughter could do it, why not Dave Fischkin's?

For a very brief moment, I considered Freud.

Freud be damned, I said. And it felt good.

Brooklyn or bust!

There was something about maids. They always picked the wrong time to tell you their own problems, as if you didn't have enough of your own.

"Ma'am," Guli said, "I need to go home."

"Guli," I said, "trust me. Brooklyn will feel like home to you."

"Ma'am," she said, "I changed my mind."

I had spent an entire two days getting her a temporary visa. She had bragged to all her friends that she was coming

with me to America. Now suddenly she was the only Filipina maid in all of the Manhattan Luxury Residence, in all
of Hong Kong perhaps, who didn't want to emigrate.

"Mommy," Danny said, tugging at my skirt, "if you
leave my grandma all by herself, will she die in jail?"

DISPATCH FROM THE WAR AT HOME I'm on my way out of the house, headed to Boutique U. It is a beautiful fall day, clear and crisp, the kind of day that makes you believe you can overcome anything, even the politics of academia.

I pick up a neighbor's *Newsday,* which is really ours but is always tossed at the next house. I wonder if they count both families as subscribers?

I stop a minute to peruse its pages, to see if there is anything I can use in class. Nothing better than teaching journalism students from the day's actual newspaper. *From Drums to Digital* has nothing on that.

I gaze at the front page, fondly remembering my own days as a reporter.

Then I see it, promoted in a box at the bottom.

Viewpoints: A Hockey Dad and the First Amendment, page 34.

And there it is, opposite the editorials.

A photograph of Mulvaney in front of the very rink from which he was ejected, wearing one of his son's jerseys, looking at the ground while waving a hockey stick above his head, violating his very own *cri de coeur* from the stands: "Head up, stick down, Jack!"

The headline is even worse than the photograph.

CHAPTER TWENTY-NINE
A Man Does Not Need a Maid

Guli, the few possessions she owned packed in one of Stanley Market's best fake Louis Vuitton duffel bags, stood with me in the hall, ignoring my pleas. I'd left the door to the flat open. Danny, in front of the television where I'd planted him, sang along with some dumb purple dinosaur.

"Where will you go?" I asked her.

"Home, ma'am."

She pressed the down button.

When the elevator arrived, Mulvaney walked out.

The dinosaur crooned on mindlessly.

Mulvaney stared at us, his eyes seasick blue and dewy, his breath smelling faintly of Guinness, which for some reason they now sold at that Brit bar he suddenly loved. Had they ordered it special for him?

"Going already?" he asked, looking at me.

"She is," I said as Guli jumped in.

The door closed and she disappeared. Perhaps forever.

"I'm next," I continued, hard.

He looked back at me, hard now himself. "What am I going to do without an amah?"

"Clean up your own mess," I seethed. "Do all your own shopping. Learn, perhaps, how to make wise purchases."

"Barbara . . ."

"Do not 'Barbara' me," I said, shaking. I felt as if I might cry. But was it because I was about to leave a husband?

Or because I had just lost a maid?

MORE THAN ZERO TOLERANCE: CHANGING THE FASCIST/COMMUNIST HOCKEY PARENT BEHAVIORAL CODE
by James Edward Mulvaney, Jr.

Recently, at a local ice arena, I had the distinct pleasure of explaining the realities of life to a referee and then a rink official. As an American, I believe this is a liberty to which I am well entitled. As a Long Islander, I think, "Just let them dare try and take it away from me." Liberty is a driveway, a lawn, a garage—and the right to say what you want when your kid's well-being is in jeopardy. When some jerk of a ref, for example, gives him a completely undeserved penalty.

Let's get the facts straight. Even with basic human rights aside, we parents pay thousands of dollars to these rinks so that our kids can play hockey. That makes us their bosses, doesn't it? It makes the rink, and its refs and officials, our employees. When have you ever heard of employees writing a code of behavior for management? For the owners? That doesn't even happen in the NHL.

Certainly there will be those who believe that if I had a disagreement with these two poor excuses for human beings, I should have expressed them in a different forum. Well, to paraphrase one of my heroines, Janis Joplin, "Freedom—if not used in a timely fashion, at the height of the moment, for example—is just another word for nothing left to lose." Strike while the iron is hot, I say. Strike when there is the possibility of a goal.

I did mention, didn't I, that my husband has never written a book?

There will also be those who claim that anything more than zero tolerance is dangerous. There again, I say, let's get the facts straight. Let's get the numbers straight. In all of America—and it was not, by the way, on Long Island—there has only been one homicide involving a kid's hockey game.

If there was another, I would know. I used to, after all, cover homicides for a living.

CHAPTER THIRTY
Las Vegas Nite East

J ewish guilt.

You'd think that after sleeping with any number of Irish men, and marrying one of them, I would have used up all of my Jewish guilt. You'd think that after leaving my parents and their shul to go to college upstate, still a tender teenager, I would not look back for an instant. That after reporting stories from the midst of wars in Northern Ireland and Latin America, that after surviving childbirth in two foreign countries and the highly uncomfortable realities of being a Gweilo in Hong Kong, that after gathering the courage to leave a man, even though he was almost shot in the head in Tiananmen Square, I would be hardened to the troubles my mother had made for herself.

But I wasn't.

As I packed a small bag for the short side trip by ferry to Macau, I wondered if maybe, after all this time with Mulvaney, I'd acquired some Irish guilt, too. Or was it what Danny had said about his grandmother going to prison? That, too, nagged at me as I boarded the boat, thinking I would just do this one last thing before I claimed my rightful place back home, as the new guiding force of Congregation B'nai Israel and its Perpetual President.

I found my mother perched on the immense stone knees of an Egyptian monarch in the lobby of Pharaoh's Palace Hotel and Casino, which, according to the billboards, "provided gaming and atmosphere aplenty, just minutes from the Macau Ferry terminal." Although my mother did not, as I had suspected, have her own mangy mutt in tow—a miracle that rivaled the Red Sea parting—she herself, in polka-dotted cheong sum, resembled, if it can be imagined, a purple Dalmatian.

"Mother," I said, "this is not funny."

She pretended to pinch the pharaoh's hard cheek, her eyes glittering with mischief. "He promised to let my people go."

Was he even the right pharaoh? Entertainment facilities did not make such distinctions. For all we knew, he could be King Tut, the boy prince. Technically, though, a pharaoh all the same. Boy princes, for all the obvious reasons, had begun to interest me lately.

"Where are the Mulvaneys?" my mother asked cheerfully as she waved to a few gamblers on their way out.

Mulvaney, my husband, had offered to stay in Hong Kong with Mulvaney, my son. You couldn't take a two-and-a-half-year-old on a late-night ferry to Sodom and Gomorrah, could you?

As for Mulvaney, my father-in-law, he was supposedly at

home in Rockaway. But I made a mental note to check the Manna From Heaven Bar that I'd now spotted alongside the gaming tables.

"No Queen Asta?" I asked my mother.

"Her name is Asta, thank you. Not Queen Esther," she said, as she slid off Pharaoh's lap. "And she's coming with your father after he locks up the shul."

"Mother!" I said, everything suddenly falling into place. In Flatbush-Midwood-Flatlands, I remembered, it would soon be Las Vegas Saturday Nite.

"Research!" she confirmed, handing me the latest version of one of her famous brochures: "A Nite of Oriental Gambling at Congregation B'nai Israel of Midwood. Dinner Included: Kosher Chinese from Moshe Peking, Brooklyn's Best."

We were interrupted by a European man in a tuxedo who kissed my mother's hand.

"*Boa noite,* Ida. *Até logo!*"

She shook her head at him and opened an empty sequined purse.

"Sorry, buddy, all washed out."

"Mother," I sighed.

"He said he had a system," she explained.

"And you believed him?"

My mother smoothed her cheong sum and righted the diamond-studded Star of David around her neck. "Barbara, I'm surprised you would ask. What has happened to your sense of possibility?"

It was a long, blustery ferry ride back to Hong Kong. I refused to speak to my mother, so she busied herself showing pictures of her grandson to hungover Chinese gamblers. When one of them brandished a switchblade, I pulled her back. Another man sneezed on us, hard.

"And the people at the Chinese laundry on Avenue J had such nice manners!" she said, unfortunately not to herself.

"Mother!" I said as a group of tattooed and pierced teenagers, triad hopefuls, stared us down. "Everyone here speaks English."

"Well, of course," she replied. "It's the universal language."

DISPATCH FROM THE WAR AT WORK Later, at Boutique U., I ask Leisure Suit for help with the Communications Department chair.

I've heard she claims her ancestors came to America on the *Mayflower*.

"Fluttering Lash," I say, trying out my new name for her.

"Who?" he asks, as if he's never heard a disparaging moniker in his life.

"The chair," I say.

"I can't interfere with faculty," he says.

Now, after all these years as a newspaper editor, he's decided to become a hands-off boss?

"But she wants to stop publication of the newspaper," I say. "What about freedom of the press? What about the reason her relatives came here in the first place?"

"You shall have it," Leisure replies, digging into his rolltop desk for more blank diplomas to throw in the air. "I will remind her that we at Boutique U. hold freedom of the press near and dear to our hearts. You run that newspaper. I will protect you."

"Thank you," I say.

"Nice viewpoints piece by Mulvaney," he says.

CHAPTER THIRTY-ONE
Heat and Song

At home it was chillier than on the ferry.

Mulvaney was asleep in our bed. I opened a fold-out couch for my mother, warned her not to wake Danny, and told her she could play with him all the next day if she wanted.

What the hell, I had no maid anyway.

She fell into a light snore. I went to Danny's room, where, for days, I'd been sleeping on the trundle of his red, white, and blue junior bed. Now, too tired to pull it out, I snuggled in next to him and dozed off with my hand on his forehead.

I woke feeling as if we were in a fireplace.

"Danny," I whispered, while he slept on, "you are one sick kid."

How sick, I hadn't realized until I put the thermometer to his ear.

"Mommy," I said, shaking my own mother awake. "Danny has a temperature of one hundred and six."

My mother, still in cheong sum, jumped from the unfolded couch. I stuck the thermometer in Danny's ear again to make sure I had not read wrong, and quickly dialed our Gweilo pediatrician in Repulse Bay.

A Brit, but I liked him anyway.

"Cool him down," though, was all he said, making me wonder if there wasn't something to ethnic stereotyping after all.

My mother felt her grandson's forehead with her hand, nodded at me, woke him slowly, lifted him gently, warned him softly: "Sweetie pie, your bath will feel cold like the pool."

In the gray tiled bathroom—Danny's own—the icy water ran into a navy blue tub. "The only thing to do," she said, looking at me with a rare apologetic expression.

Danny's screams woke Mulvaney, who arrived as the vomiting began.

"Dan my man," he said softly, as he held his son's small forehead above the toilet bowl.

When it was over, he ran a cold washcloth over Danny's face. "I've seen a lot of men puke, but never as good a man as you!"

I looked at Mulvaney.

He looked back at me.

"This isn't my fault," he said.

"I know," I replied, wondering if it was mine. If I hadn't stood so close to the man on the ferry. If I hadn't brought those germs into Danny's bed.

*   *   *

All night it went on like that. We gave Danny baths. We took his temperature. As the sun rose, we all pretended to be puking with him and we all felt like it. I had never heard of a kid being that sick.

"I have," my mother said. But she had seen so much worse than any of us. "Still," she said, her hand back on his forehead. "He is down to one hundred and two."

At nine we took off the third pair of Ninja Turtle pajamas he'd been in that night, changed him into a pair of Stanley Market chinos and a Ninja Turtle T-shirt, and hailed a taxi to Repulse Bay, where the doctor said that yes, ear infections could be this bad. But the worst was over. We returned to more guests. My father, chomping down, worried, on a Phillies Panatella, and Queen Asta, who jumped up and licked my hand sympathetically. Had I misjudged that dog for all these years?

The antibiotics worked quick and hard, making Danny whimper.

"We need to sing," my mother said.

She was in the midst of a rendition of *"Bei Mir Bist du Schön"* that would have made the Andrews Sisters weep when thirteen floors down we heard . . . could it be . . . the faint sound of bagpipes?

And the aging but hearty voice of an Irish tenor.

"Oh Danny boy, the pipes the pipes are calling. . . ."

"My other grandpa . . ." Danny smiled for the first time in a day. His eyes grew wide. "The Real Mulvaney," he said, as if he were a magical being.

"Honey," I said, "Grandpa is in Rockaway."

The sound disappeared as suddenly as it had come. We were tired enough to imagine anything. Then the elevator swished open on our floor. The pipes were outside our door. So was the tenor: *". . . when summer's in the me-eh-doow . . ."*

A very large man in a very large kilt—Dan Tubridy, the proprietor of Pier 92 on Jamaica Bay—pushed open our front door.

"Bei mir bist du schön," my father-in-law sang, although with his Queens Irish-Yiddish accent the lyrics sounded more—to my tired ears, anyway—like "Buy beer with best name."

Still, Dan Tubridy, the Mulvaney family bartender, followed along on his pipes.

Days later, all calm, the Real Mulvaney sat with me on the terrace of our duplex and gazed disapprovingly at our view. Apartments in Central and, even better, on the Peak, looked out at the harbor. Tai Tam Bay, though, offered other splendors.

"Suburbs!" he sniffed, as if the panorama of turquoise waters, teak vessels, and a bevy of pirouetting windsurfers thirteen stories down was a strip mall in Ronkonkoma.

"I think it's lovely," my mother-in-law, Eileen Mulvaney, called from inside. Since there were so many relatives already visiting, she'd figured she might as well come, too. "So much nicer out here and less crowded, too."

"You should marry her again," I said to my father-in-law. "You're the perfect couple. You agree on nothing."

"How can you celebrate Chinese New Year if you can't see the fireworks?" the Real Mulvaney said to no one in particular. In response, my mother-in-law came out and sat with us. Mulvaney came, too, holding Dan tight—he was not allowed on the terrace without a grown-up. My mother, father, and Queen Asta, back from a shopping extravaganza at Stanley Market, joined us, as did Dan Tubridy, still blowing occasionally on those pipes.

I wondered if the terrace would hold all those people. Miraculously, it did.

It was a cool winter evening, the best kind of Saturday night. It was cloudy but not cold, not if you were from New York, anyway. Still, the richest of the Cantonese women, the ones married to local mogul/aristocrats, would have their mink stoles on tonight. Maybe even their mink coats. There might even be a few Gweilos wearing them, too, including the expats who'd soon be driving up to the American Club across Tai Tam Road. This whole place was a show; it rivaled Las Vegas for artifice. How it would fare in '97, as the latest addition to the People's Republic, was beyond me.

And Macau would be handed over, too. . . .

On the terrace over Tai Tam Bay, the Mulvaney-Fischkin show resumed. More Yiddish songs. Even more Irish ones. And Tin Pan Alley versions of both, all accompanied by bagpipes.

"*When New York was Irish . . .*" the Real Mulvaney sang, as lights went on in apartments all over the Hong Kong Manhattan.

Urged on by the Real Mulvaney and my mother, who, as always, convinced my father to back her up, we celebrated Chinese New Year in a suite at the Marriott, overlooking the harbor. We charged it to *Newsday*.

"Business expense," the Real Mulvaney assured us.

"They have to expect you to entertain," my mother agreed as Queen Asta purred like a cat and my father puffed thoughtfully on a Phillies Panatella and offered to tell an expense account joke, being that he was an accountant.

We invited everyone we knew to view the traditional and spectacular holiday fireworks.

"Can't see these on Tai Tam Road," my father-in-law said, unable to resist. "Here you get the big picture, the big story."

Danny, inspired by the colored rockets and enormous bursts of light and glitter, stood and offered to sing "Twinkle, Twinkle Little Star." In English—and then in Cantonese.

Yat seem yat seem siu sing sing.

He was applauded by most of the foreign correspondents in Hong Kong that night. And by all four of his grandparents. And one dog.

And Mulvaney and I?

Well, we put our decor disagreements, deeply rooted though they were, to rest so that we could once again—tentatively—lie down together.

We had a kid. We were too tired to fight.

DISPATCH FROM THE WAR AT HOME Letters to the Editor in support of Mulvaney's hockey father piece are arriving, I am told, by the bundle at *Newsday* headquarters, which is no longer in Garden City but on a road in Huntington that has nothing on it except cemeteries and industrial parks.

Thanks to the Internet and Newsday.com, the letters arrive from all over the country.

The only complaint regarding Mulvaney's piece is that "Me and Bobby McGee," the song that Mulvaney butchered to make his point, was written by Kris Kristofferson and merely sung by Janis Joplin.
Kris Kristofferson himself is actually the letter writer who complains.

The paper, though, does not run a correction.

"Mulvaney," I say, "they need a public editor. Like the *Times*."

I think he is too full of himself to react, but suddenly his eyes foam with anger, the way I remember they did when we first met.

"Public editors," he fumes, "are worse than PR men. And ya wanna know why?"

"Why, Mulvaney?" I say, weary already.

" 'Cause nothing'll get you a good story like shenanigans, and what is the very thing public editors are put on this earth to eradicate?"

"Shenanigans," I agree, now exhausted. "Maybe what we really need, Mulvaney, is a public editor to follow *you* around."

Jack arrives and proudly hands over an invitation from one of his coaches for a "Pizza Party and Jim Mulvaney Plaque Presentation."

A spokesman for USA Hockey, which oversees the kids' side of the sport, writes to *Newsday* to say that "Mr. Mulvaney is incorrect. The code of conduct, Zero Tolerance, is actually a national policy, written with the input of hundreds of hockey parents, a number of whom serve on our board. And indeed, the NHL has one now, too, based on our example."

But it dampens no one's spirit. No correction is run for this, either. Leisure Suit's replacement, it turns out, has a kid who plays hockey.

And then, yet another letter arrives.

Perhaps Mr. Mulvaney has raised some issues this country's youth athletic programs should address.
>   *Sincerely,*
>   *Ret. USMC General Thomas P. Duffy*
>   *President, Long Island Hockey Rink*
>   *Officials Association*

CHAPTER THIRTY-TWO
What the Heat and the Song Wrought

In the playground of the Manhattan Luxury Residence, the mothers offered reassurance. "The second one is always larger than the first," they said in unison, relishing their little taunt.

Indeed, Jack Mulvaney weighed in at nine and a half pounds, breaking all records at the Matilda and War Memorial Hospital on the Peak in Hong Kong—all family records, too—and convincing me for eternity that the urge to compete is an inherited trait.

Suddenly I felt myself surrounded by a multitude of Mulvaney men. Each one in a different mood.

Mulvaney, the father, was ecstatic.

He could not have been more triumphant if he had produced that large child out of his own body. Fathers, I realize, are often like this. My husband even more so.

Mulvaney, the infant, was enraged.

Jack spent his first days screaming to high heaven. Why, I asked myself, would a baby with so little experience on earth cry so hard? It's not as if he's had any major life disappointments lately.

And finally—and most worrisome—Mulvaney, the three-year-old, was glum.

Danny had suddenly become the glummest creature on earth.

"Mulvaney," I cried out. "Do something!"

My husband considered this, his eyes flashing baby-boy blue. I'd been waiting for him to descend into a jealous funk as well. But he hadn't when Danny was born and he wasn't in one now, either. Mulvaney had apparently gotten all of that out of his system with Caridad, the baby who wasn't our baby. Maybe that's why he bought her in the first place.

"Danny my boy," he said, pulling the kid onto his lap. "You have to handle this logically. Jack is getting all the attention. All you need to do is be a typical male and go for his jugular. His weak spot."

"Mulvaney!" I said. "No violence."

"Find something you have that he doesn't," he told Danny.

"Remember Cain and Abel," I warned my husband.

Ignoring me, he took Danny's hand and led him across the living room to the battery-operated swing, which was vibrating heavily as it heaved back and forth. When it came to electronic swinging, Jack was already a pro. But now his father stopped it dead.

"If that kid screams, he's yours," I said.

Jack only looked up. To announce, perhaps, that he would meet any challenge.

Mulvaney dropped Danny's hand and gently opened

Jack's mouth. "Look inside, Dan my man. This kid, unlike your fine self, has . . ." He paused. *"No teeth!"*

"Jack has no teeth?" Danny asked with obvious interest, although still sounding a bit gloomy.

"Not a one," his father confirmed.

My three-year-old bent over his brother to get a closer look.

"Mommy," Danny said, his eyes suddenly a wondrous brown, "my brother has no teeth."

"He doesn't, honey," I agreed, wondering what we would do when Jack acquired some.

"I want to call Grandma," he said.

"What time is it in Brooklyn?" I said, half to myself.

"Las Vegas Nite time," Danny said.

Who told him about that?

"Better try Daddy's mommy," I agreed.

In Garden City, it was the same time as in Brooklyn, but it might as well have been a different planet.

"Grandma," Danny said, "Jack has no teeth." As he held the phone to my ear, I heard my mother-in-law gently laughing and, with a nod, told him to get back on.

"You are a very good brother to notice such a thing," my mother-in-law said as I listened from the kitchen extension. "And as he grows teeth, as all babies do, I want you to watch them and make sure they are okay. Can you do that?"

I tilted my head out and looked across the shining teak floor, over the raised dining room and down into the living room, where Danny nodded his head vigorously.

". . . And I want you to tell me everything you see," she added, as her grandson, now a delighted, transformed young man—for the moment, at least—hung up the phone.

I hoped that all would go smoothly, that having two children was the same as chasing two great stories at the same time. You viewed both with equal vigor—and love—and understood that sometimes one needed more attention than the other.

And sometimes the stories themselves needed attention. I hadn't written one in months. But since Guli had disappeared—into nowhere apparently, even the other maids hadn't heard from her—I'd been unable to muster the energy to hire, or even interview, a new amah. Was this, too, the Mulvaney curse?

When I had the two kids at the Manhattan playground now, I sometimes wound up chatting with the other maids, more interesting than a lot of the expatriate moms, many of whose dreams revolved around postings in Orange County, California.

"Mulvaney," I said, "there's more to the Philippines than we know."

"And who told you that way back in Mexico?"

Eventually I hired another amah, hoping desperately for a normal employer-employee relationship. In an attempt to develop this, I spoke to her as little as possible. As a result, I wrote more than I ever had when Guli was around. Maybe it was Guli, not the kids, who had stopped me from doing that. I'd felt guilty after every discussion with Guli. Guilty that she came from a poor country, guilty that I was leaving her with my kids to make a lot more money than she ever dreamed of having, meager though we all thought a reporter's salary might be.

I wrote more about the Vietnamese boat people and the Chinese takeover of Hong Kong, and Danny started at the Montessori school in Hong Kong. Three afternoons a week.

Although Danny liked it, Jack loved it, even though he didn't go.

When he woke up from his nap—he took very short ones—our new amah would take him there on the Manhattan Shuttle Bus as the school day was ending. Then she'd wheel him to the school entrance in his Aprica stoller, just as the two- and three-year-olds came rushing out.

And when they did, Jack squealed with delight, as if these were his own friends.

Mulvaney went to Bangladesh, where he wrote about people so poor they dug rocks from the river and sold them. He wrote, too, about a loan program that enabled women to start their own small businesses.

It was a dry country—in terms of alcohol, anyway—but in Dhaka, Mulvaney went to the local newspapers. There he found friends and a bottle of scotch.

I stayed home and tried to find out what rich people would do when the Communists came.

But they all had the same dual answer. A safe one, though. "Leave and stay," they said. An apartment in Hong Kong, another in Vancouver. And all the money offshore.

Globalization.

I hadn't heard from Guli since she'd left. Then a letter arrived, postmarked from Manila.

Dear Ma'am
I have seen your name in Newsday!
No surprise! I am not in New York but in my country. My new boyfriend is a DHL man who brings me all the papers from the states.

Love to Danny,
Guli

"This is the one that almost caused a People Power Revolution in the swimming pool?" Claire asked when I read the letter to her.

"Yep," I said. "But you never know who people really are. . . ."

"Everyone uses DHL now," she mused.

Then, just as I had typed my best story in months—I'd finally found someone in Hong Kong who was both rich and effusive—the Real Mulvaney appeared. He arrived unannounced and alone this time, having made his own way from Kai Tak Airport. "Cabbies here all speak English," he bellowed in greeting. At the sound of his grandfather's voice, Danny clomped down the stairs, the red lights on the heels of his new, improved, non-Ninja sneakers—his first non-Ninja sneakers—flashing like a fire engine.

"I know," I said as I kissed him. "It's great."

"Great?" he harrumphed. "These people are afraid to speak their native tongue!"

My father-in-law, I remembered, had been taking Cantonese lessons.

"Maybe the driver didn't understand you," I suggested.

Adult Ed of the Rockaways.

"Damn Brits!" he said as he bent down to examine the small, but no longer smallest, Mulvaney before him.

"Dan my man, how ya doin'?"

"Can you take my brother back?" Danny asked, woebegone yet again.

I looked at the Real Mulvaney, but he waved his hand like the Wizard of Oz. "It's not that you need one less brother," he proclaimed, rummaging through a crumpled, carry-on Waldbaum's shopping bag, apparently all he'd brought. "Nope. Not one less brother. Just one more weapon."

He pulled out a plastic Ninja Butterfly sword and brandished it in the air.

I should have known. Create more Mulvaneys, get more testosterone.

The arms deal had barely concluded when my husband stomped in, carrying our flailing, kiddie-pool-soaked infant. He rushed Jack to his swing and set it on "fast."

Now I had four of them. In the same room.

Fortunately, my mother-in-law arrived the next day to restore some balance. She unpacked and went straight to the U.S. consulate to make certain that the same naturalization rules applied as in Mexico. "Jack Mulvaney can be President of the United States? This is correct?" she asked with steely authority. Satisfied that it could happen, even if her second grandson had been born in a British territory that would be handed over to the Communists in a few years, she caught a plane back to Kennedy Airport, where a limousine waited to take her to Garden City.

"She's one tough broad," I said to Mulvaney.

"Family's full of them," he agreed.

DISPATCH FROM THE WAR AT WORK Fluttering Lash
barges into my classroom.

"Waiting in the wings," she says, breathlessly, "we have
a guest speaker! A former journalist . . . A famous one,"
she adds, throwing me a suspicious glance. "One of the
world's foremost . . ."

Names flash through my brain. With North Shore
matrons like her, you never could tell. They all have rich,
famous neighbors. I'd heard she'd been quite a hot
number in her youth, too. The Doña Venusa Alcalde de
Poder of Long Island's Gold Coast.

So who could it be? Dan Rather? Too young. Walter
Cronkite? Too old. Daniel Schorr? Really too old.

Suddenly, in the doorway, there is a flash of blue.

"Mulvaney," I say, "what are you doing here?"

"Our guest," Fluttering Lash continues, "recently wrote
an absolutely marvelous viewpoints piece on a human
rights issue that is affecting all of Long Island."

My husband winks at me.

I do not wink back.

She waves her hand toward him and Mulvaney walks—
fast—to the front of my class.

"And here," Fluttering Lash continues, "is one of our
country's foremost advocates of a right I hold near and
dear to my heart: freedom of the press."

"Watch me save your job," my husband whispers in
my ear.

PART THREE
For Attribution

CHAPTER THIRTY-THREE
Deep Background, the Global Version

Thanks to the Novelist-in-Exile and his *rabiblancos*—in Panama and Great Neck—Manuel Noriega was ousted by American forces in December 1989.

Not, though, without what we today politely call "collateral damage."

Hundreds of locals—soldiers and civilians—killed and wounded.

If only they'd had Zero Tolerance back then.

House Rules for Invading Countries.

Even Mulvaney thought Panama was over the top.

Although when it happened, he did call in all his old notes from that interview he stole from me. Okay, he called in some of mine, too. Miraculously, we shared a byline. With each other . . . and with all the other reporters on the

story. Even when Mulvaney and I wanted to be alone together, we couldn't pull it off. Not even in print.

But if you liked crowds, crowds of reporters that is, this
story had them. So many, in fact, that it sent the paper's
layout editors into a tizzy over what to do with all those bylines. They settled for a large box of names planted in the
middle of page three. Not graceful, but it did its job.
"*Newsday*'s Panama Teams: At Home and Abroad" included our successors in Latin America, a few of their
stringers, and a plethora of local reporters whose stories
went on for pages, as if there were no other news at home.

The reporters on Leisure Suit's "at home" team hadn't
merely interviewed every Panamanian supporter on Long
Island, they'd interviewed every Panamanian, as well. Most
of whom, it seemed, lived in Suffolk County, although I
wouldn't put my money on that being true-true. "My finest
moment as Foreign Editor in Ronkonkoma, my finest moment as an American," Leisure Suit proclaimed, as if he
himself had engineered the coup. In celebration, he ordered a large Carvel cake for his minions, a new management tactic of which we'd heard he'd become quite fond,
even though what everyone really wanted was a raise.

Or, at the least, a drink.

Manuel Noriega, meanwhile, rotted away in a hot
Florida cell, America's only prisoner of war at the time.
Stuck there like that, it must have occurred to him that he'd
strong-armed the wrong country.

Post-ousting, the Marcoses of the Philippines were delivered in a U.S. government plane into unincarcerated exile
in Hawaii. A veritable luau. They'd stolen more from their
people than Noriega could have ever imagined, but Imelda
knew how to get to the heart of America. Early on, she'd
made lots of friends in Hollywood.

And now that Ferdinand, always weak of heart, had finally succumbed, she didn't even have to put up with him anymore. True, her life in America was nowhere near as luxurious as the one she'd once had, and she did have to buy her clothes—shoes included—at JCPenney's. But considering what had happened to other former Dictator Friends of America, not merely *Cara de Piña,* she was lucky and she knew it. Rafael Trujillo, for example, had been shot dead in a gunfight on his own Dominican road, on a boulevard named after George Washington.

With her husband gone and trials over her finances not yet under way, Mrs. Marcos had plenty of free time to consort with old friends who occasionally sprung for theater/charity-ball weekends in New York, which always included a mention in the tabloids. People Power might have brought on a revolution, but it couldn't hope to produce the fizz that an Imelda item did. In between events, she was permitted occasional trips back to the Philippines, where she was both reviled for her excesses and adored for them—and where she threatened to run for president herself, if only to destroy "that troublemaker" Cory Aquino, heroine of the People Power Revolution and the New President for the New Philippines. A woman surrounded by sloganeers worthy of the *Newsday* advertising department.

Top among Aquino's sins, from Imelda's viewpoint, anyway, was that the new president had stopped her from burying Ferdinand in the Philippines, next to his recently and equally dead mother. A familiar cadre of fallen politicos, relatives, and "sworn-in-blood" friends—the types who survive a revolution and then refuse to acknowledge it—lobbied hard to "bring Ferdinand home to Mommy." To prove that they meant it, they put her body in a brand-name refrigerator modified with a see-through top for safekeeping and viewing. It was anyone's guess how long Doña Josefa Edralin Marcos would rest in peace in a Frigidaire.

Imelda had never really liked her mother-in-law. But a cause was a cause, particularly when it involved politics. Not to mention home appliances.

Naturally, something in all of this captured Leisure Suit's attention.

Or perhaps it was the letter from Imelda, asking if "as a darling of the media," he could do her one small favor and "assign" one of his staffers "to fetch a few items" from the confiscated estate she'd once owned in Muttontown, on the glittering North Shore of Nassau County.

"Great story!" he said. But it wasn't her attempt to co-opt the newspaper that got him.

"Who cares about that?" he told us on yet another trans-Pacific phone call.

Instead, what he wanted us to do was go to the Philippines and interview "natives." See if they, too, yearned to live on Long Island.

"Make sure you ask whether they would prefer Suffolk," he advised.

Mulvaney and I humored him, as we usually did by that point, and began plotting our own stories.

"The place is full of them," my husband reminded me.

An archipelago, practically Polynesian in its beauty and outlook, even though it had been overrun, often at its own request, by America . . .

A country once poised to be an economic giant. Richer than Japan. Now, plundered and still reeling from the excesses of a greedy little emperor dressed as a president and his wife who had too many shoes and, in a less publicized finding, several hundred black bras.

As in Mexico, the extremes would be easy enough to find.

In Manila, people lived at the city dump and scavenged to stay alive. In elegant neighborhoods in the same city mansions survived, as they usually do when there is any money left at all. The saddest victims of Manila were the members of the working class. Many of them, promised a new world by Marcos, had gone to college, graduate school, and beyond and were now maids in Hong Kong. The money in Saudi Arabia, however, was even better. But mostly the men worked there.

"Can we come with you?" asked Danny. "Me and Jack," he insisted, speaking for his brother, who couldn't do that yet—and whom he now actually liked on occasion. "Can we visit Guli? She told me you can eat little balls of jelly there."

We knew he missed her.

In hope of distracting him, we told him we'd take our current amah, too.

DISPATCH FROM THE WAR AT WORK "Didn't I sleep with you last night?" I mutter as Mulvaney begins his guest lecture in my classroom. An uninvited guest. By me, anyhow.

Most of the students don't know what to think. Reporter Mark, though, laughs hard and turns on a tape recorder. "For accuracy," he mouths in my direction, pointing to the machine. I nod back.

"Wow," I think, this kid's really making progress.

Fluttering Lash glares at him, and me, as she tries to locate old Mulvaney stories on the class computer that she can't work.

To be fair, Mulvaney says all the right things, even if some of them are lifted from Jimmy Breslin.

"To be a great police reporter, to get the story, you have to walk," he says. "You have to get wet. The best stories happen in the rain. Or in walk-ups. You have to walk into people's houses. If it's a four-floor walk-up, then it's a guarantee that the story will be on the fourth floor."

Reporter Mark raises his hand. "I thought you were a reporter on Long Island. Don't you drive everywhere?"

"It's a metaphor," Mulvaney replies, surprising me yet again.

CHAPTER THIRTY-FOUR
Philippine Holiday

We brought our new amah to Manila and gave her time off to see her family there. Then we headed north, to get a feel for the country—and take the boys to the beach.

Running to our connecting flight, one of Danny's light-up sneakers came off.

"Danny," I said, "you lost your shoe again."

"I lost my amah again, too," he said as I tied his laces.

When we arrived in Ilocos Norte, Danny insisted he was not going to the beach.

"Okay," Mulvaney said, "how 'bout we take you and Jack to see a bad guy's cold dead mother?"

Danny seemed to like that idea. I didn't love it. But I did think it might distract him.

In retrospect, it might not have been our finest parenting moment.

*   *   *

In a small courtyard in Ilocos Norte, the region where Marcos was born and raised and where the late Doña Josefa Edralin Marcos was now being kept fresh, Danny peered through a transparent top at an angry, ugly, prune face.

She looked worse than I'd expected. But then again, she was dead.

"I think she is waving to me," Danny said, and from the tone of his voice it was hard to tell whether he was petrified or fascinated.

But he waved back.

Jack, from his stroller, did the same, copying his brother.

Later, back at the Fort Ilocandia Resort Hotel, a looming, Spanish-style redbrick bastion erected in "better days" by the Marcoses, a call was placed to Ida Fischkin in Flatbush-Midwood-Flatlands.

"They put some kid's grandmother in a refrigerator," Danny reported. Like his father, he believed that no story, no matter how gruesome, should go untold. "I would never let them do that to you."

He handed me the phone. "I heard they froze her after an unauthorized trip to Macau," I said, but my mother just laughed.

"I hope that's not your best story," she replied. "It's already been on CNN."

The next morning, Danny agreed, reluctantly, to try the beach.

It was wide and clean, more like Long Island than any beach in Hong Kong. As Jack lay giggling on his stomach, his hands and toes feeling the smooth sand, Danny dutifully began work on a castle. But he'd barely begun when four bearded men on gleaming white stallions galloped up to us and circled, tightly wrapped red head scarves streaming behind them. The riders pulled their reins. As they did, their horses, wearing saddles as stiff as new sports jackets, jerked uncomfortably. Then, as though the men and their horses were lost in their own conversation, each rider shook his head, too. Strange. Yet they all smiled at us, wide and welcoming, with large, bright teeth studded with metal replacements and gaps. I picked Jack up to see the horses. He watched them curiously. Mulvaney lifted Danny in the air and he laughed and clapped as if this show was just for him. There was no trace of the dour child he had been moments earlier.

The riders pulled their reins again, reversing direction and showing off muscular backs, both human and equine. Then they turned, smiling.

I looked at Mulvaney and we nodded at one another in satisfaction. We felt then that we were at the height of our own powers, impervious to any hazards the world had to offer. We were successful, good-looking, still young. The privileged grown children of parents who were aging but active—and far enough away so that they did not offer advice on a daily, or even weekly, basis. We had two great, healthy kids—and we were foreign correspondents, goddamnit. Leisure Suit would send us "anywhere in the world."

The riders circled again. I felt exhilarated by these exotic surroundings. Back in Brooklyn the only horses my friends and I had known were the broken-down ones that took us, slowly, on trails bordering the noisy traffic navigating potholes on the Belt Parkway.

I thought of myself then.

And now.

My reverie was interrupted by the man in the lead, taller than the others and with stronger features. He offered Danny a ride down the beach.

This I hadn't expected.

The surf crashed hard.

"I don't know," I said as Mulvaney put him down.

"Mommy, puuuhleease," Danny whined, tugging at my leg.

Jack raised his hands toward the horses, too. I handed the baby to my husband. No sense tempting him, too. No way was Jack going up there. No way at all.

"I am a father, too," the man in charge said. His men, he added, motioning to the other riders, were all hill farmers who worked at the hotel during the tourist season. "We go home once a week to our wives." He laughed. "More than enough."

Could be a good system, I thought. Send them away, let them get into trouble someplace else, then bring home the money. Stories, too. As long as the trouble stayed down the mountain while the stories—and the money—came up.

Those wives probably had a ball when their husbands were gone.

"Puuuhlease," Danny said again. He gazed at the horse and his eyes, brown like mine, shone. I remembered how sick he had been when I got back from Macau. How, slowly, he had learned to love Jack.

"We'll go slow. We'll stay on shore," the man in charge said.

I looked at Mulvaney, who taunted me in blue: You scared of this? Of some old horses on the beach?

"Kids here do this all the time," my husband said.

Not kids this little, I thought.

"You come, too, ma'am," the leader offered. Then he got

down and gave me his horse. "This one's gentle. You and your husband can take the boys yourself."

The second man adjusted his red scarf and pointed to the space in front of him on his saddle. "I'll get down, too."

They were so friendly. How could they be Ilocanos, who were known for their reserved—even lackluster— demeanor?

"Mommy!" Danny said.

I looked at Mulvaney, clutching Jack gently now. But I remembered how reckless my husband could be. "I'll take Danny," I said. "You stay here with the baby."

"When did you ever ride?" my husband asked, amazed.

"Every Sunday on the Belt Parkway," I said.

So there *were* still things we didn't know about each other.

Mulvaney, to my surprise, nodded that he would do as I asked.

"Jack, too!" Danny said.

"Next year," I replied tensely. I raised my foot into the stirrup. Mulvaney put Jack down and gave me a boost up. Then he put Danny up against me and I held him tight.

"Wave goodbye, Jack," my husband said. As the horse in front of us neighed and trotted away, Jack began to cry. I looked back. "Someday you'll go faster, Jack," I heard his father say.

"Go, boy!" Danny said, giving his steed a playful pat. "Giddyup."

Danny and I and the men who seemed not to be Ilocanos, we cantered at a respectful pace up and down that beautiful Philippine beach, and I wondered what I had found to frighten me at all.

But when we got down and I looked up to thank the lead rider, I noticed he had a hole in the side of his upper arm, as if he'd been hit by a speeding rock.

*   *   *

At dinner that night, the hotel manager presented us with a complimentary bottle of good Rioja and told us, as he brought Jack some mashed mango and patted Danny's blond head, that the *halo-halo,* a national dessert straight from a candy shop shelf—prettily colored pieces of hard gelatin, fruit, and crushed ice in a parfait glass—would also be on the house.

"Beloved James," the manager said to Mulvaney, "the Fort Ilocandia is honored to have such an important guest. We are honored to have a *Newsday* reporter at our establishment."

"You have two," I reminded him.

DISPATCH FROM THE WAR ABROAD The story we missed:

In the 1990s, while the world and its journalists were paying more attention to atrocities and politics and political atrocities in other places—including China and Hong Kong—Islam grew in the Philippines. It continued to do so into the new millennium. The country's Office for Muslim Affairs reported that more than 110,000 Filipinos "reverted" to Islam from Christianity over one three-year period.

Philippine Muslims will not say "convert," for they believe that their religion was the original—or, at the least, the more original—belief of their homeland before the Spanish came, mucked it up, and turned everyone's head with the drama, pageantry, and overblown authority of the Roman Catholic Church.

"We were all Muslims here once" is what the "reverts" say.

In their own Philippine dialect those "reverts" call themselves *Baliks,* or returnees. Sometimes they say they are *Balikbayans,* a term that also describes returning emigrants. In Judaism, someone who was born Jewish but not religious and then took on the orthodoxy is a *baal teshuvah.* A returnee, too. How odd that those terms—*balikbayan, baal teshuvah*—have the same sound, the same syllable count, the same ring, as if they are cousins in the family of language.

In the Philippines, the influence of the church, of the Spanish church and Spanish missionaries, was so strong that for many years, there was another, more widely used saying: "The only good Muslim is a dead Muslim."

Eventually, those Muslims got very tired of hearing this. Other angry people joined them. The history of violence is often far more simple than we imagine.

CHAPTER THIRTY-FIVE
Who Won?

Although we didn't see the horsemen anymore, Danny came to love the beach, and we decided to stay an extra week. Leisure Suit, suddenly, was in no rush to hear from us. Back on Long Island, a couple of key environmentalists had released data showing that Nassau County's groundwater—its *drinking* water—was twice as contaminated as Suffolk's.

Finally, someone had figured out how to get that editor interested in the environment.

And finally, it seemed, the Mulvaneys were at peace.

Jack even took a few long naps.

But after a few days Danny cried for a nap, too. He was three and we'd thought he had stopped taking them. We tried to discourage him, afraid he would be up all night.

But he cried and fell asleep and, as we'd predicted, woke us before dawn.

So began a cycle we kept saying we should stop, although it seemed to have a will of its own. Each afternoon Danny napped longer, as if he was not only resting, but stocking up on rest.

At dinner, though, he seemed his usual self, engaged and engaging and only a little bit odd, not any more so than his parents, anyway.

The first afternoon that both boys napped, Mulvaney and I did what married people do when their children suddenly fall asleep in the middle of the afternoon.

But you couldn't do that every day, could you?

When they fell asleep the next day, I asked Mulvaney if he would watch them while I took a short walk. I walked for an hour and arrived home just as Danny was beginning to stir.

The following afternoon, Mulvaney told me he was going to play a few holes of golf. He came back hours later, long after the boys had gotten up and cried and eaten and played and bathed—and long after I began to wonder about the inherent inequities of being a woman.

Or the length of the average round of golf.

"I am going out for a walk," I told Mulvaney the next day, as Danny purred himself to sleep.

He looked at me with the blue of betrayal.

"What?"

"I am," I said, "going out for a walk."

"I was going to play golf," he said, steadfast.

"You can't," I replied.

"And why not?"

"Because I am going for a walk. You played golf yesterday." That man could not keep track of any schedule. "I am going for a walk," I repeated. "A long one."

With that, *he* stormed out the door.

We did not speak the next day, except about matters regarding our sons.

At naptime, Mulvaney asked me if I wanted to go for a walk.

"Nice of you to offer," I said, meaning just the opposite.

So we sat on separate sides of the large wood-paneled room and read different books.

Halfway through a chapter, I put mine down and left. I got into a hot taxi outside the hotel, rolled down a window, and told the driver I wanted to ride into town.

When we were almost there, I asked him to turn back and go up the mountain instead.

A photograph of Ferdinand and Imelda Marcos set in a plexiglass medallion hung on a rearview mirror. The driver continued straight. "There are many mountains in our country, ma'am."

"The ones where the farmers who work at the hotel live," I said as he slowed the car and, with one hand, put a cigarette in his mouth and lit it with a Bic. Did that mountain have a name? I had no idea. I hadn't seen it; you couldn't from the beach. All I knew is what the men on those horses had said—that they went up there once a week to see their wives.

But they'd said it as if there was more. I'd seen that look on the faces of any number of people who had stories that they wanted to tell but were not sure they should.

Those farmers, I was sure, had a story.

A story Mulvaney didn't have.

"Farmers at the hotel?" the driver asked. Although he hadn't sped up, we were almost in town.

I nodded. "They wear red scarves."

"Ma'am," he said, in a voice that chilled me. "There are

no such people. There is no such mountain." I swore I felt
a tug.

"Then just take me up the first mountain we pass," I
said, hearing the will go out of my voice and feeling very
much like a mother of two.

When the driver took me to town, I didn't argue. Instead, I
wandered the streets, walked into a few sari-sari stores,
Philippine versions of Latin American bodegas. I wondered
if I should stop in a café that had wooden blinds in its windows, and then I didn't. As I walked, I wondered why I was
letting go of this story. I passed a shop that sold papier-
mâché animals and large wooden cabinets and chests, the
kind of furniture that, with customs and duty, would cost
more to ship to Hong Kong than it would to buy. It all
looked too big to ever fit in an American living room. We
might have one someday. I went back to a sari-sari store
and bought Danny a coloring book. The paper and ink
were cheap and the picture on the cover was faded, as if it
was an antique. But it was a picture of a jeepney, a funny
local hybrid vehicle, and there were more inside. Not quite
Jeep or jitney, made with parts not meant to fit together—
as if they were used simply because they were around.
Which originally, they were. The first ones were made after
World War II from surplus U.S. Army jeeps.

At the edge of town where the driver had let me off,
more taxis lined up. Taxis galore. Some in better shape than
others, but plenty that could make it up a mountain.

I got into the first one. "Fort Ilocandia Hotel, please," I
said.

*   *   *

At dinner, Jack gurgled at the other guests while Danny colored a jeepney and tried hard to stay in the lines. The Rioja was good, too. We had a second bottle.

"This afternoon . . ." I said.

"Yes," Mulvaney replied, stiff despite the wine.

I hadn't planned on telling him anything. But his anger, still, after all these years together, made me want to say more. To do him one better.

"This afternoon," I said, "I tried to go up the mountain."

"What mountain?" he said. But his eyes betrayed him. He already knew.

"Where the horseback riders live."

His blue eyes turned white.

"Did you go?"

I shook my head. "Are you listening, Mulvaney?"

"And?"

"Taxi driver wouldn't take me."

"Those men don't work here," my husband said.

"I know."

"How?" he asked.

"The driver told me. How do *you* know?" I asked.

"Golf," he said.

"Golf?"

"Yeah, I've been playing with a local judge."

"A Marcos guy?"

"They all are here. Or were."

A source he hadn't shared. If you couldn't trust your husband to share a source, whom could you trust? It wasn't as if we worked for competing news organizations. We were supposed to be in this together. Would we ever be?

"Why didn't you tell me?"

"I was going to," he said, his eyes watering. "But we weren't talking."

Danny had moved on to color a palm tree purple. Leaves

and all. Maybe this was what he had inherited from my mother. Jack threw his napkin on the floor, laughed when a waiter picked it up. Then threw it again. "Jack," Danny said, "don't be a poop."

"Shush," I said to him. But he grinned at me, like a kid who knew he was safe.

"So who are they?" I asked.

"Muslims from the South," he said.

"And?"

"You know what the Flips say. 'The only good Muslim is a dead Muslim.' "

"Yeah, people say that about Jews, too. Aren't these their own Muslims, anyway?"

"Yep. But some of them are troublemakers, with a capital *T*."

"You told me about this in Mexico."

He nodded. "Years of disenfranchisement in a Catholic country. It had to happen. And they're co-opting a few disenchanted former Marcos cronies to help them."

Sounded like an unnatural alliance. But who was I to talk?

"Mulvaney," I said, "it's a great story."

"No," he said, eyeing the kids. "It's a dangerous one."

I had a phone number for one of our new amah's relatives. The only one with a phone. I could get her back here to watch the kids while we went up the mountain.

"The really bad ones," Mulvaney said, "are going to get to the point where they don't care whom they kill, even if it's their own, just to take over."

"Mulvaney," I said, "what's happening to you? Aren't you the same person who couldn't get enough of a good homicide?"

"Yeah," he said. "But none of them were ever my own. . . ."

"We're only reporters. They're not going to kill us. We wouldn't be able to tell their story dead."

"The world," he said, his eyes now like steel, "is changing. And while we might not be in the center of it, we are a little too close for my taste."

I looked at him, amazed.

"This, Barbara, is not the Felons Club in West Belfast. It's not Managua. It's not even Tiananmen Square. We are not doing *this* war zone. Not now. Not ever. Do not even think about it. We are not going up there at all."

"Then *I* will."

"Don't you dare."

"Don't *you* dare tell me where not to go."

The next morning Leisure Suit ordered us back to Manila to report out a feature on Lea Salonga, who was opening in *Miss Saigon* on Broadway. "She's back home for a quick visit," explained Mulvaney, who'd taken the phone call and seemed all too enthusiastic about this dumb feature, making me wonder if he didn't suggest it to our editor, just to get us out of there.

"Leisure Suit doesn't usually want anyone to cover Broadway," I noted. "It's in Manhattan."

"You should be celebrating," he said, throwing two plaid shirts and a sweaty, coffee-stained *Barong Tagalog,* a Philippine *guayabera,* in his bag. "The Manila Hotel is one of the best in the world."

The next day, back in Manila, I did just that. I celebrated having time to work. When the boys napped, I sent Mulvaney to play more golf—he seemed to be developing an alarming interest in putting a little ball into a little hole—

and while he was gone I worked the phones. I called every source I'd met elsewhere in Asia who came from the Philippines and a few of Mulvaney's as well. But try as I did, I couldn't piece together the story of the men up the mountain. The best I could tell Leisure Suit, if he wanted a budget note? *Religious Rebels, Possibly Extremists, Might Be Doing Something in Marcos's Mountains: Fischkin Gets Scoop While Mulvaney Enjoys Local Recreational Facilities.*

I didn't bother to call him.

"You'll have to go up there," said one highly placed government official. "Those people will tell their own story; the things we can't say."

I'll come back soon, I told myself. Alone.

DISPATCH FROM THE WAR ABROAD In America, we barely noticed what was brewing. We were quicker to see it in the Middle East, in India, in Bosnia. But not in the Philippines, our godchild country. Is that because we only see the Philippines as its history relates to us—as a backdrop for our brave General MacArthur? We tend to forget that the Philippines is also the Filipino people. Guli worked for us a year before she told us her father had fought in World War II as a Philippine national, one of many who were promised American citizenship after the war but never got it.

We did notice it eventually, though. But not until American missionaries were taken hostage by Islamic fundamentalists who made their base in Mindanao, in the South.

We were already back on Long Island by then, immersed in our own problems. But when that happened, I listened for some mention of Ilocos Norte. I didn't hear any.

Some say that the surge of Islam in the Philippines was created by Ferdinand Marcos.

That could be true.

Marcos stole from his own country, causing an economic downslide, causing droves of his countrymen to find work in Saudi Arabia, where, as good guests, they took on the beliefs of their hosts and brought them home. It was the men who had been to Saudi Arabia who seemed to be converting to Islam at a much higher rate.

But conversion to Islam was also reported as a trend among another group of economic refugees from the

Philippines: maids in Hong Kong. Did they come up with this on their own? What were their influences? They worked in a Buddhist country, many of them for Christian employers.

Were they attracted to their countrymen in Saudi Arabia, kindred spirits who refused to wallow in the poverty at home? Or is Islam just the place where the downtrodden turn these days?

Guli, as far as I knew, had been a devout Catholic. I'd even heard from the other mothers at the Manhattan that she had baptized Danny herself, because we wouldn't. She took him to the Catholic church in Stanley, they said, and threw water on his head. Just in case . . .

CHAPTER THIRTY-SIX
A Boy Who Talked

In the lobby of the Manila Hotel, Jack, in blue Dr. Dentons, and Danny, in Teenage Mutant Ninja Turtle pajamas, listened as Lea Salonga played Tagalog lullabies on the lobby piano.

"Sige mamaya," Danny told her.

Until later, Miss Saigon.

DISPATCH FROM THE WAR AT HOME "All done," I say. "The end."

Jack looks over at my laptop the way his father does and taps his fingers, not-so-lightly, on the kitchen counter, also like his father. "Mom," he says, "I've written book reports longer than that last chapter." He stops, clears his throat. "In first grade."

Have I told you that my son Jack only reads short novels?

He resumes his tapping. Danny sometimes does that, too.

"You have to tell the rest of the story," Jack insists.

Danny. This, I know, is what he means.

I am at the point now where it happened, where I have to write it. But faced with that story, the worst one of our lives, I am beginning to think Mulvaney could be right.

"This is fiction," I tell Jack. "Maybe that truth is a different book."

"Yeah," he says as he turns the kitchen garbage can sideways. "And this book is not entirely false. Everyone who knows you is reading this to see what you made up and what you didn't. And the rest of them are trying to guess."

"So?"

"Mom. If you leave out the part about what happened to Danny, they will think you are embarrassed. Or they will think that his own mother can't explain it, or won't."

Sometimes, he sounds just like me.

"Maybe they will just think I am a refrigerator mother." People used to say that "cold" mothers caused autism.

"Well, I've heard of a refrigerator grandmother. But not any of mine."

"I can't tell it short," I say.

He slashes a hockey puck into the kitchen.

"You have to. Think of it as a quick shot into a goal." The puck hits inside the can. "Painful to set up and a relief when it works."

CHAPTER THIRTY-SEVEN
Descent

On an evening shortly after we returned to Hong Kong from the Philippines, I looked over at Danny and wondered why he was scribbling. His lines had no direction. Usually he liked to at least try to color inside the lines, even if his view of color had nothing to do with realism.

Danny's teachers at the Montessori school said he seemed distant. Even more so than usual. At the end of the year, they had a costume party. It was spring, nowhere near Halloween. But who cared? We were in Eastern Asia.

Danny wanted to dress like a doctor.

"It's because he remembers being so sick," my mother said when she called.

But in a playground on the edge of Stanley Market, Danny was a doctor with no bedside manner. The other children went on the slide and swings. Danny stood alone, holding his white plastic doctor's case.

I remembered when his father had played at being a doctor. As a grown-up, not that it mattered with Mulvaney.

Unlike his father, though, Danny was not triumphant. With his bag, Mulvaney had fantasized patients. Danny, simply, had none.

He started to come home from school with his shirts in shreds.

"Danny," I told him, "if you stop chewing your clothes, I will take you to Ocean Park and you can ride the cable cars up and down the Repulse Bay hill as many times as you want." I thought about that day, more than a year ago and before Jack was born, when he rode the cable cars so happily with his father and me. When we were the last to leave the party.

The Mulvaney spirit. Danny didn't seem to have it anymore.

Maybe, I thought, he's still getting used to having a brother. That will pass.

"Cable cars all day long?" he asked.

I nodded.

And he stopped chewing his shirts.

Or at least I thought he did. He must have. I didn't see them in shreds anymore.

So we rode.

And, foolishly, Mulvaney and I thought it would be smooth sailing—or riding—from there.

The pediatrician didn't make much of it. "He's not stupid," he told us. "He's just worried about the world at large."

Funny how the world at large can cease to matter.

In fact, Danny's own world stopped. Just stopped.

Within months, Danny stopped talking. Not a word, not in any language. He stopped playing, too.

He started to put weird things in his mouth, things that made raw jellyfish seem as normal as Cheez Doodles. He developed an inordinate interest in ropes of all kinds. Once he had one—a jump rope, a venetian blind cord, an electrical wire, a garden hose—anything ropelike—you couldn't take it away from him without a major tantrum.

Ropes were his line back to something. To life as he knew it, perhaps.

And so, no matter what stories you hear from anyone else—that Leisure Suit had grown disenchanted with us, that he ordered us back because our expense accounts were too large or too weird, that we'd spent too much on that Chinese New Year's party in Hong Kong, that we had stopped finding stories—we came home for Danny.

We stopped being foreign correspondents for *Newsday* or anyone. We moved back to Long Island—to Long Beach, where Mulvaney had lived when our romance began—even though we'd said we never would. We needed the comfort. We needed relatives. We needed the schools, the Long Island schools, where no one expects that parents *won't* complain. With Danny, we suspected—correctly—we'd have to complain a lot.

We needed a driveway, a yard, a lawn. There might be a cure in those.

We thought we needed American doctors, too. Until we saw how little they could do. The ones at Yale collected data, shook their heads, and said it was a "rare subvariety of autism called Childhood Disintegrative Disorder." Kids who regress that much do not come back, they said.

We tried to write as best we could.

We tried about 375 therapies, none of which brought back our old kid, the one we'd lost in Hong Kong.

We pulled him in and out of schools, camps, recreation programs. Out of the ones that said he couldn't behave and into the ones that understood that the way he behaved was part of his disability.

"Maybe I could use that excuse," Mulvaney said to me one night, more tears in his eyes.

"Don't you dare," I replied.

Sometimes Danny got thrown out of programs. Sometimes, to get what Danny needed, we had to threaten to sue. The Real Mulvaney was a great help with that. My mother-in-law, too. Grandpa was the lawyer and she—in the life she lived on her own, separate from her children and grandchildren—was a special education teacher.

She'd gotten her doctorate while we were in Mexico.

Generally, Mulvaney and I didn't think too highly of fancy degrees, but that his mother had one was something we loved.

Something we needed, too.

People thought that one of us would write a book about Danny. But back then we were too tired. Or we needed a different topic.

Finally we bought into the simplicity of behavior modification tossed with a generous helping of humanity. Trying things over and over again. Rewarding good behavior in small bits. Common sense, not a miracle. Not really a cure, either. Not for us, anyway. Danny made progress. Slow progress, but progress all the same. Speech, though, for him, was a thing of the past.

"If we could just get rid of the Mulvaney curse," my husband said.

"Mulvaney," I told him, mustering the last shred of courage I had left, "every family is cursed in their own way. No sense trying to fight it."

It was the first time I said it, but not the last.

Danny cost a lot more money than most kids, with all those therapies and cures. Even for the simple ones, you needed to hire someone. If you did them yourself all the time, you'd go nuts. So I no longer discouraged Mulvaney from trying his get-rich-quick schemes, even if one of his ideas was to open a restaurant that served fried bugs, Mexican-style.

We moved to Orange County, California, where Mulvaney went to work for a different newspaper while I wrote my first book. Nonfiction. And not about Mulvaney. That would come later. The one about Danny may come yet.

In California I reconnected with some Gweilos from the playground of The Manhattan and explained to them how life had changed for us.

It was there, too, that Mulvaney won his Pulitzer Prize for exposing a corrupt fertility clinic. Well, I thought, at least he got some bad doctors, even if they weren't the ones we wanted to get.

The ones we'd wanted to get, I'd come to realize, weren't bad, just the bearers of bad news instead of miracles.

Vengeance rarely drives award-winning journalism, anyway.

In California, Danny seemed to like nothing better than riding horses in San Juan Capistrano, cowboy country. Just like the Philippines.

*   *   *

Eventually, we came back to New York and Mulvaney became an editor—yes, an editor—at the *Daily News.* I suppose we could have lived in Manhattan then. But we still needed the suburbs, for the same reasons we needed them when we came back from The Manhattan in Hong Kong.

We could have lived in Connecticut, too. Or New Jersey.

But it was my idea to go back to Long Beach, which had many virtues—although I always wished it could be someplace other than Long Island.

But it was my idea.

Yes.

Confession is good for the soul.

I thought familiarity would be, too—and I do suppose I was right.

For Mulvaney, the *Daily News* didn't work out. There are some reporters who aren't meant to be editors. And there are some *Newsday* reporters who only appreciate how good their old paper was when they go to work for new ones.

So Mulvaney became a private eye.

We bought a handyman's special on the water, admired the neighbors' contractors—at least I did—and hired our own.

Some days, they're still around.

Renovation for us is like romance, an activity we seem unable to stop. It is its own story.

DISPATCH FROM THE WAR AT HOME "Well," Jack says, "it could have been longer. And you forgot to tell it funny."

"Okay," I say. There are worse things in the world than having a teenager who doesn't talk.

"You forgot how it made us all closer," Jack says. "And you forgot what Grandma did, too."

"Which grandmother?" I ask.

"Both. But Grandma Ida is funnier."

"Okay," I say again.

"Maybe you should try something other than first person," Jack suggests. "Or if that's too hard, you could talk in someone else's voice. Baby steps might be better."

Is this what happens to nice children when they become teenagers? They turn into literary critics before your very eyes?

"Jack *Mulvaney*," I say. "Wouldn't you be surprised if I did both at the same time?"

CHAPTER THIRTY-EIGHT
The Last Night of the World

*A*t first, the women merely admired one another from afar.

Imelda Marcos, Ida Fischkin noted, liked her jewelry large, glittering, and colorful. Even her diamonds were yellow and pink; and Ida took this as a good sign. In Ida's book—which she believed she might actually write someday—flamboyance and generosity went together and damn the fools who said that Imelda had stolen a fortune from her country.

In her own little world, some would have said the same about Ida. That she'd once taken money from Las Vegas Saturday Nite to line her own pockets. But that modest fact-finding excursion to Macau had been for the good of the shul.

And Las Vegas Nite Chinese-Style had been an unprecedented success.

It always amazed Ida that a little bit of initiative could be misconstrued as criminal activity.

In the lobby, theatergoers hummed the tune to "The Last Night of the World." Lea Salonga, as far as New York was concerned, had a hit in Miss Saigon. *Even if she was a Filipina playing a Vietnamese.*

Imelda Marcos noticed the elderly Jewish woman right away. That woman is on a mission, Imelda thought, pleased to discover she could still do that, figure out a stranger in a split second. I might be the widow of a deposed dictator, she whispered to herself, but I haven't lost my touch.

She had, after all, been in the political realm for decades, since the day she cried when at first they refused to name her— the former Rose of Tacloban—Miss Manila, as well.

As the woman began to walk purposefully toward her, the aging beauty queen smiled.

Ida Fischkin, whose name Imelda Marcos would soon learn, wore a one-piece evening gown with a striped bodice and an intricately flowered skirt, all in primary colors.

"Nice print," the Former First Lady of the Philippines said when the Perpetual First Lady of Congregation B'nai Israel of Midwood took her hand. "Pucci?" she asked, even though she knew Emilio didn't do stripes. Maybe, though, he should. This woman might be old, but she had style.

"Nah," said my mother. "I'm from Brooklyn."

The conversation proceeded from there.

"I am a fan and a supporter," Ida noted.

"So kind of you," Imelda said. "Are you enjoying the show?"

"Oh, of course, we're huge fans of Lea, too," Ida continued. "She and my grandson are old friends."

Imelda looked impressed.

"About my grandson . . ." Ida said.

"Ida," Imelda said, after she'd heard the story, "the check is as good as in the mail."

DISPATCH FROM THE WAR AT HOME There was once a terrorist named Bruno Bettelheim. At least that's the way I think of him. He was unwavering in his misguided beliefs, rash in action, and he damaged a lot of people.

You need a better definition of terrorism?

Bettelheim was a fake psychologist who, in the middle of the supposedly progressive twentieth century, advanced a theory—somebody else's—that autism was caused by "refrigerator mothers," mothers who were cold to their children. This caused them to withdraw.

It sounds absurd, doesn't it? Mothers as cartoon characters.

SpongeBob SquarePants and the Refrigerator Mother.

By the time Danny was diagnosed, the notion of the refrigerator mother—in most of America, at least—was nothing more than a ghoulish reminder of how science can go awry. Good thing. If someone had told me that I had caused Danny to stop talking, I might have bought it, if only to have a way to explain what happened. In our family, we still don't have one.

I might have bought that I should not have been covering stories at all when he was a kid. I might have forgotten to tell the doctors that when I had a chance to go up the mountain, I didn't.

Every mother thinks she has been a bad mother in her time. During the Bettelheim years, only the strongest mothers didn't believe what he said.

I'd also like to go on record as saying that while refrigerator mothers are a myth, I have, in my lifetime, seen at least one genuine refrigerator grandmother. And for a while—a short but desperate one—I toyed with the idea that what had happened to Danny was all her fault.

Blaming Doña Josefa for the latest incarnation of the Mulvaney curse seemed as plausible as any of the other theories.

There's a lot more research going on now. Better research. And while it would be fun to say that Imelda Marcos helped finance it, I think that is just another Mulvaney-true tale, albeit one told by my mother. Even if it *is* true, it wouldn't change my feelings about what the Marcoses did to the Filipino people. But if you are fighting a war, even a war at home, you take sustenance wherever it is offered.

CHAPTER THIRTY-NINE
The Present Threatens

Whenthe World Trade Center was bombed the first time, in 1993, we both thought it would be the worst act of terrorism New York City would ever see.

But that was the war abroad.

Four years later, we were still fighting the war at home, and dizzier than ever. At our lowest point, on a Saturday at the tail end of winter, right after we moved back from California, we called out the troops based on a faulty conclusion. Frightening how easy that was to do.

It was early March, but so warm we felt as though we were inside a weatherless bubble. Like at the mall.

Speaking of malls, there are certainly any number of settings in which Long Islanders alert themselves to the possibility of crime—and the far reaches of the Roosevelt Field Mall parking garage is definitely one of them. The movie multiplex in Valley Stream, where there have been genuine off-screen shoot-outs, is another. Let us also not forget the spate of horrific assaults in diners throughout Long Island that happened in the early eighties, even if most people *have* forgotten them by now. Those of us on Long Island know it is best to be wary of the gates at LIRR crossings. It hasn't happened recently, but years ago a car-load of teenagers sped through them as they were closing, and a train crashed into them. Only one survived.

But what happened to us—or what we thought was happening to us—occurred on a dead-end street perpendicular to Reynolds Channel in Long Beach on the South Shore of Nassau County. A street that Skippy Carroll, a legendary and former local police captain, called "the safest block in the world."

Granted, when he said that, he'd been in the process of selling us an expensive house on that very street, which—to employ understatement—needed a lot of work. Still, it was hard to argue with his view that "ya can't get outta here widout sumbudie seein' ya."

That was what clinched the deal for us. Danny still needed to be watched most of the time. He liked to wander, and we were never sure that he'd find his way back to us. In California we'd lost him once or twice. But only for a few minutes, although it seemed like hours. Hours in which we'd imagined him dead.

At one end of Dalton Street in Long Beach there was a big fence in front of the water, one we knew he couldn't climb. On the other side, it was a long block. And even at the intersection there was hardly any traffic.

But on the day after we moved in—in the midst of the chaos of boxes and furniture—Danny suddenly disappeared from the yard, fenced-in though it may have been.

And Jack was gone, too.

On my watch.

Don't panic, I told myself as I jumped into my car and drove down Dalton Street.

No kids.

Think, I said.

It's a new house. They are probably in their rooms.

Then Mulvaney received the e-mail.

He is not at his best when faced with a ransom note.

"Come here and read this!" he ordered.

"Mulvaney," I said, "this is not the time."

I rushed upstairs. No kids. Rushed down again.

"Read this!"

I did and shuddered. E-mail was still new enough in those days that people took each one with a measure of seriousness.

"This is not some silly little PR stunt!" he ranted, banging on the computer, his eyes drowned in blue.

Didn't I look worried enough?

"If you hadn't hired that maid in Mexico, we never would have been cursed!"

"Mulvaney," I said, "you were cursed before I married you."

There was, I believed, a long list of people who would swear to this on a stack of Bibles.

Soon our house filled with more cops than we'd had at our wedding.

Really it was just the local police department, but it seemed like more. Maybe I could just see all the cops we'd ever known in their faces.

They hovered around one another and around Mulvaney, examining the e-mail he flashed on the screen, scratching their heads, and toying with their mustaches, the ones who had them.

I grabbed a pile of recent photographs, handed them out, and begged for them to drive around the neighborhood.

They nodded at me as if I were deluding myself.

"Ma'am, whoever took them hid them."

"Get out of my house," I yelled, and they backed away. Maternal rage is not something with which a reasonable police officer wants to tangle. I ran out to the car to go myself, shaking so much I wasn't sure I could drive.

A cop—which one was he, from what country?—slid beside me and took my keys.

"We will look, if that's what you want," he promised.

Leisure Suit called from Huntington, from that road that had nothing on it except cemeteries and industrial parks.

Did we want him to do any investigating, he asked.

"Yeah, yeah, yeah!" Mulvaney shouted, too upset to say what he had said so many times before: that Leisure Suit couldn't investigate his way out of a paper bag. "Yeah, yeah, yeah!" he repeated, too upset, even, to mention his own Pulitzer Prize.

Minutes later Claire arrived, toting a supersized soda cup filled with martinis.

The Real Mulvaney, who had sneaked in, gave her a bear hug and demanded her cell phone, even though he generally viewed such "newfangled contraptions" as totally unnecessary.

"I'll call Tubridy," he said, walking out the side door to get better reception. "He'll trace the e-mail."

From a bar in Rockaway?

"Pier 92 doesn't have a computer!" I called out after him. Tubridy didn't believe in *them*. Yet.

"Dan Tubridy," my father-in-law yelled back, "can trace anything from anywhere."

Well, if you can't call the family bartender at a time like this, who can you call?

A few minutes later the Real Mulvaney was back, standing over the computer, studying the missive.

"This," he insisted, "could be many things other than a ransom note. I don't think it's real either. Maybe it's from Nigeria."

I started to weep.

Claire looked me hard in the eyes.

"Don't worry," she said, putting her arm around me. "Your kids are brats."

I glared at her. Was that supposed to mean I wouldn't miss them?

"Danny," I said, "is not a brat. He has a developmental disability that causes certain behaviors."

"And Jack?"

Well, he, I had to admit, could be a brat. A new stage I figured he'd shake by the time he was thirty-three.

Hopefully, I'd see him again before then.

"Listen to me and listen good," Claire said. "I think that whoever took them will soon find it was an idea hatched during a moment of temporary mental apparition. . . ."

"What?"

"O. Henry," she said. " 'The Ransom of Red Chief.' "

At that a Long Beach detective got up from the couch where he'd parked himself and recited:

"It looked like a good thing: but wait till I tell you. We were down South, in Alabama—Bill Driscoll and myself—when this kidnapping idea struck us. It was, as Bill afterward expressed it, 'during a moment of temporary mental apparition'; but we didn't find that out till later."

Mulvaney looked up.

"Long Beach Middle School," the detective said, elbowing my husband. "And a photographic memory, of course."

I myself felt too old for surprise endings.

If only, as in the story, someone would pay us to take them back. . . .

Outside, a DHL truck screeched to a stop. My mother got out and stomped through our open front door.

"That nice deliveryman gave me a ride all the way from Brooklyn."

I started to cry.

"I figured it would be quicker than the railroad," she said, dropping her macramé handbag from the sixties.

"Barbara," she said.

The bag shook and Queen Asta jumped out.

"Mother," I said, "dogs aren't supposed to live this long."

"She's mythical," my mother replied.

She then drew herself up as if she, too, was the sum of all the stories ever told about her.

"Loving your children is secondary. Believing in them is what counts. In comparison to believing in your children, loving them is a cinch."

DISPATCH FROM THE WAR AT HOME A typical present-day conversation in the Mulvaney-Fischkin household:

"Something or someone cursed Danny and I won't stop till I find out who it is," Mulvaney says.

Still.

"You won't," I say. "Danny's cerebellum is probably too long." That is one of the latest "theories." After we're all dead, they might even be able to prove it. "Or there was too much mercury in his vaccinations, or too much in the fish I ate. Or he inherited a bad gene from one of our numerous crazy relatives. Or he is allergic to gluten."

"Gluten!" Mulvaney says. "Aha!"

"Gluten," I reply, "is a food product! It is not a leveler of curses!"

If Danny could talk again, he might say that he has failed to cure his parents.

My husband still wants to get rid of the curse.

And—some days—I still want to get rid of my husband.

I won't.

But I will go up that mountain.

"I won't be satisfied with myself as a journalist if I don't," I tell Mulvaney. These days, more than ever, it is a story that needs to be told.

"It's not that good a story anymore," Mulvaney scolds. "It's just a burp now compared to the Middle East. And if you do it, you will be killed. Killed over a burp."

Wasn't he the one who, years ago, announced how key the Philippines was in all of this? Wasn't he the one who said it was an underreported story?

"Mulvaney," I say, "that's not the way I see it. It's a story I almost got and one I have a responsibility to tell." Who knew what they were planning to do to the world, or even a small part of it, on the top of that mountain? Who knew what they were still planning?

"You have a responsibility to your children to stay alive," my husband replied.

I remember that when we were in the Philippines, he said the same thing to me.

But I had chickened out myself, first.

"Mulvaney," I say, "if everyone thought that way, a lot of important stories wouldn't get told."

CHAPTER FORTY
The Future Beckons

The first thing you should know about me, Jack Mulvaney, is that I am good at math.

I might study accounting.

I am also quite funny. About that, I am confident.

Sometimes it takes a couple of generations.

I also do not imagine that there are curses floating about, just waiting to find me. And, already, I have no trouble seeing myself as a parent. I'm probably not going to have to buy a baby and then give it back as a way of getting used to the idea.

Yes, my mother still reads to me. But only her own writing.

I like it. Kind of.

She does, though, have trouble with endings. Since I

don't—you just put an equal sign and you're finished—I've been known to help her along.

I try to reassure her, too. "Mom, I don't think your readers expect logic."

She looks at me like she is going to yell.

"Just wrap it up, Mom! If you can't, I will."

Being a fifteen-year-old hockey player helps. Three periods and it's over.

To O. Henry: My apologies.

To My English Teacher: No, I didn't find this on the Internet.

Here is the story I would like to tell my own children about what happened the day Danny and I temporarily disappeared:

We were picked up by two ne'er-do-wells, out to make a small fortune from our parents.

Let's call them Bill and Sam. (When it comes to making up new names, my mother has a point. Why bother?)

I, though, am not Red Chief.

That is a part made for Danny, war whoops and all. You can, you know, whoop without speaking.

I am not his horse, either.

I am a cowboy. Unlike a lot of cowboy types of yore, I am quite talkative.

Afraid? No, I wasn't afraid. I am never afraid when Danny is around.

He is, as you know, fast, durable, flexible. His arms and legs, anyway. And he has great balance. Those are still his most important strengths. I heard that when he was little, he broke things a lot. He still does. But he himself stays safe. Like my mom says, "Danny doesn't get hurt. It's the rest of the world."

Bill and Sam were very nice to us at first. I'm told there were horseback riders on a beach in the Philippines who once fooled my parents like that. They drove up to our house on Dalton Street and said they had been sent by my parents' friends to take us for a drive—and then a boat ride! Danny, being afraid of nothing, always ready for an adventure and not too particular about who provides it, hopped into the back seat. Since it was my job then—as I fear it always will be—to follow Danny, I did just that.

As we drove, Danny found the one tiny spot where the upholstery was weak—this is another one of his amazing skills—and he worked it quickly until he could lift out a lump of stuffing.

Bill and Sam had a rowboat waiting for us at the public dock in Lido Beach, on a day too warm for winter. Still, the dock was deserted. They rowed us out to a spit of land in the middle of Reynolds Channel. We could almost see our house from there. And we were having so much fun that we waved.

Danny sat quietly in the boat until we landed, and then he got out and ran without fear. He ran into the sea and those guys who took us thought he would drown or freeze. If they wanted their money, they needed to keep us alive. He ate seaweed and they thought it would kill him. He picked up a raw mussel—Irish famine food—opened it, downed it whole.

"Yuck," they said. For tried-and-true bad guys, Bill and Sam had very weak stomachs.

Finally, when Danny was ready to go home, he bit one of them so hard he drew blood.

In the end, they dropped us off on Park Avenue, in front of East End Pizza.

If my kids ask me whether we got a regular pie or a large, I will of course say large.

Have you ever known a Mulvaney who didn't engage in hyperbole?

"A large pie," I will say. "And for free."

We were, after all, heroes.

R&R—A BREAK FROM ALL THE WARS The very last of the
authors of *Naked Came the Stranger* is retiring from
Newsday. The very last Man Who Did. The last one of
those former Garden City stars who, between reporting
real stories, wrote a porn novel together.

All current and former employees have been invited.

Leisure Suit and I arrive at the party together, direct
from another world: Boutique U.

The room is filled with reporters and people who used
to be reporters: the ones, like us, who just left, the ones
who took buyouts in recent years—and the ones who have
decided to brave journalism in the age of the Internet.
The ones who became editors and, the bravest of all, the
ones who stayed on to find and write the stories that still
needed to be told, no matter what the technology.

"They are all the same to me, all made of the same fine
cloth," Leisure Suit says, and I nod. "They, the people of
the Gloomroom," he continues. Gloomroom. That is my
word. I look at him, surprised that he knows it. "Nassau
or Suffolk, it doesn't matter, they are the people with
whom I will always feel comfortable."

I am further surprised to see my former editor and
current university president sipping a beer, since Leisure
Suit was one of the few among us who never drank. It
seems, though, to calm his fidgets and loosen his tongue.

"You and I, Mulvaney and Claire, we will be outsiders
everywhere but a newspaper newsroom, a Gloomroom.
Every place, including and particularly the university. The
people of academia have their own inbred gloom. But
theirs is not ours."

When Mulvaney and Claire arrive, we sit together like a

family of four. We need nothing, not even sources. We always thought we needed nothing except sources. Now we are our own.

As the speeches begin, every bone in every one of our four bodies relaxes. Our old colleagues talk about stories. Not about championing causes but about telling stories for the pure glory of it. They talk about irreverence in the face of seriousness, about dissecting a sad story, sometimes with ruthlessness, so that you can tell it well.

Before we leave, Leisure Suit announces that soon he will be gone from Boutique U., too.

"Not to go back to newspapers," he says. "They are done for me, although I wish they weren't."

Instead, he is going to fix yet another troubled university. A big one.

"I actually like being an Interim President." He shrugs. "It's the closest job I can find to being an unreasonably fidgety editor."

"And, like a newspaper story," I say, "it has a beginning, a middle, and an end."

"Interim," he agrees.

CHAPTER FORTY-ONE
Jack Mulvaney-True

Mulvaney-true always starts and ends with a grain of the real truth, but if you want to tell the absolute truth—and still be a member of the Mulvaney tribe—then you have to tell two versions.

The true-truth of that day we disappeared is that Danny wandered off. And for the first time, I followed him. I'd wanted to do that for a long time.

When Danny disappeared in California, he got all the attention. Even in absentia. Even when he disappeared for a minute or two. My parents would begin to cry over him immediately. It seemed kind of cool. Would they, I wondered, cry over me like that? One day I pretended to disappear so that I could watch and see what they did. But I blew it. My mother called out "Jack!" and I answered her from the front closet. Again, I realized that being Danny had its advantages.

Every time he disappeared, he came back with this look on his face as if he'd had a great adventure. It was everyone else who was in shreds. I wanted that, too.

What I got instead was responsibility. At seven, at six. Even at five. Those were hard years for my parents, worse than they are willing to admit. They needed my help.

Jack! Keep Danny out of the refrigerator!

Jack! Keep Danny from knocking down the lamp!

Jack! Keep Danny from running into the street!

Really, they needed to relax. Danny is easy; it's always amazed me how in the early years so many of our "helpers" quit. If only they had learned to follow these two simple rules:

1. Play follow the leader.
2. Danny is always the leader.

You start with that and then you build. In moments of great desperation, you can always count on Cheez Doodles. In fact, by the time I am done with this story you may never forget Cheez Doodles. But if there are none around, let him eat what he wants, within reason. He is a person in constant motion; he burns it up. Leaves, by the way—yes, leaves, they have lots of vitamins—are fine as long as he gets them from the ground and not our neighbors' trees. Onions from the ground are okay, too. Someone else's soda bottle is not great, but I never saw him get sick from it. Guck on the ground—any kind of guck—is another story.

Oh, and if he starts to scream, duck.

If he runs into the street and you grab him, keep your arms away from his mouth. If you couldn't talk, you would bite people, too. I learned this the hard way. And Danny was the one who was worried about my teeth?

But it's okay. Now that he is eighteen and I am fifteen, he is much better. He doesn't talk, but he doesn't fight over ropes, either, anymore. These days they tell me I am the difficult one. Can you believe it? Worse: My mother—when she gets on her high horse and tries to convince me she is writing literary fiction—says that Danny is a metaphor for our times.

"Mom," I say, "what exactly do you mean by that?"

"Well," she huffs, "it should be obvious. The world has been transformed into something unrecognizable. People need to learn to deal with it."

"Mom," I say, "you ain't no Steinbeck."

I am expanding beyond O. Henry. In high school you have to read a few novels or they won't let you play hockey. I know what you're thinking: *Tom Sawyer*. That's okay, but when I read it I wondered why everyone says that funeral scene is so original. Fortunately, there are lots of *truly* famous authors—do not tell my mother I said this—who have written really short novels. I like *Of Mice and Men*, for example. The girls are impressed when I talk about what it means to someone like me who has Danny for a brother.

Let my mom think Danny is a symbol of our times. All I think is that I am his friend for all times. Maybe I should have been the teller of this story from the beginning.

On that day—the day of the great, ahem, "kidnapping"—Danny just started walking and so did I. I followed him through the narrow blocks of the canals of Long Beach, streets where, as the years passed, I would know lots of people. But I was only seven then, and we had only just moved back from California. And to tell you the truth, as long as you don't try to ask Danny any questions, he seems as normal as anyone.

So I guess if anyone saw us, we looked like a kid and his little brother taking a walk.

Which, in effect, is what it was. It all depends—as Ms. Mancusi, my English teacher at Long Beach High School, would say—on perspective. We walked in a bit of a circle since Danny likes them, passing the bridges over the canals and an old white house with pillars which, according to my mom, belonged to a movie star named Clara Bow. Silent screen, I think.

I was careful to keep him from tearing leaves off trees and/or stealing hoses from front lawns.

We turned and went back through the east side of the canals. When we passed our block, Dalton Street, I tried to get Danny to go home since it seemed like something exciting was happening there. Wow, I thought, look at all those police cars on our very own street. Funny, isn't it, the things that occur to a seven-year-old—and the things that don't? Not that it mattered. Danny would have none of it. He just kept walking and, well, I couldn't let him walk alone because even on those small canal blocks there is traffic. And besides, what would he do if someone asked him a question?

We made our way down Pine, turned left on Neptune, and marched right into the playground of the East School—and then out again. Being that it was a Saturday—and warm—the place was packed. Danny likes slides; he sometimes sits in the middle of them, as if it reminds him of something. But he only likes parks if they are empty.

He walked farther toward Park Avenue and so did I.

I held his hand as we crossed Neptune, which was a bigger street than I was allowed to cross. We walked another block or two and then Danny stopped dead in his tracks.

I tried to figure out what it was. We were in front of a big house. Nicer than the others on the block, old, white, stucco, and set back from the road, with a boat on a trailer in its driveway.

Danny, it seemed, wanted very desperately to get on that boat.

"What is the big deal?" I asked, trying to keep up with him as he climbed up the boat's side like some Transformers toy with suction cup feet. "It's not even in the water."

Then I saw it.

Orange like a crayon-colored sun and stuck behind the captain's wheel in clear view: a large bag of Cheez Doodles.

"Bingo," I said to myself as I followed Danny up, except I used the steps of the ladder hanging over the edge.

I thought he'd leave when the bag was finished. But he wouldn't budge. He just sat there as if there was something more. Well, there always is. . . .

He opened the tops of seats until he found it.

A whole case of them.

Whoever owned this boat really liked Cheez Doodles.

We sat in that boat until they were finished.

It was our sailing trip; we sailed over Park Avenue in Long Beach that day, watching from our perch on a sea that included the other neighborhood yards, the traffic in front, the trucks double-parked down the block in front of Guy and Company, the hairdressers, Colleen and Shari's coffee shop, King's Pharmacy, the Lido Kosher Deli, East End Pizza—where years later I would imagine they gave us a whole large pie for free—Lazy Day Books, Mr. Tom and Teresa's dry cleaners, and next to it the Associated supermarket and more. . . .

The ocean was only a few blocks away. But who needs an

ocean? In life you can make do with less and have more fun.

And although Danny never said a word, we talked that day and told one another secrets that neither of us has ever told anyone again.

And when the Cheez Doodles were gone and our hands and faces were completely orange and our bellies ached but our brains were filled with each other's stories, we walked home hand in hand.

At our house, we met every cop in Long Beach.

DISPATCH FROM A CORRESPONDENT ON ALL FRONTS

Fluttering Lash summons me to her office to discuss my future at the university. She has, she says, neglected to ask me to specify my qualifications to teach would-be young reporters.

"No problem," I say. "Twenty-five years in the news biz!"

"Uh, we're sorry," she replies. "But what we really need is someone with a Ph.D. in Human Ecology."

Uh-oh, I think. Human Ecology. A favorite term around Boutique U., particularly since everyone who says it means something different. Loosely translated: Man interacting with his environment.

Or woman with hers?

On the professor's desk, I see a copy of the latest edition of the school newspaper. Front-page story: *Jim Mulvaney, Former Pulitzer Prize–Winner, Slams Communications Department Theorists,* by Reporter Mark, Editor, *Boutique U. News and Views.*

"And really, dear," she continues, waving the paper in my face, "the things that go on in a classroom are family matters. We keep them to ourselves."

So much for the First Amendment.

"Human Ecology," I reply. "Does that have anything to do with getting people to recycle?"

I spend the time I have left reviewing important lessons.

"Save your reverence for the man or the woman on the street," I say to my students. "Particularly if on the street is where they live."

Self-important journalists, I tell them, are insufferable. . . .

"I didn't ever mean," I say, "to be one here."

"Irreverence," I continue. "A number of you have

delighted me with yours. But don't leave it here. Take it with you to the real world."

"Authority figures, government officials, politicians, movie stars," recites Reporter Mark, and I nod again.

"Professors, too?" someone asks.

"Including yours. And don't forget that when you think you have asked the last question, ask another."

"Professors' husbands, too?" asks Reporter Mark.

"Some in particular," I reply, contemplating what this kid could dig up on him. "Which reminds me, making things up is fun. No reason not to do it. You just can't call it journalism. Journalism is true-true. And it's accurate. Every word."

Reporter Mark nods. I lift the current copy of *Boutique U. News and Views*, point to that front page. "For example," I say gently, "you can't be a *former* Pulitzer Prize–winner, unless, of course, they've taken the award back." Mulvaney, far as I know, still has his.

"Sorry," Reporter Mark says.

"But an honest mistake or a careless one can be corrected in the next edition. If it's a bad mistake, though, they might take back your Pulitzer. If you make stuff up, they'll definitely take it back."

Not Mulvaney's, though. He may have made up his entire life, but never anything under his byline. That I will grant him.

I pass a few sentimental hours in the university library, filled as it is with obscure but useful books, all of them bound with identical, leatherette covers.

Well, this is a boutique university.

Thinking that I will never be here again—and I did kind of like it—I peer at the tiny golden titles.

One I have not seen before—but should have—jumps out at me.

A Short History of Famous Curses.

I take it off the shelf, check the table of contents and the index, and breathe a sigh of relief. Dozens of curses named for their perpetrators—and their victims. No mention, though, of any named Mulvaney.

That settled, I peruse the introduction.

> *. . . For example, the Curse of Tutankhamen—King Tut—the one that threatens a premature death for anyone disturbing the grave of the boy king of the Valley of Thebes—is a tale that starts, as the bent truth so often does, with a reporter looking for a good story.*

Wow, I think, turning to that chapter.

> *It is 1923 and the adventurer charged with guarding this newly discovered archeological find is far more worried about graverobbers than spirits. He tries to scare them away with a wind-up gramophone and three records, including the triumphal march from Aïda. When that doesn't work, he decides to make up a curse. The Curse of King Tut! Then this adventurer-turned-PR-man locates a newspaper reporter desperate for a front-page story. . . .*

Spin.

The curse of King Tut was spin.

And in 1980, the adventurer/PR man confessed all to . . . another reporter, of course. To a Fleet Street veteran who in quick, flashy prose—*"Tut, tut to Tut"*—told the tale.

"You believe this?" my husband says after I rush home that evening to show him. "You believe they made up the curse of King Tut? They made it up just to fool some reporter?"

"Mulvaney," I say, "they made it up to keep people away. And to do that, they had to manipulate the press. . . ."

"And the press wanted to be manipulated."

Belatedly, something occurs to me. All these years as a reporter, trying to remember to ask the next question . . . how many times did I forget to ask the most important one?

"The Mulvaney curse," I say. "When did you first hear about it?"

"Ancestors. When I was in Ireland before you came . . ."

Before he had me kidnapped.

"I saw relatives. They told me," he said.

"The ones," I ask, "who lived near the Blarney Stone?"

At Boutique U., Reporter Mark leads a demonstration of students, "the Committee to Save Fischkin."

"There's a real war going on," I remind them. "Save yourselves first."

But they persevere and are granted an audience with Leisure Suit's successor, who, being a Permanent President, says he needs time to think.

In May, as the semester ends, I pack up my office, the writing haven where, really, I didn't get too much writing done.

Then I go home.

I pack up Jack for hockey camp. He and the Real Mulvaney fly to Buffalo and drive to Guelph.

I pack up Danny for his own camp. Camp Loyaltown at Hunter Mountain, where there is something "wrong" with every kid—and some of the "kids" are sixty years old. No one, though, makes too big a deal about it. The enormous theme-park pool is filled with gaiety and swishing fountains, and sometimes when we visit we see Danny, all two hundred muscular pounds of him, as he is thrown across the water by a couple of sturdy and/or resilient young men from Eastern Europe. I look at them and wonder if this is what the people of my mother's shtetl looked like, the place that was ravaged but not decimated by a pogrom. Or are they related to the farmer who, risking his own life, hid my mother—and could do that because he himself wasn't Jewish? Those counselors—because they are not disabled themselves—make me think of saviors, of "righteous Gentiles," like Raoul Wallenberg and Oskar Schindler. And my mother's farmer, the one who gave her shelter after the Cossacks passed and she came out of the haystack.

Invariably, Danny lands back in the water with giggles of immense relief, as if he has overcome grave danger to get from one side of the pool to another, like an immigrant seeing the Statue of Liberty for the first time. He bobs up and makes his way back through the throng, looking for more "hard times" to overcome. He has always loved pools. When we visit him at camp and see him in that one, I wonder if he can remember the others from his past life. The ones in which he not only splashed but spoke, too. Does he remember the pool in the backyard that was like a park on the Plaza de los Arcángeles? Does he remember the pool at The Manhattan, the one he jumped into without fear, the one in which his amah led an act of civil disobedience?

Does he remember speaking?

And does it matter whether he remembers or not? He now looks to me like one of the happiest teenagers I have ever seen. Certainly not anyone who is cursed. Although if anyone in the family has been cursed, it is him. And yet

he himself is the one who seems to view it as a
transformation.

As if to say: Mom, this now is me.

My parents don't come up from Boca for the summer.
"Too many new fund-raising projects," my mother
explains, and I shudder at the thought. My mother-in-law
leaves, too, renting an apartment in Paris with a woman
friend her age. And no, she says, this has nothing to do
with Gertrude Stein. It has to do with finding a life for
yourself when your children are grown but your husband,
or even your ex-husband, isn't.

The house is quiet, as it usually is in summer. But this
year the quiet is eerie. Is it because Mulvaney and I are,
temporarily, not bickering over the veracity of curses or
anything else? Or because I have aged beyond fifty?
Soon—except for the occasional in-law visit—it will be
like this all the time. Jack will be in college in two years.
By then, if our war at home goes as planned, Dan will
have moved, with a few of his camp buddies, to a house
nearby. Supervised living. Not a bad idea for anyone in
this family. Danny already has a job and I'm betting
he'll have more. No one can lift a heavier box or unload
a dishwasher faster than he can. A life plan has been
devised for him, too. It's been noted that, under the
right circumstances, he might, someday, like a
wife.

Not a complete victory, I agree. But an honorable
resolution to the war at home.

Quiet. Mulvaney and me. Isn't this what I wanted?

Just in case it isn't, I get my passport renewed.

*   *   *

"I see what you were saying about the curse of King Tut," my husband tells me.

Why does he argue with me if weeks later he's going to wind up agreeing with me anyway? For the sake of it? To see if he still can? Is this mellowing-with-age Mulvaney-style?

"A great story," he repeats. "That they made up the curse. But the stories people believe most are the ones they make up."

I look at him. He no longer has a beard like the one he grew so that he'd look like he was in the Irish Republican Army, even though he was only covering it. He doesn't always shave, though. The stubble is turning gray and it charms me, makes me think we have too much history for me to walk out. History and fiction. We have fiction, too.

We have seen people live, seen people die, seen a child lose his language but, ultimately, not his zest.

We have grown older, but still managed to learn a thing or two from our parents—and someday we might even admit it.

And we have made up a lot of stories. But we found a lot of real ones, too.

Look, I say to myself, we have lasted with each other until now, until Mulvaney's beard turned gray.

But that's not the only answer to the only question.

"I think," I say, "that I miss being a newspaper reporter. Telling the truth."

"I have heard all your stories," I tell him a few days later. I regret it instantly.

"I have many left," he says, and I can hear his voice shake.

"I doubt it."

"I think I have heard all of yours, too," he says.

"Mulvaney," I announce, "I am going to rent an apartment. To work in."

When the kids are gone, I will move there. It is one room. A desk, a stove, a bookcase, and a pullout couch.

"Don't you dare," he says, blue eyes raging red.

"Don't you dare tell me where not to go," I say.

In the middle of the night, I leave a note on the refrigerator.

"Gone to the Philippines."

PART FOUR

Today's News

CHAPTER FORTY-TWO
Debate

At Kennedy Airport, before dawn on a Sunday in the dead of summer, 2006, the peace is interrupted by the heels of a security guard reporting to work. Then another. I have two hours before my flight leaves to sort this out. With any luck, Mulvaney will sleep late. Unlike most people, he sleeps more calmly now than he did when he was young. He has, perhaps, stopped dreaming.

I check my cell phone for messages, but the kids are at camp. I consider my marriage. And then consider not considering it. From a knapsack I haven't used in years, I dig out printouts from the websites I began searching at midnight.

U.S. State Department

The terrorist threat to Americans in the Philippines remains high, and the Embassy continues to receive reports of ongoing activities. . . . In view of a number of security-related incidents and the possibility of future terrorist attacks and other violence or criminal activity, Americans traveling to or residing in the Philippines are urged to exercise caution and maintain heightened security awareness. . . .

Well, they always make those memos sound as bad as they can, to keep nut-jobs and do-gooders away from trouble spots where they'll only have to be rescued by American consular officials. No reporter ever got anywhere by listening to the State Department.

Still, times are different now. And with so many obvious dangers, it's too easy to overlook the subtler ones. There was that old friend of ours, the one we met for the first time in the Dollar Store—a great hack, our age, but he seemed to have lived a million lives. He died in Baghdad, but from a heart attack.

U.S. citizens in the Philippines are urged to defer nonessential travel to central, southern, and western Mindanao and the islands of Basilan, Tawi-Tawi, and Jolo, located in the Sulu archipelago in the southwest of the Philippines, due to military operations against kidnappings and other criminal activity.

But I am not going south. That's not only the most dangerous place, it's the most obvious, too. I am going up the mountain. To report the story I found, from the mountain I found. Or almost did, by the beach in Ilocos Norte.

. . . It is possible that other locations in the Philippines, such as beach resorts, could be attacked.

I put the printouts back in my knapsack.

Contemplating long-term marital irritation might be more relaxing.

As I imagine my husband waking and finding my note, I turn off my phone and board a flight to Ninoy Aquino International Airport in Manila.

DISPATCH FROM THE PLANE But you have been through so much together, people say.

You have led such interesting lives.

All of which is true. But marriage is marriage, anyway.

That, though, is not the only reason I am flying out of here. I still need the next story. Or the one that, as a young mother, I had had to forgo.

Who were those people on the mountain? Who are they now? I don't know if they are very bad or very good or just okay. This, I suppose, isn't that much worse than American intelligence on any given day. All I do know is that they are some kind of story and that knowing, and telling what I know, might just add a speckle of illumination to the maze of confusion that has become our world. But isn't that what each story really is?

Out of practice, I try to remember the name of the mountain. Did it have a name? Maybe I never asked. That would be twice, at least, in one reporting career that I failed to get the name of a place I needed to know.

The last time I'd done that, it was Caridad's mother's *campo* town. For years my mother showed me photographs of Caridad and how she'd grown, letters her mother wrote, too. But as a charity case—hopefully a recovered one by now—she was long ago transferred to a temple, not a shul, in Suffolk County. I should have written that story, too. But I didn't.

I've spent a few years writing the story of my husband and me, the fictional one, anyway, and I think I could write it five more times and not fully understand it. Perhaps that is the real Mulvaney curse—that since we met, what we have been to each other is characters in a story we don't quite know how to end.

But what if it turns out that we *need* to be each another's characters? Then we have a bigger problem. We are running out of scenarios and backdrops. We should replenish our repertoire.

How many times, after all, can Mulvaney get thrown out of the hockey rink?

And how many times can I write it?

CHAPTER FORTY-THREE
The Old Source

I check in to the Manila Hotel and glance around its large teak lobby for Lea Salonga, hoping she's not there. Too many memories. Cole Porter tinkles from the baby grand piano and a cocktail waitress rolls post-dinner cigars on her bare thighs for a table of Japanese businessmen.

Night here but morning in New York.

Upstairs, in a room that smells to me of damp tropical air, *halo-halo,* and luxury, I shower and change into a long skirt and a short blouse, clothes for an evening on the town. I place a call on the hotel phone—mine doesn't work here—to Camp Loyaltown. A long wait but finally a counselor is summoned. He giggles when I ask for the latest news, then says that one of Danny's cabinmates tried to eat a frog down by the lake. The frog, he says, is fine, as is

Danny, who has not yet considered this local delicacy. "He might," I say.

I call source after source until I find one who hasn't emigrated, died, or changed phone numbers. He'll meet me at the bar in Malate in an hour.

Downstairs, chardonnay in hand, I walk into the Executive Services Center and send e-mails to the Real Mulvaney and Jack, still in Guelph.

"No guarantee they will tell you a story you can use," my source says.

The mountain, he claims, is just a hill. It doesn't have a name.

But someday, I think, it might.

We shoot more pool as the bar fills.

"You might find an old Marcosista or two, hiding, in the mix," the source says, echoing my husband.

I take note of this, since the source, a thin slip of a man now bald, was one himself once. A Harvard-educated Filipino version of a *rabiblanco*. Consequently, he managed to survive awhile in the Aquino government.

Storywise, this is better than I'd thought I'd get but still insubstantial. I take a bad shot and a long, slow sip of rum. "After all the murders and kidnappings here, after all the religious strife, you can't tell the bad guys from the good ones?" I say. Now I am wondering about the wisdom of this whole idea. I can just imagine winding up with a bunch of peace-loving people who have gotten together to study the Koran. What kind of story would that be? A feature maybe. But who would take it?

Who was going to take anything I wrote? I'd gotten on that plane without time to call any newspaper editors, not that I'd worked for any of them in years. And most of the editors I'd worked for were now long gone anyway. Here I was, being a reporter out of habit and marital disharmony. Nothing more. And I was also, perhaps, about to interview the wrong people in a country where the death rate for journalists was now almost as high as in Iraq, depending on who was counting and how.

"Even your country can't tell the good guys from the bad," says the source.

I put down my stick. "You win," I say, wishing I craved putting the right ball into the right hole in something besides real life.

We move to the bar, where we are joined by an investigative reporter who has seen it all. "Don't worry," she tells me. "Most of the reporters killed are freelance radio reporters, block timers." Block timers are people who buy their own time on the air and then let their opinions explode. Not that safe a thing to do anywhere, anymore. But if you want your voice heard . . .

Upstairs, at the local Foreign Correspondents Club, I get press credentials just in case I actually do have a story.

Back at the hotel, I open an e-mail from my father-in-law.

"Your son is speaking French like a Canadian hockey player."

And from Jack himself: *"Je suis joueur de hockey. Love, Wayne Gretzky."*

Well, it's a start.

I spend the next two days looking for sources, finding a few. None of them, though, do any better than the old Marcosista. Feeling uninformed in a world that supposedly has too much information, I land at the Laoag International Airport and hail a taxi to the Fort Ilocandia Hotel. I take a deep breath and say to myself that if anything happens, the kids are already teenagers.

At the hotel, I step out onto the beach, remember the way it was when I felt that as reporters—privileged American reporters—we were above the fray. Only here to cover it.

DISPATCH FROM THE WAR ABROAD In Belfast, our first war, they'd had Catholic taxis and Protestant taxis and you could have gotten killed by merely taking the wrong one into the wrong neighborhood. In America, people thought they knew all they had to about Northern Ireland. But they didn't know that. They knew that the place was crawling with Irish Americans running guns. But did they know the Sandinistas were there, too?

Who, I think, is here in Ilocos Norte?

CHAPTER FORTY-FOUR
An American Reporter

Outside the Fort Ilocandia Resort Hotel, I get into a taxi and tell the driver I want to ride into town.

Halfway there, I put my left hand, with its Claddagh and wedding rings, on the back of the front passenger seat and ask him to go up the mountain instead.

With a screech, he stops the car in the middle of the road and turns to look at me.

"Which mountain?"

"The mountain where the farmers who used to work at the hotel live," I say.

"Ma'am, there are no such people." The driver's English is slow and careful. "There never were."

"I'm an American reporter!" I say. Or at least I used to be. In the days when that more or less guaranteed access—

and immunity. "I saw them," I continue. "The farmers who wore red scarves."

A photograph of Ferdinand and Imelda Marcos set in a plexiglass medallion hangs from the rearview mirror. Here in Ilocos Norte, some things never change.

"That was many years ago, ma'am. People like that," he says, "are all back in the South now. In Mindanao."

"My story," I say, "is here."

He shrugs and sighs. "You'll need a different car, then."

He drives me into town, to a body shop, and goes inside. "That one," he instructs when he comes out, pointing to a rusty pickup. I get out, walk over, open the door, smile at the driver. He is wearing a red scarf and he has a face I swear I can remember from a horseback ride on the beach fifteen years earlier.

"Ma'am," this new driver says, "do I know you from somewhere?"

"Nope," I reply, remembering, too, a truck in Mexico.

The red-scarved truck driver reaches over me and pulls a black shade down on the passenger window. For effect, I tell myself. Nothing else. I can still see out the smudged windshield and the driver's window, although as we ride off I notice that the back window is covered by a black shade, too.

The driver nods at me. I watch an obscured view of the sun shining on lush, thickly wooded mountains. The green, but not the altitude, resembles Ireland. Higher than the Basque country, too. My head pounds first. Then my stomach.

"Stop," I ask the driver, holding my hand over my mouth.

The man in the scarf nods gently, as if he has seen this before.

I step down, admire the view, throw up. I look again at the mountains, still beyond us, find a large leaf and wipe my face with it, hoping it isn't poisonous. From below, other leaves rustle and a thick red and black coiled snake unwinds and slithers toward me. When I get back in the truck, the driver nods, kindly, as if I had only gone for a walk. As if he had all the time in the world.

By the time we reach our destination, I feel strong again. Ahead, I spot a small colony of thatched huts. We drive closer and the thin, sweet air clouds with the smell of wood smoke.

"*Merienda?*" the driver offers. A snack. He grins wide with perfect teeth and steers me to a yard in front of the first hut, where a large black kettle simmers on an open fire. "Adobo?"

I nod.

A typical Filipino chicken dish. Maybe there really is nothing here. The driver motions for me to sit on a rough wooden bench with no back. Just a frame of thick tree branches with a seat crafted from slats still protected by bark.

"Khadya!" the driver calls.

A woman in a plain cotton skirt and a thin, white, un-tucked long-sleeved blouse, her mouth and head covered with a scarf, comes out of the hut and sits on the ground in front of me, as if she wants to look up and examine me, like a specimen.

I am covered in a similar way, with clothes bought in Manila at the old Marcosista's urging, but I think they make me look like nothing as much as a *rebbetzin* in the Catskills.

I have a scarf in my knapsack, too, but no one asks me to cover my face. No one seems disturbed that I haven't.

Slowly, other women, faces covered, come out and sit on the ground. More men join them, all with those red scarves, except for one. He has silver-gray hair, a pink Ralph Lauren Polo shirt, a Rolex watch that might have been a Hong Kong fake but a good one, nonetheless. Around his neck he wears a short, thick filigreed gold chain. A thinner one circles a wrist, and on the other he wears a silver ID bracelet with his name engraved in script. Can't remember seeing one of those since junior high school.

Well, I think, at least I found another former Marcosista.

He moves closer until he stands in front of me, playing with his ID bracelet and smiling. His face wrinkles up as if he has spent decades on a golf course.

"Write that we will be back," he says.

"Who," I ask, "is 'we'?"

In reply, he shakes his head. "Guess the worst."

This, I hope, is Marcosista-true bravado.

A few red scarves join us. Dour-looking men. Had they once rode up to me and my husband and child with huge smiles? I see the leader, the man with the scarred arm.

The rich Filipino, waving his ID'd hand, gestures in their direction. "Marcos was the only president who ever understood that they are the first Filipinos." He bends down, lights a cigarette, and throws the spent match in the woodpile under the simmering adobo.

"They may be the last Filipinos, too," he says. My nausea returns. I look in his eyes to see what I can glean.

"Marcos," I say, certain that he was on that side, and a few others.

He nods. "Maybe President Marcos stole a little. But we were not a country in chaos then. Very poor with a few rich may be bad. But it is better than having leaders who do not lead, who do not hold the country together."

He bows and disappears into a hut, followed by a sea of scarves, pickup driver included.

The women remain.

First they stare. Then they tell me stories—many stories—

all of them about disenfranchised lives. About how they are not vengeful, only living their own lives, their own religion.

Some of them are lying. Of this I am sure. But there are also grains of truth.

"I was nothing in Hong Kong, just a maid," says one of them. "I could watch people's children but not swim in their pool. As if I would make the water dirty. Here I am something. The people who rescue you from oblivion, you can live with them through curses both real and imagined."

Through a veil I see eyes that, in the darkening light, I think I recognize.

"Guli," I say.

"That is not my name."

You could, I reason, build a story from this. If you get out in time. Not a new story; Filipino reporters have already told it many times. But it could use a few more tellings.

Time to go.

"Driver!" I call into the hut. But from there, only silence.

A woman stands up, then another and another. They make a circle around me, as if they are holding me tight. The circle tightens yet more. I try to walk through it, but the woman who Guli has become holds me back. I try again. They hold me back tighter.

That tug. I feel it again, years later, as strongly as before.

My kids at home.

And the family curse. I think about that, too.

This circle can't be real, either, I reason. Why would they want to keep me here? If I go, I can write about them.

But although they tell some rational stories, these are not rational people.

From down the mountain a car accelerates, makes its way into sight. A limousine. A black limousine. Up here, of all places.

Mulvaney, I think. Or hope. Must have cost him a fortune.

When I met Mulvaney on Long Island in the early eighties, he drove a BMW held together by duct tape. The Thunderbird he drove a year later in Belfast had duct tape, too, along with other idiosyncracies.

But what is this? Prom night in enemy territory?

The circle holding me back is closing inexorably. I look at the woman who says she is not Guli, but she stares through me and raises her hand as if to salute. I see that she holds the hand of the woman next to her by her thumb and forefinger, the weakest spot, as I'd learned when Danny was younger and angry and when sometimes I had to break his grasp on me. I slice my hand through hers and it opens. Had she meant it to do that? I push out of the circle and run to the car.

The man who rolls down the driver's window is not Mulvaney. He is a Filipino, as is the man next to him on the passenger side.

"Get in," he says.

I look back at Guli, who nods as if I should listen.

Does she mean me good or ill?

There comes a moment when a reporter gets into the right car or the wrong one. It's not a decision anyone can make well.

I open the back door to the limousine. Mulvaney hands me a paper cup and pours black liquid in from his own. I love the way he pours wine, but just now I am glad to see him pour anything.

"Rum and Coke," he says. "Best I could do."

"Well," I say. Then I take a gulp.

"They told me I could ruin it if I got out of the car. But I was watching." He closed his eyes. No color at all.

At the Manila Hotel we drank Château Margaux and fell into bed, taking up where we'd left off the last time. When was that and where?

"Why so glum?" Mulvaney asks when we are done.

"It's not you," I say. "It's that we don't have a story."

"We don't have an editor, either," he says.

"Or a newspaper," I agree.

That's when we look at each other and say the same thing.

"Let's write it."

Budget Note
Ronkonkoma/Foreign Bureau
Unexplained International Intrigue

Asia Correspondents Fischkin and Mulvaney report from a mountain in Ilocos Norte in the Philippines where members of the country's long disenfranchised Islamic community have gathered into a small satellite village, joining forces with at least one former powerful, and still unindicted, Marcos supporter. International law enforcement sources, including two Interpol bureau chiefs, have said they are watching this phenomenon to see what develops.

We take out our laptops and write in bed. While we do, I wonder about Mulvaney and me. What will happen? Maybe we can date. We never really have.

"Mulvaney," I say, as the keys clack on, "I didn't really need to be rescued."

"I didn't rescue you. I missed you."

"Mulvaney, to find me you had to have left right after me. I was only gone for a morning."

"Your refrigerator note," he said, "indicated it could be longer."

"Do you remember the refrigerator in Ilocos Norte?"

"Marcos himself is in one now," he says. "Too bad we didn't have time to go."

"There are a lot of stories here," I agree.

"Everywhere," he says.

As we fall asleep, the phone rings.

Leisure Suit.

I pick it up, put it on speakerphone.

"Where are you?" I ask.

"Cambridge, Massachusetts," he says.

I look at my husband and our mouths drop open.

Leisure Suit coughs into the phone as if he is smoking a pipe. "I think, though, this is to be my last Interim Presidency."

Well, yes, actually. Where could he go from there?

"Heard you guys have a scoop. Maybe more . . ."

"You don't work for a newspaper anymore," I remind him.

At this our former editor coughs again, although with more conviction. "They say good stories bring back the dead."

"You game?" Mulvaney asks.

"I am," I reply, and we shut off the lights.

DISPATCH FROM THE WAR AT HOME Back on Long Island, I check Leisure Suit's new blog—the one that he hopes will convince someone to buy him his own newspaper—for our story.

The byline reads "Jim Mulvaney." There is no mention of me.

"Damn," I say, throwing my laptop on the floor.

Never share a byline. Men often forget to add your part of it. Why don't I ever listen to my own advice?

Then I remember, these are different times.

I e-mail Leisure Suit and insist that he restore my name.

"Certainly," he e-mails back.

And quickly, it is done.

I feel a familiar energy at my back. Mulvaney has been standing behind me, watching while I type.

"Didn't I tell you," he says, his eyes as blue as when he was young, "that we'd always have another story to tell?"

Acknowledgments

As Ida Fischkin might say—and probably did—it takes a village to make a book.

Like most things in life I could not have done this without my beloved—really, I mean it—husband, Jim Mulvaney. Living with a protagonist is not easy. But easy isn't my style.

Nor could I have written this book without the support of my brave, handsome, dashing *and* nondelusional sons, Daniel and John Mulvaney, better known as Danny and Jack. Both agreed to lend their names and their own grains of truth to this story. Guys, I love you. And of course, I love Danny's teachers and guides, starting with Anthony Butler, Josip Kostovic, Paul and Karen Cullen, Chris Brown, Regina Santo, Patty Tomanelli, and Mary Tatem, and the many, many others who have assisted us along the way and still do. Without them, I would not have been able to write this with an easy mind.

The real Real Mulvaney must be thanked for being a character in all of his manifestations. I am also grateful to my brother-in-law, Patrick, now the proprietor of Mulvaney's Building and Loan, the finest restaurant in Sacramento, California. My own brother, Ted Fischkin, gets thanks again, as a great confidential source. One also shouldn't write acknowledgments without thanking the family bartender. So, Dan Tubridy, this one's for you.

I am also grateful to two of my former students, both of whom I should have thanked last time, but forgot. They are Mark Ginocchio, now a reporter and columnist for the *Stamford Advocate.* And Tom Westerman, now a Ph.D. student in History at the University of Connecticut.

You can't write a book without a quiet place to think. For arranging a wonderful alternative location, I thank the staff of the Long Beach Public Library. Many thanks also to my dear friends, Anita and Steve Jacobson, and Mimi and Lester Bernstein, who also so graciously gave me space in their own beautiful and peaceful abodes.

With so many locales, I needed fact-checkers and tone advisors, as badly as a real *señora* needs a maid. And so I am grateful to Frankie Drogin, Peter Eisner, Tricia Joyce, Patrick Kelly, Dianne Klein, Carolyn Lesh, Lesley Lewis, and Carol Stabile. They all spent a great deal of time scouring my manuscript for mistakes. If I made any, it is because I did not take their advice.

Senior Editor Tracy Devine at Bantam Dell at Random House is, simply, the best editor I have ever had. As further proof of Tracy's brilliance, I offer this: She asked Kerri Buckley, now an Assistant Editor, to work for her. Many thanks also to Deputy Publisher Nita Taublib, and to Barb Burg, Susan Corcoran, Chris Artis, and Shawn O'Gallagher, with apologies for whatever I have written about PR "Men."

Frank Weimann, my agent, is a master of brevity. In that spirit: Frank is great.

Our neighbor, Anthony Libardi, designed beautiful promotional materials. And he couldn't have done it without his own protagonist, Beth Cohen.

I'd also like to thank Charles King, for suggesting book ideas—even though he is a psychologist—and for helping us through the hard times that all who raise children with autism experience.

I am indebted to the book, *Bizarre Beliefs,* by Simon Hoggart and Mike Hutchinson (Richard Cohen Books, 1995) for alerting me to the journalism angle regarding the Curse of King Tut.

I've left people out. Certainly they will let me know. My friends are like that, thank goodness. A drink on me for anyone who can prove they were slighted (even "Mulvaney-true" evidence will be accepted).

About the Author

As a journalist, BARBARA FISCHKIN covered stories in New York, Latin America, Hong Kong, Dublin, and Belfast, and is the author of *Muddy Cup: A Dominican Family Comes of Age in a New America* and *Exclusive: Reporters in Love . . . and War*. She lives in Long Beach, Long Island, with her husband, who continues to be Jim Mulvaney, and their two sons.

Visit the author's website at www.barbarafischkin.com.